REB

A TASTE OF JASMINE

CHAPTER 1

The sound of Jasmine's laughter echoed from all directions, as the wind whipped up and across the base of the mountain, snow swirling around her with each gusty blow. As she walked away, she looked over her shoulder one last time. As the wind came to a slight pause, the faint outline of a barred door could be seen through the trees surrounding the area. Inside of this ancient looking wooden door, stood three very upset people, us!

A locked cell is always a terrible place to be, given the fact we were all in one, made our situation all that much more grand. Only thoughts of freedom ran through my head, as I looked around in my dark, damp, surroundings. I couldn't believe Jasmine did everything she did to us tonight, I knew she was evil, but apparently she was more evil than I'd imagined. Everything was for her own gain, a master plan if you will, with us being her pawns.

I watched as Jasmine walked into the treeline before she finally transported herself away from us, the moonlight shimmering off of her long dark hair, with her walking the way she did, that annoying joyful bounce with each step. I turned, looking at Darius, who suddenly ran to the back wall of our cave cell. Suddenly he began running his hands over the walls grey rough surface, finally placing his ear to it, listening carefully, before he began pounding on it.

"Quigley!" He yelled out. "Can you hear me? Are you ok?"

There was no reply, my thoughts began turning dark, as I started to think Darius was possibly loosing his mind, he was speaking to a rock wall after all.

Jupiter still lay on the hard dusty ground, bloodied from his battle, slowly recovering from his injuries, I felt absolutely powerless. Powerless to escape, powerless to help my loved ones, and above all, powerless to remember why I'd done so many horrible things to people. I mean, I remembered doing everything I'd done, vicious things, but I couldn't understand why, or even how I could be that way to anyone. In my eyes I saw things much differently than they really were in reality.

Playing such a terrible prank on my own son for his birthday, treating the man I love the way I have, or how I've plotted to kill people, it's just not me, I'd never be that way to people, for the life of me, I couldn't understand why I had been. There was not a thing I could ever do to correct any of these horrible acts, how do you say you're sorry for the past twenty five years? How do you explain that something unexplainable seemed to distort the way you were, but you remember doing everything?

I suddenly felt something I'd never thought I'd feel again, as a tear slowly filled my left eye slowly, a large tear could be seen building up, before finally streaming down my face, with me letting out a slight uncontrollable whimper. I clasped my hands over my face, preparing myself for a good cry, only removing them to look for a place to sit down, finding a good sized rock behind me to use as a chair.

I was just about to sit down, when from outside, I could hear a rustling sound in the nearby woods. Suddenly, Thomas placed his face upon the bars of the cell door.

"Hey! I found you, awesome. What are you guys doing in here anyway?" Thomas asked. "We've been looking everywhere for you, what happened?"

"I'll tell you what happened," Darius said as he turned from the wall. "We were tricked! We were all tricked! Jasmine killed Quigely, putting his body in a world within our world called Nod, the entrance is the wall behind me, she's the evil everyone's been worried about, not my mother. My mom's part of a great cycle, with my birth being one of her tasks. See, Quigley uses my body to get himself a new one, which is like the reset button to this cycle that occurs every seven thousand years. This is a thing that has to happen every so often, as evil begins to rule over the Earth over time. For reasons I won't even attempt to explain, Quigley has the task of being the balance between good and evil. Quigley's married to Jasmine, but there are six women that live inside Nod, with five of them being his other wives, as well as currenlty being pregnant by him. The sixth woman is my wife, her name's Life. She's been my wife many times, in fact she's my wife in every single life I live, as I am not like them, I'll eventually die, so I'll be able to be reborn. The Elders are not what everyone thinks they are either, they're actually the grown children of Nod, they're all inside their mothers right now as we speak, just waiting for their rebirths. Jasmine has taken advantage of this cycle, using her knowledge of it as a way to kill Quigley while he was still his weakest, after separating from me."

"Wow dude," Thomas said in a shocked voice. "That's *really* a lot to take in, this has been a very bad night for me as well, kind of a nightmare to be honest! First, I lost my pack of cigarettes in the woods, then, as I'm looking for it, I end up falling down a really steep hill, landing in the river at the bottom of it. A big brown bear just happened to be down there fishing at the time, it wasn't very happy about me disturbing it's dinning table. That thing threw me around for about ten minutes, jumping on my back, biting my head, flipping me all over the river. I hit a bunch of rocks, they really hurt man. I finally managed to get away from this beast, finding you guys locked in this mountain jail cell. To top off my evening, I never found my pack of smokes, just not having a good time tonight, doesn't look like you guys are either. Well anyway, where's the key to this place? I'll let you all out if you give it to me, no worries."

"Jasmine took it with her," Darius replied. "The key will return eventually, but I don't really know when, or where at, Quigley never really told me that, so I'm doing some guess work."

"So," Thomas asked curiously. "Just how do I get you out of there without the key? Did you just plan on waiting around for it? Or did you want me and the others to go and get it? You tell me what you want, I'll make it happen. You know, odd, for some reason I can't feel any of your powers right now, are you guys like normal people or something?"

"In this cell," I replied. "Our powers seem to not exist, like some kind of magic forcefield or something."

"Is there anything I can do for you guys right now?" Thomas asked, as he looked at Jupiter's bloody face. "Jupiter looks injured, do you need medical supplies?"

"No!" Jupiter, spoke out as he sat up and began wiping the blood from his face. "We don't need anything like that, but if you could go and find Julian, JC, or Von, I'd really appreciate that."

"Alright, no problem," Thomas replied as he turned away from the cell. "I know where they were just a few minutes ago, I'll get them at once."

"Thank you Thomas!" I spoke out, in a surprisingly friendly voice. "I wanted to tell you something, I just wanted you to know that I'm very happy I made you a part of our family, I'm so very sorry for any pain I've caused you."

"WOW! Really?" Thomas said totally surprised. "I think that's the first time you've not treated me like I was some kind of idiot. Thank you, for your apology, I didn't feel very wanted until now, I thought you were just a cold hearted person all this time."

"Like I said Thomas," I spoke out once again. "I really am sorry, I never mean't to treat you the way I did, I just don't know what came over me, I'm truly hoping you can forgive me for my actions towards you."

"Alright," Thomas said as he smiled awkwardly. "You're forgiven, I hoped you'd eventually see that I wasn't such a bad guy, apology accepted."

Thomas quickly zip sped away, just a blur of him in the moonlight, could be seen, as his speed was so fast, snow kicked up in the small clearings air, with him soon disappearing into the trees, snow falling to the ground as he passed by them.

"You know," I spoke out as I watched him disappear, turning, staring at Jupiter. "I really don't know why I didn't like that guy, in fact, there's quite a few people I don't know why I didn't treat better than I did, including you Darius. I haven't been a very good mother too you, in fact, I haven't been a very good wife either, have I Jupiter?"

Jupiter, who'd been on the ground cleaning himself up, slowly stood up, cringing in pain as he did so, coming forward into the light. As his face cleared the shadows, the look on it was one of total surprise, yet happiness filled his eyes.

"Maria, I wouldn't call you the epitome of wives, you have your good points as well." Jupiter spoke out as a smile crossed his face. "It hasn't been all bad baby. You seem different now though, like when I first met you, before you were changed. I'm not going to lie, I like it, I've missed this side of you, more than you'll ever know."

"I know what you mean," I replied. "I remember doing everything perfectly, but until now, I didn't realize what all I'd really done. I can't explain, it's like I've lived two different lives at the same time. I always believed I was doing all of the right things, never wrong in my decisions. Now I see what I was really doing, I never would've done half the things I remember doing. I'm so sorry for all the misery, especially all that I caused to you my love. I've treated you like I was superiour to you, like you were beneath me or something, I'm deeply sorry, I never realized I was doing that."

"Hunny," Jupiter spoke out as he grabbed me tightly in his arms. "You don't have to say you're sorry, not now, not ever. I'm the reason you changed in the first place, and I saw the change in you instantly. I might've fell in love with the human Maria, but to be honest, I kind of liked the vampire Maria as well. Yes, you've spoken to me in some pretty severe ways, that's only because I let you, maybe it's because I secretly like it, so forceful you can be, pretty sexy baby. I love you Maria, believe me, if I didn't, I would've said goodbye long ago. I know the real you though, I knew one day I'd get to see the real you again and here you are. I could always understand what you were trying to do, even though just about every single plan you ever came up with turned out to be a disaster. Never say you're sorry though, we've had a blast together, have we not?"

"Oh, yes!" I spoke out with a huge smile on my face. "I'm so happy I found you Jupiter, you've been such a good man to me, even from the begining of our relationship, always showing me more respect then any woman could even dream of. My plans have been major disaster's, but you've always been there to bail me out, I feel like such a fool."

"Do you guys need a room?" Darius suddenly asked, as he walked towards the big rock by the door of Nod. "I'll be over here if you need me. It's cold in here and I'm pretty tired, it's been a long week, not trying to be rude or anything, but I think you guys might need to talk. I really don't want to know anymore private matters, Quigley filled me in on enough, believe me, when I say I've had my fill of that for awhile, it's an understatement. You guys just don't know, I really wish I didn't either."

"Get some sleep son," I spoke out. "I have no idea what you're talking about, but I know one thing, I love you Darius, I really hope you know that. I never mean't to do the horrible things I've done to you all of your life. I ingored you as a child, I never spent time with you like a normal mother would. I was selfish and then to top it off, just thinking of the horrible birthday party I threw for you, just makes my stomach turn. I'm so very sorry, for everything, I've been a terrible person to you, I'm surprised you even love me. I promise though, from here on out, I intend to make up for everything, every single day of my life, I hope you can forgive me, but I understand if you don't."

"You know mom," He said as he laid down on the hard dirt floor, propping his head up on a small rock, using it as a pillow. "Don't worry about it, what's done is done, I look forward to you making things up to me, but I forgive you, I don't think you could help it, I have a feeling Quigley had something to do with it."

"Maria," Jupiter spoke out happily. "I've waited a long time to hear you apologize to Darius, you never seemed to realize the things you caused him. I was the only one that seemed to take care of him for a really long time, that is until your parents took over. I'm not going to lie, I like this you much better, I mean, I know I said I like the other you, which I do, but I've missed this side of you for a very long time, I thought I'd never see the girl I fell in love with again. Once I changed you, watching you become an evil person like you did, wicked thoughts running through your head all the time, you'll never understand how much that tore me apart inside. After all, I did this to you, I deserved the treatment you gave me."

"I can only imagine what you had to go through," I spoke softly. "I can't believe that being in this dungeon took away our powers, which, made me finally open my eyes, seeing things for how they really have been. I never would've thought that such evil could be inside of me, I've always had only good thoughts and intentions, funny that I should end up the opposite of who I am."

Jupiter laughed for a moment, suddenly grabbing me, pulling me up to him closely. Looking in my eyes for a few moments, before kissing me on the tip of my nose.

"Oh Jupiter," I giggled. "You always know how to make me laugh".

Jupiter smiled as he leaned forward the rest of the way, softly kissing me. Running his finger's through my messy looking hair like a comb. He stroked my hair over and over again, smoothing it out slowly, before finally parting lips.

"We might as well sit down," Jupiter suddenly spoke out. "I think we're going to be here awhile, might as well get comfortable."

We found a spot up by the wall, sitting down in the dirt, watching as dust particles filled the air from our sitting upon it. After sitting down, I snuggled up to Jupiter, in an attempt to get warmer, as I was actually starting to feel cold. This was a feeling I completely forgot about long ago and I really wished I wasn't feeling it right now.

"Are you getting cold Maria?" Jupiter asked as he picked up my hand in his. I shivered slightly, as I looked at him, his hand was even colder than mine. "I'm getting cold, so just wondered."

"Yeah, I'm getting cold," I replied. "I wish we had a fire or something, it must be twenty degrees in here, but at least there's no wind blowing. You know, I've only been to this mountain three times, yet it's always like a blizzard outside, I thought it was suppose to be summer right now."

"It's always winter here Maria," Jupiter replied as he ran his cold fingers through my hair. "There's no such thing as summer on this mountain, I'm surprised the trees grow as well as they do, it'll get to sub zero temperatures at times, with it never getting above freezing."

"Well, winter sucks," I laughed as I closed my eyes, snuggled up nice and tight against Jupiter's warm muscular chest. "I'm glad I have my teddy bear here with me, keep me warm hunny."

"I'll do my best," Jupiter replied, as he snuggled up to me even more, wrapping his arms tightly around me. "We'll be alright, I promise."

"I hope so," I replied, softly as sleep suddenly overcame me.

CHAPTER 2

Thomas finally arrived to where he last saw Von, Julian, and JC. As he made his way through the thick forest undergrowth, he couldn't see them anywhere. He looked around for a minute, scanning through the trees around him, before finally using his powers to locate where they were at. He quickly zip sped towards another small clearing, finding them burning the left over bodies from the battle. The sickening smell of burnt flesh lingering in the air, made him slightly gag.

"Hey, everyone," Thomas spoke out as he came to the fire. "I found Maria, Darius, and Jupiter, they're in a jail cell, which is part of the mountain we're on, sadly, someone named Quigley died, we need to go to them now, they need all of your help."

"Quigley? Dead?" Von spoke out. "This can't be! Why didn't you just use your powers to open the cells door? What happened to Quigley?"

"Someone named Jasmine killed him and believe me, I already tried my powers, door won't open," He replied. "My powers couldn't do it, but yours might. You and Julian have been vampires for a lot longer time than I have, plus, I'm not as strong as either one of you, maybe your powers can open the door."

"YOUR POWERS WON'T OPEN THAT DOOR!" Jasmine's voice suddenly rang out from the dark thicket, with her slowly making her way towards the light of the fire, a key dangling from her fingertips, sparkling from the fire's light. "ONLY THIS WILL!"

"Jasmine!" Von quickly spoke out. "Why have you imprisoned them? What happened to Quigley? Just what's going on here?"

"I'll tell you all what's going on here," Jasmine quickly replied in an evil voice. "I'm ending something I started a very long time ago and you're all going to help me. I'm your new master, be happy, I've gotten rid of Maria, the creature that would've destroyed you all. With her imprisoned as she is, it won't be long before she's no more, as well as Jupiter and Darius. So, now, I'm going to ask nicely here. Who's with me here? I promise I won't destroy any of you at this moment in time, if you're not with me, but I'll eventually hunt you down, you'll just never know when I'm coming for you."

"I'M WITH YOU!" JC rang out, as she suddenly walked in Jasmine's direction. "I was just created, I don't want to be killed by you, Maria, or anyone else for that matter, I like this new life I have."

"Good, good child," Jasmine said with a grin. "Who else? Julian? Von? How about you Thomas?"

"Um, well," Thomas stammered. "I was just created as well, but I don't really want to get in the middle of anything. I know this may sound messed up, but at least I know I'll get to enjoy this life for awhile. Knowing you'll eventually stalk me out, is kind of just like a natural death, I'll never know when you're going to come after me, so that's actually cool. I want that route, not knowing when I'm going to die, it's actually reassuring to know it's coming eventually, so hunt me down later lady."

"So be it," Jasmine said as her smile quickly turned into a frown. "I'll remember you said that, once you've seen this."

Suddenly Jasmine placed her hand on Thomas's shoulder, with Thomas looking like he fell into an instant trance, not moving a muscle. Finally after quite a few moments, Thomas began blinking his eyes once more.

"I'm with you Jasmine!", Thomas spoke out as her hand released it's grip on him. "I knew she was evil, but now I know how she truly feels, I know everything she thought, like I was actually there watching that fight. If you don't mind though, I think I want to leave now."

Jasmine extended both of her hands, placing one on Von, as well as on Julian's shoulder, they were both soon entranced such as Thomas was. Instantly images filled their minds with information, every single thought Jasmine ever picked up on from Maria found their way inside of them, moments later both of them returning to reality.

"Sorry Jasmine," Von spoke out. "I already know these things, you couldn't imagine what all I know, I cannot support you. I know who you truly are, and I know what you're capable of as well. I'll happily wait out my days knowing I played no part in whatever you're about to do. I have only one master I obey!"

"I'm sorry Von," Julian quickly spoke out. "I'm not going to help anyone that killed my Maggie, she could've helped her, she chose not to, she does want to kill us, all of us, you could hear her thoughts just like I did, she's not the person, or friend I always thought she was."

"I'm sorry you can't see past the things Jasmine just showed you," Von spoke out. "There's more to the eye than the beholder can see. I wish I could change your mind my friend, you really don't know *why* Maria is the way she is, I DO! My allegiance has been and always will be only to Quigley. Maria is Quigley's tool, therefore, I will support her. Death is a welcomed treat my friend, someday you might understand that, until then, Jasmine, you say you'll be coming for me, well, I promise you this, I'll be waiting."

"So be it then," Jasmine spoke out, as she turned, smiling at her trio with a satisfied look on her face. "I got who I really wanted tonight anyway. Good luck getting that cell open though, I highly doubt anyone here could take this from me, I've been waiting seven thousand years to get this key, I sure don't plan on letting anyone have it. Well my friends, it's time for us to go, say goodbye to Von everyone, it's the last time any of you will see him alive."

"See you later Von," Jasmine said as she slightly giggled, grabbing her three new minions by their arms. "Nice to know you."

Suddenly, this strong smell of Jasmine entered Von's nostrel's, moment's later a wormhole appeared behind her, with Jasmine, as well as the rest of them, turning around, quickly stepping in, disappearing in the twirling blue and white colored void.

Von stood there for a moment, as the wormhole disappeared, finally shaking his head at the three of them in disgust, instantly transporting himself in front of the cell's door. He wanted to make sure to surprise everyone, so he yelled out through the door, as his hand began banging on it furiously.

"Hello? Anyone home?" He joked. "Knock Knock! Visiting hour has begun, hope you feel like a chat."

"Oh, thank god," Jupiter said as he jumped to his feet. "Quick, use your powers to gather firewood, we need lots of it, Maria, and Darius are almost froze to death, hurry!"

The happy look on Von's face quickly turned into a concerned one, as he immediately, without hesitation, began scouring the woods edge of every loose branch laying on the ground. Using his powers, he concentrated and all of the loose wood began flying in the air out of the woods, landing directly at the door. Von quickly began feeding the wood through the bars, having to toss the bigger pieces away. Jupiter quickly made a large pile of wood in the center of the cave, as close to his family as possible, until he had one large enough for a descent fire.

"Check this out Von," Jupiter said, as he walked back to the cell door. "Use your powers to light a piece of wood on fire, give me a good fire please, then pass it through the bars."

"I can do that my friend," Von replied. "You know, you don't have your powers right now right? If you touch the fire, it's going to be a bad thing."

"Yeah, I know that," Jupiter replied with a grin. "Ready when you are."

Von picked up a medium sized piece of wood, igniting one that would easily fit through the bars, with Jupiter grabbing just beyond the fire. Ever so carefully, yet swiftly, did he pull it through, flames still going strong. He carefully carried the flaming stick to his wood pile, the lite glow of the fire casting it's rays upon the ground made the floor light up with an eerie glow. Placing the stick just right at the bottom of it, Jupiter stood there for a moment, watching the flames as they finally began to slowly spread, before finally coming back to the door.

"Keep the wood coming, we're going to need a lot more of this stuff." He spoke out. "Thank you Von. It shouldn't take too long for this place to start heating up. Go ahead and get a good bunch of wood, I'm going to get Maria, and Darius a little bit closer to the fire."

With that said, Von began doing just that, as the wood once more began flying out from the forest. Branch after broken branch all finding their way directly at his feet. Jupiter walked over to where Maria lay, she looked so frail, so fragile. Slowly he bent down, picking her up off the cave's cold floor. She was unconscious, feeling very cold to the touch. He quickly carried her over to a nice area, which was now putting off pretty good heat, gently placing her on the ground, kissing her as he did. Upon getting her head on the ground, he went over to where Darius had laid down, picking him up as well, carrying him like a baby, placing him in a nice warm spot, next to his mother.

"I love you both so much," Jupiter said as he stood over them looking down. "Please be okay, I can't lose either one of you, I'll die inside if I ever did."

Wood began landing on the cell floor, as Von continued to feed it into the cave. Jupiter quickly began walking back and forth, gathering up a few more arm fulls, tossing them on the flames each time he returned to the fire, quickly getting roaring flames to appear, with the glow of them fully lighting up the entire cell.

Jupiter could finally feel a difference in the cave's temperature, as it quickly heated up to a nice warm tolerable cave. Jupiter once again came over to Maria, bending down to her, he placed his hand upon her face, feeling her skin, making sure she was warming up as she slept, doing the same with Darius. A feeling of relief came over him, as they both felt warm to the touch, with Maria even having a slight grin appearing, as he huddled down next to her and began stroking her hair.

He stroked her hair for a few minutes before he stood back up, making his way over to the window, watching out for flying pieces of wood, as Von was relentless in his stockpiling effort.

"Von," He called out through the cell's small barred opening.

"I have another favor for you to do, one that's about as important as the wood."

"What's that my friend?" Von replied as he quickly appeared at the window. "I'll be more than happy to do another favor for you, but you'll owe me a favor in return."

"That's fine, a favor for a favor, sounds good," Jupiter quickly replied. "I think we're going to be needing some food really soon, human food, water as well, we don't seem to be immortal in here, I can already feel myself growing extremely hungry, I have a feeling that Maria and Darius will be just as hungry as I am when they wake up."

"Food huh?" Von joked. "You know, I figured you'd get hungry eventually, but I never would've thought *you,* of all people, would ask for human food. I figured you guys would've wanted some of the bagged blood from inside of Lars' castle instead, I was just getting ready to go and get it."

"Wow!" Jupiter said surprised. "You guys still have bagged blood in the castle? That stuff would be very old by now, in my normal form that would sound lovely, right now though, I could use a Big Mac and some fries."

"Sounds yummy," Von replied. "I've never tried one myself, anyway, we never emptied the lab's freezers when Maria stopped allowing people to go to Lars' castle, some of that stuff is even older than your son, I think I'd rather have that than a Big Mac, think of how fine it's aged over time."

"Doesn't sound good right now," Jupiter said as he looked at the ground. "You know, she wouldn't have forbidden people from going to the castle, that is, if she wasn't positive that Lars was living there. She did mess him up pretty bad, you know, with the half a leg, half an arm thing she had Quigley do to him. Believe it or not, that was actually her way of giving him the castle, without being nice to him about it. She wanted him to live his days out all by himself, no visitors, no friends, no life, in constant fear of her ever finding him."

"Wow!" Von spoke out. "That's pretty harsh, even for Maria, you know, she really did change once you turned her. I fully enjoyed the girl she once was, watching her slow evolution into the Destroyer has been disturbing, to say the least".

"The Destroyer?" Jupiter said very confused. "What are you talking about? Maria isn't this Destroyer, to be honest, ever since we've been in here, she's been acting like the same girl we both met twenty five years ago. We have no powers, so whatever was controlling her isn't effecting her anymore."

"My friend," Von spoke out in a very calm voice. "I'd love to stay and chat, but all I'll say is this. I want to be the last person she kills, that is, before she kills you as well. This is the favor I'm asking for, in return, of course food and water will arrive shortly, I'm going to go get some here in a moment. Just remember my friend, *who* she is can't be changed, who she has to destroy is all predestined. We *will* all die, I only ask to die immediately before you do."

"I really think you're wrong about the whole Destroyer thing," Jupiter replied. "But if that's all your asking for, then, agreed. If Maria goes on this huge killing spree, killing well over five thousand vampires, I'll make sure she kills you, immediately before she kills me, of course, like she'd ever want to kill me, but ok my friend, you have a deal."

"Fair enough," Von spoke out as he began smiling a happy smile, slowly fading out of sight. "Be back soon."

Jupiter's attention once again focused back on Maria, as well as Darius. He stared at them momentarily, before once again throwing a few more pieces of wood on the fire, watching as the sparks flew up in the air as the wood landed. It had to be at least eighty five to ninety degrees in there by now, but he wanted to make sure they were plenty warm enough.

With the sound of the wood landing on the fire, Dairus was the first to awake, laying there for a few moments, before rolling over, with him getting to his feet. He walked over to the big rock, leaned on it and began just staring at the wall.

Jupiter stood there, looking at Darius, his perfect looking blonde hair all dirty now, not really knowing what to say to him. He felt like he didn't really even know him anymore, like something changed inside of him as well.

"Hey Sporto," He suddenly called out to Darius. "Are you going to be alright? I mean I know Quigley put his soul inside of you and all, but I'd think you'd be happy to be able to get away from him, it must've drove you mad having his crazy self inside of your mind like that. I couldn't even imagine how bad it was for you. So don't be sad, be glad."

"BE GLAD!" Darius yelled out as he suddenly turned, now facing his father. "Be glad for what? The loss of the only real family I've ever had? You don't know who I am, I mean who I *really* am, do you? To you, I'm just your son, Darius, but to the rest of the world, I have another name, that name is Abel, Quigley, as weird as this all may sound, is my brother, he originally went by the name Cain. It's very hard for me to explain it all to you, Quigley, would be much better at it. He's got me tied up in some great big cycle, as odd as it may be, Quigley serves a greater purpose in our world, all because of the crime he commited against me thousands of years ago. I'm tasked to help him in this work, which is why he brings me back"

"Look," Jupiter said informatively. "You're MY son, the son of a vampire, I made you, you're not some kind of biblical person, just because a crazy person living inside of your head, told you that you were. To be honest Darius, you're sounding a little crazy right now, maybe you should focus your attention to our reality a little more than on Quigley's make believe. The guy loves to play his games, how do you know he was telling you the truth about anything he told you, or EVERYTHING? Don't be a fool son, he's a pretty big prankster."

"You'll see dad," Darius replied as he walked as far away from Jupiter as he could,sitting down behind the large rock. "You just don't understand, I can feel him right now."

CHAPTER 3

"What's going on here?" I suddenly asked as I sat up, wiping the sleep from my eyes, the warmth of the fire making me slightly shiver. "What are you two arguing about?"

"Maria!" You're awake, Jupiter said happily. "You need to listen to what our son seems to actually believe. He thinks his brother is Quigley, and that he himself is Abel, the same Abel from the Bible. I mean I understand Quigley was inside of him, but maybe he shouldn't believe a word Quigley told him, wouldn't you agree Maria? I mean come on, we both know he's totally nuts,"

"To be honest Jupiter," I said as I stood back up. "I'm not

saying the guy isn't crazy, but I really don't know what to think, I mean something deep inside of me is telling me he's not lying to Darius at all. I don't know why I feel this way, but I do know that I've never really felt like Darius was really my child. I mean I know I gave birth to him, but I've never felt a connection between us."

"Funny you should say that mother," Darius laughed, as he once again rubbed his hand over the caves wall. "Apparently you give birth to me everytime I'm reborn, yet, I'm never really the child you think you had. I've never really had a connection to you either, I believe it's because we've always been destined to go our separate ways. As a kid I was always more excited to see you leaving grandma's and grandapa's, then seeing you arrive. I didn't understand why I felt that way, but now, knowing what I know, it all makes sense to me, I was just waiting for my destiny to take shape, to which you were more like a vessel than a mother. I still love you though, regardless of what the reality of things may be, you're still my mom. I actually understand why you've been the way you've been towards me, you just really couldn't stop from doing it, you were pre-programmed in a sense."

"Wow," I said as I looked down at the ground. "I *really* wasn't there for you was I? I've been a terrible mother to you, I'm so sorry. I hate to admit this, but I always dreaded coming to see you as well, if that makes you feel any better."

"Not really," Darius laughed. "I guess an apology works for me though, you're forgiven, just as long as you never act that way again."

"Really guys," I spoke out, trying to make them understand what I'd experienced. "I never meant to act that way in the first place, it really wasn't me, I mean it was, but it wasn't, way too hard to explain. I promise the two of you one thing though, I plan on making things up to both of you."

"Oh Maria!" Jupiter said as he leaned to hug me. "Come on Dairus, my boy, group hug."

Darius leaned into his father's outstretched arm, with the three of us hugging each other momentarily.

"I have Von getting us some food and water right now," Jupiter said as we all let go of each other. "He should be getting back here pretty soon, so if you guys are hungry or thirsty, you won't have to wait long."

"We should try to figure out a way to get out of here." I replied. "There has to be another way."

"Nope, not at all," Darius chimed in. "This prison was designed especially for Quigley, only one way in, only one way out. Jasmine has the key, but it will return, I just don't know when. We need to find a way into Nod, then if we can save Quigley, he might be able to explain to us what's going on with Jasmine and him, why she locked us in here in the first place."

"Well don't just stand there then," Jupiter blurted out. "Everyone feel that wall, see if there's a secret trigger to open the door to Nod."

We all began running our hands frantically across the forty foot long ten foot high cave wall. Darius even getting on Jupiter's shoulders, reaching as high up the wall as possible, feeling around everywhere, yet in all our efforts, we still felt nothing in the process. The roughness of the wall actually hurt my hands if I pressed to hard on it, I wasn't used to being so frail, I felt useless. Darius suddenly got off his father's shoulders, crouching down on his hands and knees, he began looking around at the big rock, getting as low as possible, as he inspected it. Jupiter who'd been quick to get his hands on the wall, soon removed them from it. The look on his face was one of defeat, which made me cringe. Seeing one of the proudest men I've ever known with a broken look such as he had right now, made me lose it. The tears began streaming down my face, as I tried to catch my breath enough to talk.

"We're never getting out of here are we Jupiter?" I said as I suddenly choked back the tears. "I mean I know Von's bringing food and water, I can see we have plenty of firewood, so we're okay for now. What I mean is, once we step outside of this cave, I'm afraid I won't be me anymore again. So in a way, we're never getting out of here, at least I'm not."

"You look to much into things Maria," Jupiter laughed as he

placed his big arm around me, pulling me tightly into him. "I don't really care which person you are once we get out of here, as long as I get to spend my time with you, that's all that matters. Darius said the key will eventually return, so we'll just have to wait for it."

I turned into Jupiter, wrapping my arms around his neck, and buried my face into his chest, as I wasn't finished with my cry quite yet.

"*ALRIGHT, ENOUGH ALREADY, STOP YOUR CRYING,*" Quigley's voice rang out from the other side of the wall. "*Man, you really know how to ruin a perfectly good moment don't you? I was enjoying everything so much, seeing you three flipping out like that was classic, one question though Maria, why do you insist on being the brakes on my train? You just had to start crying huh? Oh well, anyway, I hate to inform you, we don't have much time before Von gets back, I have much to teach you, as time will be of the essence during our little ride, so please keep your arms and feet inside of the coaster.*"

"Quigley!" Darius shouted as he sprang to his feet off the

floor, placing his ear on the cold and rough wall. "Are you okay in there? How do I get you out?"

The sound of Quigley's voice sent shivers down my spine, quickly reminding me why I always felt the way I did about him.

"Guess he's not dead," Jupiter said as he looked at me with surprise. "Too bad!"

"Yes, I'm alive and well, thank you so much JuJu the balu," Quigley spoke out again. *"Were you worried about me Maria? I know you were Darius, but you Jupiter, how rude! Is that anyway to talk about an old friend? Wishing death on me is fine, it would be nice if Death would find me right about now, I have a bone I'd like to pick with her, it's a big bone at that, I promise! But anyway, unlike any of you, I cannot die, I'd more than welcome Death though. Darius, did inform you both of who I am, as well as who he is. If you'd like, I think now would be a good time to tell you both who you two really are. That is, if Maria, as well as you Jupiter, tell me how sorry you both are for the way you acted towards me all these years, tell me sorry, just like you told Darius,*

Maria, do it Moo Moo."

"Just how long were you listening to us? Were you ignoring us all that time?" I asked as my temper started to flare. "How long did you plan on just standing there behind your wall?"

"*Oh,*" Quigley replied merrily. "*I figured I'd do it for a couple of days, but then you had to ruin everything and start your crying.*"

"So, Quigley has a soft side," I joked. "Didn't know you even cared."

"*No, not really,*" Quigley chuckled. "*See the key can only be out of the cell for just a few hours before it automatically returns, Jasmine has a big jump on you two time wise right now, so you don't have any time for crying right now.*"

"What are you talking about, a big jump on us?" Jupiter asked. "Why do we have to go after Jasmine, you should do that, she's extremely powerful."

"No doubt," I added. "She went through both of us like we were nothing, we wouldn't be in here right now if we could beat her. If you're this all powerful entity, then you should take care of her yourself, like Jupiter said."

"Ah *Maria*," Quigley giggled uncontrollably. "*I know something Jasmine doesn't know. When I designed you in the lab, prior to placing the seman inside your mother, I made you a little special.*"

"Special," I asked in a surprised voice. "What do you mean by special?"

"*Well, here's a question,*" Quigley asked with a serious tone to his voice. "*Did you really have control of who you were before you entered this cave? I bet not, it's always hard to not distort the genes as you create a new monster. I made you enhanced, and now that you've entered this cave, when you go back outside, the beast shall finally be unleashed. Sad that I had to make you into such an evil person, but I wanted Jasmine to learn how a distorted mind thinks, so I've been distorting your thoughts with my mind, I've been doing it for twenty five years now, that is, until the moment you entered the cave. Jasmine won't know what to do when she sees you next, let alone how to fight you, once your power fully*

grows. I won't be able to mask your true strength anymore now

either, but I don't need to hide you anymore. When your powers

are restored to you, your power level will be so low she won't feel

you for quite some time."

"What the hell are you talking about,?" I yelled back at him.
"You seem to always have interesting stories, but I'll never be this
monster you speak of. Are you telling me that you're the reason
I've been such a terrible person all this time? Now you want me to
be that way again?"

"I must admit it," Quigley laughed." *I had a really fun time*

influencing your mind, what a wonderful birthday party you and I

threw for Darius. I promise you'll be this monster I speak of, but

it's not as bad as you think it is, you'll see. Because I made you so

evil before entering this cave, it'll have a reverse effect, making

you the nicest monster anyone's ever been killed by. Your good girl

attitude you're so afraid you'll lose, well that's not going to

happen, you're stuck this way, all nicey, nice. That is UNLESS you decide you'd like to be your old self again, in that case, you'll need to find that old blood sample up in the castle that Jupiter took from you all those years ago, this blood is special for you, it was taken before you were ever changed, it'll make you a fun girl again, I promise."

"Why would I ever want to be like that again?" I asked in an appalled voice. "That was like a nightmare I couldn't escape from."

"*Ahh*," Quigley chuckled. "*You just never know, maybe being a goody two shoes isn't such a good idea right now. You'll still have a job to do once you exit this cave, your mind is telling you no right now, but once you step out of the cave, you'll see things much differently, it's programmed into you, there's no way to stop it from happening, you'll see, it's a mindblowing surprise, I know how much you like those. You truly are the beast everyone's been afraid of, you just can't understand right now. Your services are much needed in this world, as evil is everywhere once more, you'll destroy this evil for me, if not only because I ask this of you, then again it's something you always do. Call yourself the reset button if you will, but not only will you destroy every vampire on Earth, but once you do, you'll also be the one who'll create the first of the next batch.*"

"Wait, wait," I blasted out loudly. "I'm like *really* missing something here, I know you're saying I'll be this monster, but *why* do I have to kill everyone? I really don't understand, plus how would I ever find them all? This seems a little on the far fetched sided, like a wild goose chase. What did you mean by I always destroy the evil for you? I've never helped you with anything to my knowledge, except to fulfill your stupid little pranks."

"*You've helped me many times Maria,*" Quigley snickered. "*You've been on this Earth a time or two, I know, I'm the one who always creates you. I always save a piece of your DNA everytime you leave this world, only to mix my DNA with yours to reactivate you when the time is right. Yes Maria, a small piece of me is in you, did you feel it? Well at least it used to be in you, that is until you came into this cave, the magic I had inside of you has now disappeared, isn't that disturbing? Well enough sex talk, back to my story. You are always the mother of Darius, even though, in a way, he's not really your child. Jupiter, I make you the same way everytime, a big lugg with a soft spot for Maria, you're always Darius's father as well as protector.*"

"So," Jupiter laughed. "I'm part of this so called cycle as well huh? Well what if I just decide to stay in this cave? What If I don't help with your little drama?"

"*Well,*" Quigley said after a short pause. "*I guess that wouldn't make you a very good protector now would it? That's fine though, do as you wish Jupiter, I'm sure she'd appreciate the help, but you're not the beast, she is, so she'll still do her job with or without you.*"

"Thanks for making me feel needed Quigley," Jupiter replied. "Of course I'll be there to help her out, I'm just saying, you seem to plan things out far in advance, just once I'd like to see what happens if someone goes against your plans."

"I don't get it Quigley," Darius, who'd been silent suddenly spoke out. "Why does everyone have to die?"

"*To be honest,*" Quigley replied in a serious tone of voice. "*With the death of the old, springs life with the new. The world itself needs to be reborn, as evil has slowly over time consumed our world. My rebirth is the beginning of the new cycle, and as with any new cycle, it's out with the old, in with the new. All evil must be detroyed before the cycle is completed, every vampire must die, in whatever fun and exciting way your vicious mother decides. I'll of course be standing at the sidelines, watching anxiously as the fun plays out, you have to admit, it sounds like a blast huh?*"

"Doesn't sound like much fun to me," Darius spoke out as he looked at Jupiter and I. "Don't worry though, I'll help you guys out best I can."

"*No can do sonny,*" Quigley replied. "*They'll be doing this task on their own, I have something else for you to take care of, it's just as important as your mothers task, probably more dangerous than hers though, but you get a present in the end. I guess it wouldn't be quite considered a present to your mom, it just* depends on who's eyes your in, you, or your moms, but I think you'll be very happy to get it regardless. Unfortunately you two won't be able to help each other out, but then again, where would the fun be in that?"

"But of course," I replied sarcastically. "Just where would the fun be in something easy? Just what is Darius suppose to do for you anyway? Just what kind of danger are you planning on putting him in?"

"*Oh yeah,*" Quigley laughed. "*Like I'd tell you all that, spoiling the surprise, actually, it's none of your business, I'll tell Darius all about it once you and Jupiter have left the cave. Really now, I mean, come on, you haven't figured it out about me yet, so I'll just have to tell you, I just really love surprises, they usually turn out to be a lasting memory of a fun filled day, or something like that, anyway, this doesn't concern you, I'm sure Darius will agree with me on this, that is, once he opens his package.*"

Suddenly, a rustling sound could be heard at the caves door, as Von had made it back, and was stuffing a brown paper bag with a big yellow M on it through the bars, dropping it on the floor.

"Anyone here order hamburgers?" Von said happily as he passed a second bag through, dropping it as well. "If you come over here, I have your drinks as well, I'll pass them to you. I do wish you would've told me I needed a car if I used the drive thru window though, I felt pretty odd walking up to it with people honking their horns at me."

"Oh man, I'm so sorry, I didn't even think about that," Jupiter spoke out as he walked over to the door, grabbing at the first drink as it made its way through. "You're a lifesaver, I'm starving. You couldn't have made it here at a better time either, my stomach was about to eat itself. I smell fries and believe me, I know how they smell, I used to hangout at fastfood restaurants when they first started popping up all aver the place, I couldn't even tell you how many fry cooks I've munched on, but I could always smell that french fry smell on them, as they always seemed to have fry oil splattered on their clothing."

"Well your very welcome!" Von said as he passed the other

two drinks through the bars. "I've hunted a few fast food places myself, I usually just got a human though, not burgers. I do hope you know, I hurried as fast as possible, I had a hard time finding what you wanted, just figured you might want to know, this wasn't what I would consider an easy task to complete."

"I know now, glad you did this for us" I spoke out as I grabbed a Big Mac box out of the sack, handing it to Darius. "I appreciate it very much indeed."

I grabbed two more boxes, handing Jupiter his, opening mine as fast as possible. It smelled wonderful, my mouth began watering for its taste just from memory of the flavor alone. Darius and Jupiter both stuck their hands out holding their boxes at me I grabbed the small red boxes full of salty goodness, pouring each of our containers of fries in the empty side of all of our boxes. Picking my burger up finally, I held it in my hand, looking at it for a moment, smelling the delicious aroma I so missed. Finally, I brought it closer to my mouth, how long a time it had been since I'd tasted real food, let alone the flavor of the thousand island dressing mixing with the awesomeness of the rest of my sandwich. Taking that first bite sent a wave of happiness down my entire body, as the flavor bursted in my mouth. A large pickle came out of the sandwich as I brought my face away from the sandwich. Opening up the top of it, I looked inside, noticing a bunch of pickles in it. I picked the pickle out of my mouth, tossing it on the dirt, as the sandwich seemed to have way to many on it in the first place. I mean, I can handle one or two pickles, but this had like ten on it. I took a second bite, picking another pickle out, before opening my sandwich back up, removing the rest of them, before putting it back together again. I reached my hand into the french fry side of my box, retrieving a handful of the french fries. The explosion of flavors from real food in my mouth were almost strange at first, but by the time I finished demolishing my fries and Big Mac, it didn't seem so foreign anymore.

"Hey!" Jupiter yelled. "You got anymore fries left? I want some if you're not going to eat them."

"Yeah mom," Darius jumped in. "Don't be a fry hog, you

took the biggest box of them, so hit me with some, sharing is caring you know."

"Alright children," Von laughed. "No fighting over the fries. I also have a pizza out here, but we'll have to pass it in piece by piece. Don't really know how long you guys will be in here, so figured pizza to be a good choice, after all, who doesn't like cold sausage and pepperoni pizza? I used my powers to keep your food hot, if you wondered, thought you guys might like a hot meal."

"Thank you Von," I replied. "You're a very thoughtful man, a hot meal was exactly what I needed."

"Not a problem Maria," Von said as he leaned in closer to the bars, looking around the now well lit up cave. "Glad to be of service. Hey, you guys didn't tell me you found the key, how long ago did you find it? Why are you still in here?"

"The key?" I asked, as Von pointed toward the rock. "Really?"

I quickly turned in the rocks direction, the sudden feeling of relief rushed throughout my entire soul, as I could clearly see the key laying on top of the rock.

CHAPTER 4

With the key now being in my hand, my thoughts went directly to what Quigley had said. I really didn't want to become a monster again, even a nice one. I'd always thought I'd want to be a vampire, but being human once again made me never want to go back to the way I was.

I handed the key through the bars, giving it to Von, who quickly unlocked the door, the clicking sound was a wonderful noise to hear, as he began opening it up for us as well. He stepped back a few feet, as the door swung open with it's distinctive creaking sound, as if afraid his magic would be taken away such as ours had.

"I'd ask you to come in," I said jokingly. "I highly doubt you'd really want to though."

"No, that's okay," Von laughed as he stepped back another couple of feet . "I'm fine right where I'm at."

"Alright, you guys got to eat,and now you have the door open," Quigley spoke out from behind his wall. *"Now it's time for the two of you to get going, Von give them a hand with everything, just like we spoke of. I guess it's about time for me to say hello to everyone before you go though."*

"You got it Quigley," Von shouted into the cave. "We'll get everything taken care of, you don't worry about that one."

Suddenly, and without warning, the entrace to Nod began to vibrate, as it started to open, causing me to stumble back a couple of feet. As it slowly lifted open, it was as if I was looking at an exact duplicate of Darius on the other side, except for the clothes.

"Goodevening sports fans," Quigley spoke out. "Tonights game is looking like a real killer."

"You look like Darius," I spoke out. "The voice though, now that I can't mistake, it's you, it's really you."

"Thank you, thank you very much," Quigley replied in an Elvis styled voice. "I knew you'd miss me, you were always so sweet on me. Do you like my new body? I'm sexy and you know it, I'm hot. See, I always told you when I was younger I was a sexual dynamo, well with a body and face like this, now do you believe me?"

"You know," I replied. "I've grown alot as an adult, in fact, I'm not even going to reply to what you just said. I forgive you for being the creepy guy that you are, we all know you have a few brain cells that screamed for joy as they made their escape from you, you just can't help yourself, we understand. Alrightly then, enough of that. Since you're now out of Nod, I'm sure you'll be able to help us in this quest you have for us, this could make things turn out a little better."

"Sorry Maria," He laughed. "I cannot and will not help you! The first task you have, making the voices stop, will cause you to cross paths with Jasmine, it's your main task to get Jasmine back to this caves entrance again, I'll be here to handle her when you arrive. Killing all the vampires of the world takes time anyway, but what Jasmine's about to do soon makes her the real priority, the woman just didn't understand I'd already gave her what she wanted, there was no need for all of this, yet, here we are."

"So, you want us to go after Jasmine?" I asked a little confused. "I thought you wanted us to kill vampires, I don't know if I know how to kill Jasmine."

"No nimrod," Quigley laughed, his eyes sparkling into a maroon coloration. "I don't want you to kill her, I don't even want you to fight her if you can get away with it. Harming her will be a bad thing right now, so fight without fighting, that is, if you can. Killing vampires will be how she'll be able to find you. She expects you to do just that, so beware, she'll be feeling for that. If you'd like, I could tell you where I put my old flesh eating virus, I actually created a special batch to be used right around now, a time lapsed virus, a virus that ONLY attacks vampires, I made gallons of the stuff, plenty for everyone to enjoy. Twelve hours after drinking, and all hell breaks loose. All I can say is, second freezer from the back."

"Can we please put a stop to this name calling?" I spoke out. "Kind of getting sick of it. In my experience, when someone keeps calling people names like you do, they tend to be whatever it is they're calling the other person. I already know you're a big doofus, just try to refrain from your usual childish behaviour for five minutes, if that's even possible. Now as for what you want me to do here, I think you need to be more specific, I really don't get what you're saying. You want me to hunt Jasmine as I kill vampires?"

"No, no, no," Quigley stammered. "I want you to destroy the vampires, without looking for Jasmine, she'll find you. It just might be a good idea to put a drop of my virus into every bottle of bloodwine you guys have back at that island mansion of yours. You know, there's a lot of people that stop by that place, let them all have a glass or two, it'll make your job that much easier. I also need you to touch my head real quick, I'll show you what the women of Nod look like. In the event Jasmine does what she's planning on doing, I'll need you to return them all to this cave, they won't be safe, you'll have to protect them from her. Keep Jasmine away from them at all cost, if she should show up, just simply transport everyone away from her and to this cave, it takes her a few seconds to track you down, if I know Jasmine and if she's mad, she won't think about where she's transporting herself to, then I'll do the rest."

"I'm so happy to see you're alright," Darius suddenly spoke out. "What job do you need me to do?"

"We'll discuss that later," Quigley said as a grin crossed his face. "Your mission is top secret, I'll get your bicycle ready for you. Would you like your helmet bicycle boy?"

"Oh come on with that," Darius yelled out. "That's really getting old now."

"Bicycle boy? That's awesome!" I laughed as Jupiter and I had a quick moment where we faced each other, laughing quietly together.   "That's a pretty good nickname there Quigley, kind of fitting since he never learned how to ride a bike. In fact there was alot of things he didn't learn, like how to study for a test instead of having mommy and daddy pay the Dean to give him a passing grade. I swear Darius, not trying to be rude at all, but sometimes I wonder if you're even our son. I mean I graduated with honors, at the top of my class at only twenty three, almost twenty four years old. Your father here was already a genetic engineer when I met him, together we make a pretty intelligent team. They say the apple doesn't fall far from the tree, but in your case, the tree must've been overhanging a cliff."

"Thanks mom," Darius said as he turned around, walking back over to the rock. "That almost sounded like you were calling me stupid or something."

"We should probably get going," Von quickly spoke out laughing. "I don't want anyone to get Darius confused here. Oh yeah, I like your idea with that virus, by the way, good thinking, hundreds of vampires show up each week there, it'll make our job much easier."

"What do you mean our job?" I asked sarcastically, yet joking at the same time. "Who even invited you Von?"

"Uh, well, nobody I guess," Von stammered, as he began swinging his foot back and forth on the ground, small puffs of dirt being kicked into the air. "I just figured you guys would want my help."

"Well of course we do," I laughed. "I just wanted to see what you'd say."

"Wouldn't have it any other way," Jupiter jumped in. "Now what fun would a killing spree be without you?"

"True," Von replied. "Yet it's you that seems to come up with the most unusual kills. Remember that skewer stick guy? I have to admit it man, you even topped my kill that night and I was really awesome with my puppy impersonation, so much fun."

"Not going to lie," Quigley joined in. "I got to see the whole thing, Von's puppy was a cute one, but Jupiter, now you my boy, you're even sicker than I am, which is pretty sick man. Very creative, absolutely loved it."

"How did you get to see anything," Jupiter said confused. "You weren't even there that night."

"Ahh, or was I?" Quigley giggled. "Let me just say, there's many things you don't know about me, but I'll give you that A for effort now."

"You *were* there," I blurted out. "But how? I didn't feel anyone there but us and our kills."

"No big deal, really," he replied. "I've been a busy boy, I know many things, things people have no idea anyone knows about, but I do. Like when you turned into that mist of a fog, and materialized behind Heather, or should we call her Lauritta? You should have seen the look on her face, believe me, it was classic. Like I said though, no big deal, I know lots of things."

I just stood there for a minute, taking in the creepy idea's running through my mind. He knew Heather's real name, I never told anyone that, he was truly there that night, how many other things did he witness over the years?

"I think I'm starting to get this now," I laughed. "You're like the ultimate peeping tom, I bet you've watched me take showers, or maybe you were watching Jupiter instead."

"I might've watched you a time or two, you to Jupiter," Quigley said as he smiled, puckering his lips, blowing him a kiss. "I did get to see you tasting the blood you really crave though, on more than one occasion. Poor Jupiter, he's like a walking feeder to you, definitely your guinee pig. Didn't you ever wonder why vampire blood made you feel more powerful than human blood, or Unicorn blood did?"

"You saw that to?" I replied, ashamed of my actions. "I couldn't stop myself, Jupiter just happened to be there when it happened. I did feel the difference though, I always seemed to be stronger than before, after each drink from Jupiter, or kill I made, my powers seemed to grow as well."

"The powers you'll get once you exit this cave won't be quite what you had before you came in here." Quigley announced. "I would highly reccommend drinking the fun girl blood I had Lars and Von make Jupiter take from you. It may be twenty five years old, but that blood is untainted *Maria*, drink it, I think you'll find your new evil self is much more fun than the old one. As you drink from each vampire, your powers will increase more and more."

"You know Quigley," I spoke out softly. "All I ever wanted was a happy life, a life spent with the man I love. I wanted a good job, a nice place to live, and above all, children. The life I ended up with, a life of violence, death, destruction, it's not what I wanted at all. I'll do as you ask me to do, on one condition, I want you to change me back into the person I am right now, that is, once this is all over. At least let me have the mind I have right now, I can't handle being that vicious person that lived inside of me again."

"I think you'll be surprised this time around," Quigley chuckled. "I think you'll find yourself to be in complete control, unlike when I kept placing my own thoughts in your head, I won't be there now."

"Well I hope not," I said as I started walking towards the door leading outside. "Guess if I've got to do this, I'd better get started, the sooner this nightmare is over, the better."

As I walked across the dirt floor, kicking up dust in the process, it made me realize how long it had been since I wasn't just hovering above the ground. Being mortal again, even for just a little while, has opened my eyes to so many things. I just hoped that by walking through that door, my eyes didn't close once more.

"Are you sure you want to do this?" Jupiter quickly asked as he grabbed me by my shoulder, stopping me just short of making my exit. "We could just stay in here."

"No, actually we can't Jupiter," I replied. "Anyway you look at it, at some point in time, we'll have to leave this cave, and once we do, if I'm pre programmed to be this killer, then really, there's no time like the present. Why wait for the inevitable to happen, I just want to get it over with. So hunny, if you don't mind, please let go of my shoulder."

Jupiter stood there for a few moments, looking into my eyes, finally releasing his grip. I didn't say anything to him, as his hand dropped away fro me. I just calmly took my next step, a step which brought me right to the edge of the door's exit. I stood there for a second, looking at the nights sky one last time with human eyes. The moon lit up the night, casting it's eerie shadows across the mountain, with a few fluffy looking clouds close to going in front of it. I couldn't feel it yet, but I could see the trees swaying from the breeze, shadows dancing below.

Taking my first step through the door, was like being attacked by one hundred thousand volts of electricity, all in the fraction of a second. Instantly everything around me changed, I screamed out in pain, as it was almost to much to bare, with my powers coming straight back to me like that. Instantly, what sounded like the voices of five thousand vampires suddenly filled my head. I could hear them all, every last one of them, their voices, their thoughts. I could even see in my minds eye what each person was doing, well at least what they were looking at, whatever the surroundings may be. Hearing their sick twisted vicious thoughts made my blood boil, they needed to be destroyed, yet, I wasn't so sure I could bring myself to hurt anyone. So violent is a vampire, I didn't want to be the monster, yet I now knew I'd truly always been one. Suddenly, I just couldn't take how everything was hitting me anymore, collapsing on the ground, landing in the cold wet snow.

"Maria, are you okay?" Jupiter asked as he quickly made his way through the door, only to fall to his knees's upon getting passed the doorway. "Oh, god, wait, too much, stop!"

Jupiter curled up into a ball for a few moments, as I watched him make fists so hard his hands were starting to bleed. After what seemed like forever, he uncurled himself, rising to his feet slowly.

"I'm, I'm alright Jupiter," I said as I gathered myself once more, the voices still growing louder in my head. "I just wasn't ready for anything like that, were you?"

"WOW!" He spoke out as he looked at his now healing hands. "That really hurt, glad it's over, was all that pain really necessary? Was that something else or what?"

"Tell me about it," I laughed. "I never expected anything quite like that, did you?"

"Hang on a minute," Jupiter said as he looked at me

curiously. "You did *change* right? I mean, I don't feel any power from you, plus you don't quite seem like your fun evil self, I thought you'd be a little more like the old you again."

"I know, isn't it wonderful," I said cheerfully. "I mean, yes, I'm changed, but I'm still me this time around. Maybe I'm not the monster Quigley said I am after all."

"Now that's the funniest thing I've ever heard you say," Quigley said as he made his way to the doorway, staying in the cave all the while. "Can you hear the voices? They call to you already don't they? They will get louder, I promise. Ha, funny, not a monster, I hate to tell you this, but you've been a monster for years now. You do hear them don't you?"

"The voices? Yes, I do hear them." I replied quickly. "How did you know I hear them? Just what do you mean they'll get louder? How do I shut them up?"

"Well," He laughed. "As you'll soon find out, the voices grow louder with each passing hour, the only way to get them out of your head, is to destroy them. You'll find out here in a little while that the louder the voices get in your head, the more you can't focus or function. If you're not quick about things, you just may go insane. Now listen to me carefully Maria, this is what you were created to do, give birth to Darius, which gives me my new body, then you destroy all vampires on earth after my Rebirth. You've done this many, many times and you're going to do it in the future, as well as now. Unfortunitely you just won't remember this conversation when you're reborn, you don't get to keep your memories, which is why you can't remember doing anything like this before, yet, you know I speak the truth. By the way, you're really good at this, I'd say you're actually the master, that is, once you finally finish becoming the beast inside of you."

"I don't want to be your monster anymore Quigley!" I shouted. "You say I've done this many times, yet I don't have a choice in the matter, now do I? You programmed me to hear these voices, what a horrible thing to do to someone. It would've been nice if I had a choice, nobody ever seems to care about what I really think, or want. Now I have to kill people to get their voices out of my head, I never wanted to have to hurt anyone again. With the amount of unicorn blood we've extracted, plus with the almost five million gallons of wine we have stored, once we mix them together, they'll be enough to never have to feed on humans again."

"See now, I figured you'd go all nicey, nice on me," he replied. "That's exactly why I made sure you'd hear the voices like you do, let's see how nice you'll become once the volume really turns up. There's only one person responsible for the voice's though, every different voice you hear all comes from the same person, they just happen all at once. Every sight you've seen, every sound you hear, just one person's mind is infecting yours. These are every hateful thing they ever said about you, how they really feel. Some of these thoughts you may find very interesting, even already know, or suspect, I think you know who this person is already to be honest."

"Oh great!" I spoke out. "You mean this gets louder? It's pretty loud the way it is right now, I don't even want to think about the volume turning up, I can barely hear myself think the way it is.

I really have no idea who your talking about though, I don't recognize the voice."

"Oh, goody," Quigley giggled. "It's started then, think Maria, think, you'll figure out who's the voice, but you haven't much time before it gets to loud to bare, you guys should get going, maybe setup some kind of game plan for some serious mass killings. I know what I would do first, let's see if you guys can figure it out. I think Maria will though, she's pretty intelligent now, sometimes though, well, sometimes, Jupiter, you know this, she can be so stupid! Nice to see the smarter version of you finally back, the other you was fun though, be nice to see the two of you finally get together. As a wise man once said, let's get this *party* started."

With that said, Quigley walked away from the cell door, towards Darius. I stood there for a few moments before finally walking away from the door, as for some reason, I wasn't floating like normal. In fact, I didn't feel very powerful, or quite like the master vampire I once was at all.

"We should take Quigley's advice," I suddenly spoke out.

"Let's go up into the castle, and gather up his virus. We can go to different area's, contaminating all bloodwine, as well as all bagged blood, I think Quigley's saying we should through a huge party, everywhere. Thousands of vampires rely on the bags to feed on, we'll give them a special batch. We should go to Paris, DEP, as well as the island, and contaminate everything there as well. Maybe invite everyone we know, to invite everyone they know, to the island for a huge unicorn bloodwine festival, all you can drink of course."

"Guess that's a good start," Jupiter said as he looked at me. "You have a good idea, we can get rid of many people without even confronting them, I think the voices in your head will grow silent much quicker that way."

"Well gentlemen," I said with a grin. "Lead the way and as Quigley just said, let's get this party started."

With that said, Von, Jupiter, and myself began heading up the long path on the side of the mountain, moving all kinds of branches, and debris out of our way the entire time. Von could've just transported us, but I think he knew I was to proud for any of that, as he didn't even offer. This was an old trail, not used by many people, but finally, upon reaching the top, stepping through the last of the brambles, there it stood, Lars' former castle.

CHAPTER 5

"It's been a long time since I've been inside this place," Von spoke out as we walked through the gated entryway of Lars' old castle. "The walls never looked like this back in the day, a far cry from what this castle once looked like. It used to be the most beautiful castle around, it never looked like it aged one day, now look at it. It's completely falling apart everywhere you look, the rocks even look filthy."

We all stopped walking, looking at the beginnings of a very sad ruin. The walls, crumbling, with chunks of rocks littering the gates ground everywhere, the walls themselves were covered in vines, which grew literally everywhere, the rock looking old, as if becoming dirty with time very quickly, dark grey in color, instead of the bright light grey I was accustomed too. The arched gates were cracking, missing pieces in the middle, with it looking like the rest of it may just fall to the ground soon as well.

The castle itself looked as if it aged 300 years overnight. The once beautiful circular towers were missing pieces as well, with one tower already halfway collapsed into itself, the other ones missing their roofs, looking like they could collapse at any moment. The stone roadway all around the castle was buckling everywhere from tree roots popping up, weeds grew through any and every crack possible between the square stone pieces, they grew everywhere in fact, with hardly any path even left for us to walk on.

"I can't believe how much this place has aged," I spoke out. "This was the most beautiful site I'd ever seen at one point in my life, I'm sorry to see it like this."

"Yeah," Von replied with a sigh. "It pains me to see it like this, I have many fond memories of coming here, I was always excited to see the place, now I just want to hurry, so we can just leave, I'd rather remember it the way it was."

"I wonder why it looks so bad?" Jupiter asked curiously. "Was there some kind of magic holding the place together or something?"

"Actually Jupiter," Von said informatively. "Yes there was! Lars used his powers to keep this place together, now it looks just like it did when we first got here. See, he was more powerful than he let on, when we arrived here, he instantly fell in love with it, using his powers to restore it to it's former glory. *Many* people knew that Lars held an entire castle together with his powers, which is why so many feared him. Fearing him so much that they abided by the laws he set. This place used to be a symbol of his power, now that he's gone, I can fully understand why he kept the place so perfect all the time. I never wanted to see it look like this again, but there's many things I didn't want."

"Lars held the castle together with his powers?" I asked curiously. "I had no idea he was so strong, he felt so weak to me, I knew I could beat him, and I did."

"Not really Maria," Von announced. "Actually, Lars wasn't *allowed* to kill you, his instructions were to get you to kill him. I was to assist him in this endevour, which I did. It was all planned out from the beggining, your changing, the trip to Paris so you could feed and of course, your killing the master. This is all Quigley's doing, he's always been the person pulling the strings around here. He wanted us to make you think you were going to die, this was supposed to make your instincts kick in, instincts he implanted in your DNA. They kicked in just like he said they would, with you drinking the blood of Lars, which was just what he wanted you to do. If you remember, once you drank from Lars, the evil thoughts began filling your head even more, besides your powers increasing ten fold. Usually you don't get to drink from vampires until after Quigley's reborn, but this time around, Quigley said it was imperative that you fed from Lars within twenty four hours after being changed."

"Why was this all planned out for me like this?" I asked

sadly. "My life, everything about it, I mean, I didn't really have a life now did I? Everything seems to have already been mapped out for me and I did everything like clockwork. Do I really love Jupiter, or is that just part of the show?"

"Oh, I'm sure you love him for real," Von replied with a grin. "After all, you're kind of programmed for him, he's in your DNA as well. From what I understand, you guys always are the parents of Darius, plus, I bet you guys still can't keep your hands off each other now can you?"

"You got me there," I laughed. "But in my defense, Jupiter usually starts it.

"That I do," Jupiter perked up, quickly joining in on the conversation, as a smiled soon crossed his face. "But I never start anything I can't finish."

With that said, after walking another thirty feet or so, we came to the huge double doors of the castle, Even these majestic beauties were looking bad. as the wood itself had a big crack in both of them, stretching all the way from the ground, to the top of them, some twenty feet up in the air. Pulling them open wasn't easy either, as Jupiter had to slightly pick one side up , with it still partially touching the ground, scrapping a line in the ground as he pulled it open. As we entered the castle. The first thing I noticed was that a large piece of the very high ceiling had come crashing down to the ground, shattering into a million pieces, debris littering the floor everywhere. I could even see a small part of the nights sky in a few different places, shinning through brightly in the ceilings exposed areas.

The once beautiful double staircase leading upstairs in the center of the castle, now only had one side still intact, with many steps missing, as the other side had collapsed and lay in a pile on the floor.

"Alright," Von spoke out. "I'm sure you guys would like a change of clothes, you still have outfits hanging in your closets in your old rooms, I made sure to not have them removed for just such an occasion. I'll head down to the lab and retrieve what we need, go ahead and take care of yourselves."

Jupiter and I took a look at each other, quickly taking Von's advice as we both headed to our old rooms. It had been a long time since we last walked down this hallway, It used to be an amazing walk, but now it had a really creepy feeling to it. As we rounded the corridor, our room doors were in sight. We got to my door first, but I even didn't enter, that is, until I watched Jupiter walk away, going into his room first. I don't know what it is, but, even after all these years, I always have to catch at least a glimpse of his butt, after all, it was such a cute one.

I stood there for a moment, hesitant to open the door I knew the place would be a wreck, I wasn't sure if I wanted to even see it. I wanted to remember the room the way it was, when it was magnificent. Finally after what seemed like an hour, I opened the door quickly looking inside. To my amazement, the room looked untouched, as if it had been cleaned just today, it even had that certain clean smell it always had, even the jaquzzi was on, bubbling away.

I just stood there, spinning slowly in a circle, taking it all in. I couldn't believe the place looked so spectacular, I really expected to see a ruin of a bedroom, something that would've ruined the memory I had forever, this was the last thing I expected to see.

"Holy crap!" Jupiter belted out as he entered the room, carrying a new outfit and shoes. "How did you do this? My room looked like shit! This place looks amazing. We had some fun times in that jaquzzi over there huh?"

"Fun times," I laughed. "How about one fun time, you found every excuse in the book to not have a round two, made me feel like you rejected me because you didn't enjoy the jaquzzi as much as I did that night. I didn't do this to the room though, it was already like this when I came in. I don't remember there being a big heart hanging over the jaquzzi like there is right now, but, other than that, it looks exactly the way I remembered and hoped it would look."

"Hmm," Jupiter replied. "If you wanted it to look this way, maybe you did do this after all. Only you would hang a heart over the jaquzzi like that, Lars was able to make this castle look awesome, maybe you have that power as well, only you don't know how to use it yet, could be a power you have as the destroyer."

"I didn't think of that," I said as walked over to the jaquzzi, running my fingers across the top of the jaquzzi's water. It was nice and warm to the touch, inviting would be a better word for it. "If I am doing all this, maybe I can learn how to do the entire castle, like Lars did. I promise you this, if I can do it, I'll restore this place to the way it should be."

"That would be really nice," Jupiter said as he brushed his hand slightly on my thigh. "I know what else would be nice right now."

"I swear," I said as I began laughing my sexy come get me laugh. "That's all you think about."

"You too!" Jupiter snapped back. "Now don't tell me that seeing this jaquzzi again, feeling it's warm waters, thinking of what happened in it long ago, doesn't kind of turn you on."

"Well," I hesitated. "Maybe a little."

What he didn't know was how badly I'd always wanted a second round in it, I knew it would be even better now, as I'm a much more experienced woman than I was that night so long ago.

Jupiter grabbed the bottom of his shirt, slowly bringing it up his chiseled stomach, exposing his chest momentarily, before taking it the rest of the way off.

"Hmm," He said seductively. "I don't know about you, but I'm a dirty boy, are you a dirty girl Maria? We should jump in the jaquzzi and take ourselves a little bath."

"You know," I said with a grin. "I guess I could use a bath, so sweetie, are you going to wash my back for me?"

"Oh yes, I plan on washing many things on you," He replied with his sexy, I want sex voice. "I think you'll feel squeaky clean once I'm finished with you."

"Oh really," I laughed. "Well don't forget to wash behind my ears."

"Maria," He snapped back. "I'd never forget your ears, where else do I like to nibble? Okay, don't answer that!"

Jupiter quickly placed his mouth on my ear, gently sucking on it. Flipping his tounge, making me slightly giggle like a school girl. I soon couldn't help myself and began running my hand across his chest. The ripples of his body still excited me, just as the first time I ever touched them, making me want him even more than I already did.

He stopped the ear play, moving his lips to mine, kissing me as passionately as possible, with me rubbing my hands all over his back all the while.

"That's it woman," Jupiter said as he quickly moved away from me. "You're dirty, I'm dirty, we're getting clean."

Suddenly, and without warning, he wrapped his big arms around me, picking me up off the ground, and in an almost comical fashion, we slid into the tub together, clothes and all.

We landed back first in the water, but, as we quickly went under, Jupiter placed his lips upon mine once again. Lifting us up swiftly, bursting through the surface of the water, as we still embraced in our kiss.

"Oh my goodness, look what I've gone and done," Jupiter spoke out in a playful voice, as we parted from our kiss. "I've gotten you all wet, maybe in more ways than just one, I need to fix that, but first, we should get you out of those wet clothes."

"You're so silly," I giggled as I removed my top. "I love that about you."

"Really now," He replied as he stood up on the bench, removing his pants, exposing his huge pride, jiggling it wildly in my face. "I always thought that you loved this about me."

"Oh, I do," I said as I grabbed ahold of his Johnson, sliding my hand back and forth a few times. "I love this thing, but then again, I love everything about you."

He lowered himself back into the water, straddling my lap, placing his hands on my breasts, my body grew very warm with excitement, as I couldn't help but enjoy his touch a little too much, as it always caused the same reaction in me.

"Like that did you?" He asked with a smile shining brightly on his face. "There's more where that came from."

Jupiter scooped me into his arms, quickly spinning us around to where he was now sitting down. The warm water splashing us in our faces, making us both laugh a little at each other. I suddenly straddled him, as he had done to me moments ago, with one exception. I had his undivided attention still in my hand, which I placed inside of me. We gently got things going, as the water was a little issue for a few moments, but once we got things going, that feeling I always get, began to place me into our own little world once more.

His touch was like magic, his kisses perfect, any move, or thrust he made, placed me into an unexplainable ecstasy. I wrapped my arms around his neck, staring at him, holding on tightly as he began pounding me, harder, faster, over and over, it was wonderful. I started slamming my body just as hard onto his, as I watched his eyes gaze at my chest. It turned me on just knowing what he was staring at. I released my death grip on him, grabbing him by the shoulders, grinding my hips hard against his, causing him to throw his head back in pleasure.

The water splashed out everywhere around the jaquzzi. as it began bubbling wildly, both of us becoming more savage in our actions. The outfit he had brought was laying in a pool of water on the floor next to the jaquzzi, but it really didn't matter to him right now, nor to me.

"Damn," Jupiter moaned out, as he slowed down his speed. "You really turn me on."

"Funny," I said as I continued to grind away. "I was just thinking the same thing about you."

Suddenly , he grabbed ahold of my sides, spinning us around, placing me on the bench, with my butt on it and my back against the side of the jaquzzi. Hard thrusts began to follow, with each one taking me to my breaking point. Ever so quickly he picked me up under my knee's, placing my legs comfortably against my body, suddenly getting even deeper than before.

"OH GOD YES!" I screamed out in pleasure, not caring that my knees were almost hitting my face. "HARDER!"

He didn't hesitate to follow my instructions, as he was taking me to a new level he'd never taken me to before. He began slamming his body into me just as I asked him to, as he did, with every thrust, I began having multiple orgasms, wrapping my arms around his back, pulling him in closer all the while.

He began grinding at me, like I did him, this was too much for me to handle and I started shaking uncontrollably, as wave after wave flushed throughout my entire body. This was just to much for him to handle anymore, and with one last powerful thrust, he let out the weirdest sounding moan, which almost made me laugh, as I could feel the throbbing and sudden heat of him exploding inside of me.

We held each other for quite a few moments, neither one of us wanted this moment to end, but after once the water settled down to its normal bubbling motion, we released our grips on each other. I always hate that feeling when he pulls out of me, but that's exactly what he did next.

"Oh wow," Jupiter spoke out as he plopped down onto the bench right next to me. "I don't know about you, but I thought that was fantastic."

"I agree," I replied with a grin. "I really liked that, but then again, I always love what you do to me, you keep me guessing, that's for sure, never a boring moment."

"Well, like I've always been told," He said with a smile. "Never play all your aces, keep a few under your sleave."

We kissed once more, before we both decided our little quicky was over, Von was probably starting to get worried and would probably look for us soon.

There were no towels around for some reason, so I just started getting dressed while I was still wet. Jupiter on the other hand, looking at the ground at his soaked clothing, suddenly smiled at me and briskly walked naked to his room. I had to get away from all the water on the floor, so I went into the living area to dress. It didn't take very long before I shook all the water out of my hair, it may have still been a little damp, but it snapped back to it's perfectly combed self pretty quickly.

Jupiter didn't take very long in finding a new dry outfit to wear, he looked pretty good as well, more like the Jupiter I remember, before he started dressing like a librarian. He had on a black tux, if I didn't know better I'd say it was the same tux he wore that night long ago in Paris, only thing different was there were no snazzy colors, just a simple black and white tux, like you'd see at a prom.

"I decided to tone it down a tad this time," Jupiter spoke out as he leaned against the wall. "Been a long time since I last wore this tux, do you recognize it at all?"

"Why yes I do," I said happily. "That's the tux you wore in Paris, on our little date night. That's the night I totally fell for you, just knowing how you defended my honor, made me see a much different side of you, a loving side, one that would defend me no matter what. I knew from that day on that I could always trust you, I'm so happy to see you wear that old thing again, brings back some good memories, that's for sure."

"Well I'm glad you like it," He replied. "You know, I still look good in this."

"That you do hunny," I said with a proud smile on my face. "You know, Quigley did tell us to get this party started, so maybe I should put on a nice party dress, together, we can have a ball."

I ran to the bedroom, making my way to the closet, quickly entering it. After going through all the clothes in there, I picked out a nice Turquoise dress with ruffles on it, fit to wear to any ball, especially the one we were about to throw. I found some matching tennis shoes, which looked odd, but still kind of neat since they matched my dress perfectly. Making my way back to Jupiter upon dressing, he stared at me in awe, like we'd never seen each other dressed up before.

"Maria," He said with a smile. "You look stunning, I love those shoes!"

"Why thank you," I said as I grabbed his hand, pulling him into the hallway. "We should be getting back to Von now, don't you think."

"No need for that!" Von suddenly said as he rounded the corridor. "I figured you two would take forever, so I've taken the liberty of coming to you. I found exactly what we were looking for as well. I have everything downstairs. I made sure to grab plenty of your blood, you should drink it now."

"I'll think about it," I replied. "For now I just want to get our supplies and get going, I have a feeling Jasmine will be going to the island soon, she's in Paris right now as we speak, she's in a fight with Pierce, I can feel it. We need to get to DEP and the island as soon as possible."

"You say she's in Paris?" Jupiter quickly asked. "Then that's where I need to go right now, I have to contaminate that blood supply before she instructs everyone to come with her. Plus, Pierce is my friend, if he's in danger, then I want to try to help him."

"Not a good idea my friend," Von replied. "I don't think you'd like the outcome, anyway, we need to be stealthy about this, if you go banging your drums, you could ruin what we're trying to do here. Be mellow fellow, just add three drops into the processing unit, the disease gets into the filter, transfering microscopic particals into all of the blood supply. The directions Quigley left said that one drop will treat ten thousand gallons, so three will be overkill, but at least this way we can make sure it's all contaminated really well."

"Alright then, "Maria said as she began hurrying down to the main lobby of the castle, carefully stepping over all the chunks of rock littering the floor. "We need to get a move on, Jupiter, like Von says, keep things secret, I'm not very strong right now, the last thing I want to see right now is Jasmine, Von, I'll drop you off at DEP, you can contaminate everything there, inviting everyone to a party at the island, but at least the stragglers that stay behind can enjoy the festivities as well. I'm going to go to the island, I'm going to make a huge new batch of bloodwine, making sure every last bottle is contaminated with our little secret."

Making our way into the main lobby, we were all surprised to see Thomas hunched over our stuff, holding the virus container in his hands, looking at it all weird like.

"WHAT ARE YOU DOING!" Jupiter yelled out at him. "Put that down."

"HOLY CRAP MAN!" Thomas screamed out in fear as he turned into our direction, making immediate eye contact on Maria. "I'm sorry, I didn't know this was your stuff, I was just looking at it, please don't destroy me destroyer, not yet, please."

"Hey!" Von spoke out, his eyes glaring at Thomas. "I thought you were helping Jasmine, maybe that's what you're trying to do right now huh? Why do you have that container in your hands? I wouldn't trust this one Maria."

"Really? Helping Jasmine, I think not! Now get up Thomas," I replied as I came up with a good way to deal with him. "I'm not going to destroy you, you'll destroy yourself in due time, nevermind Jasmine, I have a job for you to do. So, I'm happy to say you're coming to the island with me, we're going to have some fun you and I."

"What?" Thomas replied with a terrified look on his face, as he quickly handed over the container which held the virus. "Here, take it, I don't want it! I'm sorry, I'm sorry! Don't take me back to that place, anything but that, you're going to hunt me again aren't you?"

"Only if you think you deserve it, do you Thomas?" I said trying to joke with him. "I just wanted you to be the host of a little party we're going to throw."

"A party," Thomas said nervously. "As long as it's not a dinner party, I don't think I can handle anymore of those. I'm not working for Jasmine though, I promise you that, I just said anything to make sure she'd not kill me. She just got done dropping me off here, I was happy to see her leave. The last party you guys had wasn't quite what I had in mind, so, as long as it's not like the last one, I'll be happy to help you."

I reached out my hands, concentrating on who needed dropped off first, as we stood there, I felt Pierce in dire trouble, then suddenly with no warning, I just couldn't feel his life force anymore, a sudden surge of power entered my body, with me hardly being able to contain the surprise entering me. Pierce was gone, that was for sure now, as I could feel the same power inside of me that I always felt from him. I decided our first stop would be in Paris. As the three of them grabbed my arm I looked at everyone, giving a big smile for all to enjoy, as suddenly behind us, a wormhole appeared with its bright blue and white swirling color. Ever so carefully we walked in, instantly it closed behind us and off to Paris we went.

CHAPTER 6

"Follow me my friends," Jasmine said as Julian and JC walked out of the castle, waving goodbye to Thomas. "Don't worry about him, he'll be just fine, I told him exactly what to do, we'll see him on the island soon enough, that is once we can finally go there. We need to get a move on, I think we'll start by going to Paris. I have so much on my plate right now, I could just explode."

"I still can't believe Maria is the beast everyone spoke about," Julian replied. "I'm not going to lie, if I hadn't seen it through your thoughts, I never would've guessed it."

"Well, yes," Jasmine replied sarcastically, "She's the beast, believe it! Now as I was saying, I think we'll go pay a couple friends of mine in Paris a visit, they won't be expecting to see their old friend Julian tonight, but they might be expecting to see me, we could use their help in putting together a little party I want to have."

"A party? Really? Are you referring to Johnson and Pierce?" Julian asked confused. "If so, I don't see how they can help. I haven't seen them in years, I'd love to catch up with them on everything, but I don't see how they can help."

"Yeah, yeah, whatever," Jasmine said as she looked in the direction of the mountain in the distance. "Well, we need to get going, I have much to do before dealing with Maria, or Jupiter, as I feel they're no longer in the cell."

Reaching her hand into her pocket and after quite a few moments of digging around in it, Jasmine soon knew for sure that she no longer had possesion of the key anymore.

"It must've returned to it's spot," Jasmine spoke out as she turned, facing JC and Julian. "We won't have much time at all now, let's go, Maria has the key by now and yes, you better hang on tight."

Jasmine reached out her hand, with Julian and JC walking to it, grabbing hold tightly, instantly they were spinning in her wormhole, which upon stopping this stomach turning ride, they were directly in front of the blood center in Paris. Their timing was perfect, as Pierce had just pulled up to the center in the limo to drop off Johnson.

"Hello boys," Jasmine spoke out suddenly as they both were exiting the limo. "Beautiful night we're having huh?"

"Jasmine!" Pierce said surprised. "And what do we owe this pleasure too? I take it you have some kind of detail you'd like us to work out for you?"

"Why yes," She exclaimed. "That would be wonderful, see I want to have a really large get together on the island tomorrow night, I was hoping you two might assist me with that."

"Do we really have a choice in the matter?" Johnson said as he closed his door. "I sense you're becoming hostile right now, your emotions are very off beat as well, somethings different about you, just can't put my finger on it, are you pregnant?"

"Not yet," She laughed. "Maybe sometime soon though, I'm glad you care so much about me. Let's not talk about my mood though, I've had a really long day here."

"Just what is it that you want Jasmine," Pierce asked with distain in his voice. "What kind of party could you be throwing."

"Oh, I'm going to throw the best party we've ever had, it'll be to die for," Jasmine replied with a grin. "So how about it guys? Would you help me get the word around? I'll make it worth your while."

"To be honest Jasmine," Pierce said, replying just as she hoped he would." I wouldn't help you even if my life depended on it. Do you forget I have the power to read and see everything in your mind? I even know you're thinking about killing me right now as well. Why don't you tell Johnson here how you plan on using this party to take the actual essence from everyone, including Johnson and I. To take someones essence will forever trap them inside of your soul, this is a horrible existence for anyone to have to deal with. It would be like an eternal prison to anyone inside of you, please don't do that to anyone. Seeing inside of your mind is enlightening, I now fully understand why your mood is so erratic, you're pregnant wether you think so or not, plus this baby shouldn't be born in the first place. I'm sorry this has happened to you, but even you believe that Quigley has to bring the baby to life, stealing people's essence to gather Quigley's energy won't work out, you know this is a bad idea so why even try this plan of yours? It won't work and you know it already, don't trap people inside of you. You'll pay a price for your actions, even you understand this.”

“SHUT UP!” Jasmine yelled out. “YOU KNOW NOTHING!”

“I'm sorry to say it to you like that Jasmine,” Pierce spoke out softly. “I wasn't trying to offend you, but I won't help you do this to anyone.”

“Offend me?” Jasmine said, as she suddenly began laughing. “Really now Pierce, you always were so proper, you didn't offend me, not at all, you infuriated me.”

Suddenly and without warning Jasmine threw some kind of electrical blast into Pierce's chest, stopping after just the one blast, giving him time to get back to his feet.

“Ahh, that didn't feel very good,” Pierce said as he looked at

Jasmine confused. "I'm sorry Jasmine, you're right, I deserved that, I'll help spread the word of your party."

"You had your chance," Jasmine replied as she used her powers to flip the limo on top of him. "I think you'll say about anything right now, but if you can still read my mind while your trying to get that car off you, then you know, if I were you, I'd be saying just about anything to me as well, but it really won't make a difference now will it? You know what I plan on doing to you tonight, huh my little experiment?"

"NOOOOOOO!" Pierce yelled as he threw the car off of him, quickly getting to his feet. "You won't do that to me!"

Pierce went on the attack, using his powers to control the earth around him, forming a large hole under Jasmine, who quickly fell in, not even trying to escape the earths grasp on her, as he closed the hole back together, trapping her in the ground, just her head still exposed.

"I think that will hold you for awhile," Pierce spoke out smugly. "At least long enough for me to disappear, take care

Jasmine."

"Bravo," Jasmine replied, as the dirt imprisoning her suddenly exploded from around her, with her instantly hovering out of the ground. "Now, as you were saying?"

"Look Jasmine," He spoke out nervously. "I don't want any problems with you, you're far more powerful than I am, I know this, I've always known it. I don't want to help you, but you don't have to make me into your test victim, there's no need for that. You already know there's no need to even try it."

"Sorry buddy, as they say, you never know until you try." Jasmine replied as a smile crossed her face. "I'll end this quick for you."

With that said, Jasmine once again hit him with an electrical blast, this one even harder than the first. Pierce rolled on the ground, trying to escape it, but to no avail. Thinking quickly, he used his powers to throw the limo at Jasmine, who so easily used her powers to reverse the limo's direction, right back at him.

The limo slammed into Pierce with a horrendous thud, with

Pierce flying across the parking lot, slamming back first into the concrete statue of Lars, which stood in the middle of the blood centers sidewalk, just past the entryway.

Pierce slowly got back to his feet, using every bit of his power, he zip sped at Jasmine, with the intention of knocking her out with the hardest punch he could throw. To his surprise, she sensed everything, simply stepping to the side of his punch before he ever even threw it. Hitting him instead with an uppercut so hard, that the shockwaves from it made Johnson stumble backwards a little, as he was trying to stay completely out of the fight.

Pierce flew backwards, his eyes rolling into the back of his head, as he once again slammed into the statue of Lars. Pierce was groggy, it became really hard for him to concentrate, but he managed to get back to his feet one last time before Jasmine did the unthinkable. Zipping over to him, she immediately threw her hand up at Pierce's chest, as she suddenly began gathering his essence. Pierce began screaming, and shaking violently, falling upon the ground. Jasmine hovered over him, making sure to keep her hand in place.

"NOOOOOO!" He begged. "STOOOOOP!"

"There's no rest for the wicked baby," Jasmine replied. "Sorry about this, but I wanted Johnson to be able to tell Jupiter what I'd done to you, I'm sure he'll be coming here soon to recruit Maria's little army, she's so predictable that girl, not very bright but predictable."

Once again, she concentrated on Pierce's essence, and after a few final blood curdling screams, a blue orb began rising out from his his chest, the look of terror filled his eye's, as he let out one last desperate cry.

"PLEASE!" He screamed to no avail, as Jasmine pulled the orb the rest of the way out of him, you could see the life leave his eyes instantly.

"Oh my god!" Johnson screamed out. "What have you done? What is that you're holding in your hands, no, my friend, why?"

"It's no big deal Johnson," Jasmine said nonchalantly. "I don't plan on doing this to you, at least not tonight, that is until after you inform my friends what I've done, then I may come and get your orb, but we'll see, no promises."

Jasmine stood there for a moment looking at Johnson, before directing her attention back to her orb. She held it close to her face for a moment, as if looking inside of it. After inspecting her prize, she placed the orb directly outside of her belly, holding it there for a moment before pushing it slowly inside of her lower abdomen area, with her body quickly absorbing it.

Jasmine couldn't help but to let out a little giggle, as instantly inside of her belly, she felt a small flutter, it felt like a butterfly in some kind of liquid, or gel, but she knew what it really was, it was the first time she's ever gotten to feel a baby kick. Pierce's essence must've had enough power to get the baby started in it's growth. She knew now that her plan was going to work, as she just felt it work only a moment ago. Her mind quickly went to the what if's, one of the first thoughts were, what if people don't show up to the party, then what? She had Julian and JC, so she could absorb theirs, but what if she needed many essences, saving them for later seemed like the only choice. Jasmine turned to Johnson with a sour look on her face, she was going to make sure he obeyed her.

"Alright," She spoke out. "Unless you want to be next here, I'd suggest a simple promise, help me make this the largest party ever, and I'll leave now, but don't disappoint me."

"I promise you Jasmine," Johnson spoke out in a nervous voice. "I promise I'll tell every vampire I know about this party, you said tommorrow night right? Well I think I'd better get on this immediately, I have so many calls and e-mails to send out it's unreal."

"Good boy," Jasmine said with a smile. "I'm glad you see things my way. Now there, wasn't that easy to do? I didn't come here to hear Pierce's mouth, I came to ask you guys to do a job for me, he just took things too far, I needed to test a theory of mine anyway, so no biggie, I figured no time like the pressence, so any questions?"

"Nope," Johnson replied. "I hear you loud and clear, you can count on me."

"Good," Jasmine said as she turned and faced Julian and JC, who'd just been standing in the distance, far from the action. "Let's go kiddo's, I feel like we just ran out of time and we have much more work to do, not really a whole lot of time to do it."

They hurried over to her, with Jasmine extending her hand out to them, once again, they hung on for dear life, as they went on another disturbing twirling ride, disappearing into the wormhole which immediately appeared in front of them.

CHAPTER 7

We arrived in Paris just a few moments after leaving the castle, just outside of the blood center. As we were coming out of the wormhole, I couldn't help but notice the limo Pierce usually drove, the thing was upside down, all smashed up looking, leaning up against the entrace of the center.

"Back so soon?" Johnson, who's back was to us, suddenly spoke as he started turning in our direction. "You just left, come back for me already?"

"What are you talking about?" I said curiously. "We just got here, I thought you'd be happy to see us."

"Oh, Maria, Jupiter, Von," Johnson said surprised as he finished facing us. "I thought you guys were Jasmine, she just left like a second ago."

"Jasmine was already here?" Von asked quickly. "Maria, we should get going very soon, I have an idea as to where she's headed next. Wow though! I must say your powers have increased substantially, I can't feel you at all now, how'd you do that?"

"I have an answer to that," I replied. "First though, I think we should find out what she was doing here in the first place, Johnson, what all happened here tonight? What all did she say?"

"To be honest," Johnson replied. "She seemed a little off, really moody, Pierce said she was pregnant, then after getting madder than she already was, she killed him, he really didn't do anything to deserve quite the severe treatment he recieved. He's not really dead though, he's trapped inside of her, she extracted his essence from him. It came out of him as a blue orb, about the size of a softball, maybe just a little larger than that, but anyway, you get what I mean. She absorbed the orb into her belly, then laughed for a moment, before asking me if I wanted to be next. So instead of being absorbed by her, I promised to help get as many vampires to the island for a party she wants to throw. I believe this party is only going to be an essence festival for Jasmine, as Pierce confirmed that prior to his demise."

"She plans on absorbing more people's essence?" Jupiter spoke out confused. "What can she gain by doing that?"

"She thinks it will bring her baby to life, as it actually could," Von answered. "Each little essence orb is a very small part of Quigley's magic, if she absorbs enough of these orbs, she just might be able to get what she wishes."

"This would be a bad thing?" I asked confused. "Think about it, with her absorbing people, it'll make my job much easier. Plus, why shouldn't she be able to have a baby? I think most women dream of the day they'll become a mother, Jasmine should be able to have that dream as well, what's so wrong with that?"

"Maria," Von replied. "Every essence Jasmine puts inside of her, traps that person in her forever. I know we're to kill everyone, but when we do it, they get released to be reborn into a new and exciting life, when she does it, they are prisoners inside of her. Regardless of the fact that everyone's getting destroyed, there is a right and wrong way of doing things."

Suddenly, once again, a new surge of energy entered into my body, causing me to take a step backward slightly.

"Are you alright?" Jupiter spoke out as he held onto me, keeping me steady on my feet. "Maria? You okay?"

"I'm, I'm fine, thank you," I replied as I collected myself, once again feeling stronger than I did after the little episode. "I think Jasmine is staying busy, she just killed someone else. Not sure who though, I don't recognize the enegry, must've been someone I'd never met before. By the way, the more energy that comes to me, the more my own body automactically masks my energy level, this is why you can't feel me."

"That's freaky," Thomas who'd been standing back from

everyone suddenly jumped in. "You mean you can feel people's energy? I can't feel people's energy, I only feel heat from you guys."

"You can't feel me or Von?" Jupiter asked him. "That's odd."

"Nope," Thomas replied. "Like I said, all I feel is heat from everyone, some of you are hotter than the others, but niether one of you are as hot as Maria is."

"Heat huh?" Von spoke out. "I've never met a vampire that couldn't feel his own kind around him, I've heard of one's like you though. Have you learned what your special power is yet?"

"No, not yet," He replied. "I haven't really had any time to do that, plus, nobody ever explained how to use my powers the right way, I've just been winging things."

"I'm sorry Thomas," I quickly replied. "That's my fault completely. If I hadn't been the person I was, I never would've ignored a new family member such as I did."

"It's alright Maria," He replied with a smile. "To tell you the truth, I've been having some fun with figuring things out. I know that my life as a vampire is going to be somewhat shortlived, so it's fun to learn as I go, but, I really wanted to thank you anyway."

"Thank me?" I said surprised. "Thank me for what?"

"For giving me the best few days of my life," Thomas said happily. "However long a time that may be really doesn't matter. I've lived such a boring life up until now, you have no idea how much I longed for something different. You really can't get anymore different than this now can you? A vampire, I'm a freaking vampire! How cool is that huh? So like I said, my life may not be for much longer, but thank you for the best time I've had while living it. I don't think you really want to kill me though, something tells me you have no choice, I hear voices in your head, all kinds of them, it's really hard to even find you in there at all, so I understand where you're coming from."

"You know, you're really upbeat about this whole thing," I said amazed. "And you're right, I really don't want to kill anyone. So, you can hear the voices in my head as well huh? It's getting pretty loud in there, really starting to bother me, we must kill them all to make the voices go away, but I was told only one person really matters when it came to them. So you're very much right, I don't have a choice in this matter, you of course will be one of the last that will have to die."

"Good enough for me," Thomas said merrily. "You should really let me at least hunt one human though, we're going to the island anyway, can we please pick up a human so I can hunt them down? Please? Come on, you want me to host this party, putting my essence right in Jasmine's reach if she decided to take it. I have no problem doing as you asked me to do, but I've been the hunted before, now I want to now how it feels to be the hunter."

"Alright," I replied. "I can respect that, I know exactly how you feel right now. I'll be dropping you off at the island, but I promise you that I'll do everything in my power to bring back a human for you to play with."

"Oh, for real?" He said with a happy surprised tone. "Oh man, that would be awesome. I want a big burly dude, biker type, someone who doesn't scare very easily, so I can practice scaring the shit out of them. I want to have fun with this whole thing, I've waited a lifetime to be a monster. I mean look at me, even as a vampire, I'm so skinny the wind could blow me down. I've always been picked on, pretty much all of my life, stuffed into lockers in grade school, de-pantsed in the swimming pool in highschool, even hung upside down at the top of my colleges flagpole. So it'll be nice to be the bully for once. Try to find the biggest piece of crap around, I don't want you bringing someone like me or anything, I want a big brute, not a whimpy wannabe."

"You're not such a bad guy," I replied. "In fact, before I met Jupiter, I liked the brainy, nerdy, skinny type of guy. Now that I really think about it, I might actually know of a place where I can find the ideal person for you. I do hope they're there right now, but it could take me a few minutes to get them alone. So don't freak out, you know, start thinking I'm not coming back, I promise you, you'll have your hunt."

Suddenly not one, not two, but three separate energy waves entered my body. It was too much going into me all at once, and a powerful blast wave came exploding out of me, causing the four of them to fly backwards, away from me, hurdling them around a hundred foot or so. Once this happened, I was able to regain control of myself, the power inside of me was far from the power I once had, but at this rate, I could become even more powerful than I was before.

"You need to warn us before you do that kind of crap!" Von spoke out as he stood back up, dusting himself off all the while. "Give everyone a thumbs up or something, but at least some kind of hint before blasting the crap out of us like that again."

"I'm sorry," I replied quickly. "I didn't mean to do that, I couldn't stop it, it just kind of came out."

"It's no different than your first drink from a human," Jupiter quickly spoke out. "Or when you had to hold in the power after you fed from another vampire? You can hold it in, or like Von said, at least warn us."

"Look," I said sarcastically. "I already said I'm sorry, I wasn't expecting three people to die at once, that's what happened guys,

Jasmine just killed three more people, I wasn't ready to take in that many at once, I will be in the future though, I'm ready right now for more energy, so see, it won't happen again."

"I'm sorry I got mad at you hunny," Jupiter spoke out as I held up my hands for Von and Thomas to grab onto. "I'll get what needs done, done here, I'll meet you at our favorite restaurant, once you finish doing what you need to do. It's not like I can travel anywhere in the world like you, so you'll have to make sure you come back to get me. I'll see you real soon though."

"See you soon," I said as both Von and Thomas grabbed ahold of my arms. "Make sure you leave a few clean bottles for Johnson to drink, we don't want him parting before his time."

With that said, once again, our wormhole emerged, with us whirling and churning away, destination DEP.

CHAPTER 8

"Alright Darius," Quigley spoke out. "I don't think standing at the doorway is going to make your parents come back any quicker. Come over here, sit by the fire, I'll tell you a little story."

"I'm not interested in your stories right now," Darius replied sarcastically. "I'd really like to know how my parents are right now, I have no powers in here, so I can't feel them at all."

"Oh mommy, oh daddy, are you okay?" Quigley snickered. "Come on now Darius, have a little faith in your parents, just wait, once your mother drinks her own blood, you're going to know it, I promise."

"Why couldn't I help them?" Darius asked confused. "You said something about a job for me to do, just what is it?"

"Well before I tell you that, I do believe I said I'd tell you a story," Quigley replied with a grin. "Now, if you want to see how your parents are doing, sit back and listen. I think you'll get a kick out of this one."

"Alright," Darius said as he walked to the fire, sitting Indian style on the floor in front of him. "I hope this isn't a long story though, I really want to know how things are going with them. Plus, if you push me to hard, I just may have to beat things out of you, we're both powerless in here, but I know how to fight, do you?"

"Alright, now where to begin," Quigley stammered, as he ran his hand across his chin. "There was once a man named Darius the Turd Eater, he ate so many turds, crap began to spill out of his mouth. Kind of like the crap you just tried to feed me there turd boy. You forget I used to live inside of you, without your powers, you couldn't beat your way out of a wet paperbag, so your idol threats are heard, but, my stories last as long as it takes to tell them."

"Alright, alright," Darius replied visibly upset. "Let's get this over with already, don't be telling me what color shoes people wore, or anything like that either, just stick to the story."

"Now what fun would that be?" Quigley laughed. "See, there

was once this man, he wore *green* tennis shoes. He liked the ladies, but only a few of them ever gave him the time of day. See this guy was kind of an asshole, a big one at that, he insulted people just for the fun of it. He grew up a normal kid, even went to college, but he seemed to always end up making people mad at him. Well this *green* shoe wearing, asshole of a man, actually found four women that dug his shoes enough, that three of them married the guy, with the fourth one being just a one night stand, while the guy was away on business in another state. Well, the one night stand was just a week before the guy got married for the first time, so of course, he didn't bother to mention that to his soon to be wife. Well this little booty call created a child, but the man and his new wife just found out that they were going to have triplet girls. The man actually had no idea of the little boy that he fathered, he couldn't even remember the woman's name that he slept with, every child he had after the boy were all girls."

"So this guy had ten girls?" Darius laughed. "I hope they don't all like to go shopping at the same time."

"Shut up, you dirty turdy," Quigley snapped. "I wasn't finished yet. So anyway, like I was saying, this guy had no idea he had a little boy, actually, nobody knew about him. This was a good thing, as one horrific night, all ten of the girls were killed by a crazy thinking psyco. Even the man himself was hunted down and after a long evening with his killer, he himself was destroyed. Now like I said, nobody knew about his bastard boy, so he was safe from the wrath that his sisters met. What the boy didn't know was that his father, as well as himself carried a very important bloodline inside of them, royalty would be the only way to explain it. Well when this boy finally tries to claim his throne, he wasn't met with smiles and handshakes, instead, as he tried to claim his rightful throne, he was savagely attacked, almost to a critical point. The attacker thought he'd hit him good enough to kill him with just the one blow, but to his surprise, when he turned around to look at his dead victim, his victim wasn't dead, he was in fact very close to taking the throne. Well the attacker couldn't let him take his rightful place as lord and keeper, the attacker had grown fond of this title, which was basically just given to him, but he wore the title proudly. He sprung at the young prince once more, this time making sure to attack with everything he had. Now this is where you come in Darius."

"Me?" Darius asked surprised. "What kind of story is this? One that you're making up as you go? I've never been around any princes in my life."

"I know," Quigley laughed. "But you will be. See Darius, I can't help with this one, I create the show, but I can't change the channel, you're the remote control I need."

"What are you talking about dude?" Darius asked curiously "You lost me back there somewhere."

"Alright, from turd head back to bicycle boy," Quigley snickered. "I have to spell things out for you way too much, have you fell on your head lately or something? You seemed smarter when you had your powers. Now, as I was saying, you *will* meet a prince in your lifetime, in fact, you'll meet him in a little over thirteen hours, don't worry about Jasmine feeling your powers either, I got that one covered. You, Darius, are going to save this prince from the attacker of the story, I just can't let you go help him until the exact moment his attacker lunges at him. You can't be the one to defeat the attacker either, only the prince will do that, so only minimal help is allowed by you. Just throw the attacker around or something, don't punch or use your powers on the guy, you're much to powerful for that, plus like I said, only the prince is to defeat the attacker. The Prince's name is Stain Casey, he's named after his father. Promise me you'll do this and we'll go into Nod right now, I'll show you what you'd like to see."

"Doesn't seem like I have much of a choice here if I want to see how my parents are," Darius said sarcastically. "So yeah, I'll do as you ask, just show me what I want to know."

"Alrighty then, it's done." Quigley said with an evil grin, as he threw his hand up in the air, opening up the door to Nod. "After you."

"I thought you lost your powers like we did when you were in this cave?" Darius asked inquisitively. "Have you had them all along?"

"Of course I have my powers," he laughed. "Everyone seems to think that just because *they* have no powers in here that *I* don't either. Well, okay, maybe I lie to people and convince them I have no power in here, but it's all in the name of the game, fun times huh?"

"You were inside of me in this cave," Darius replied in almost a yell. "I didn't feel any power from you once we entered, there's no way you could've hid that from me, I just don't understand."

"It's easy dum dum," He laughed. "How do you know I didn't erase your memories as they happened, implanting you with new ones, more memorable ones, ones where you didn't feel my powers."

"Huh?" Darius stammered. "You can do that?"

"I can do many things my boy," Quigley laughed yet once again. "I'm the conductor on this train, your mom never got to see me driving the Quigley Express, which believe me is a good thing.

You just don't want to know, she thought it was a sexual thing, long story, but very funny."

"Knowing you, I'm sure it is, believe me, I really don't want to know," Darius joked back. "You're a sick puppy sometimes."

"Yes I am," Quigley laughed as he gave Darius a thumbs up. "I take high pride in myself for some of the sick actions, or comments I must make, but then again, how much fun would the game be without a little something interesting to get in the way."

"Wow!" Darius suddenly spoke out. "I think I just figured out something about you, without you telling me for once. You say your the conductor, then you call all of this a game, you also speak of conflicts with your something interesting remark, then to top it off, you speak of actions you must make. You're the one that's causing all of this stuff to happen aren't you? You're the master of us all, I bet you already know the outcome of everything as well, I think you're the worlds greatest voyare, sitting back and watching it all play out. The little things you plant grow into much larger things huh?"

"WOW!" Quigley said in a shocked voice. "You're pretty good, I don't see how in the world you, of all people, would guess things correctly, but congrats. From now on, you'll be known as Einstein instead of bicycle boy, dirty turdy, fart snorter, or any of the other awesome names I had planned for you. Believe me, a lot of time went into picking out snazzy names for you, I had everything all planned out too, what a shame you grew a piece of a brain. I was looking forward to the whole fart snorter name, I was going to say you got the snorter name, because you liked farts so much you didn't sniff them, you snorted them out of the air, like invisable cocaine, my joke would've been awesome, good job Einstein, thanks for ruining it."

"I knew it," Darius spoke out triumphantly. "You've been controlling everything everybody does as well huh?"

"Of course I do," He laughed histerically. "Who else do you think does it? I don't help people out normally though, usually I just watch everything play out. I've been on this earth for a very long time, I got tired of being bored, so I now make my own drama, it's now a wonderful life, like one big ongoing television show."

"You're a sick man, my brother!" Darius laughed. "I actually understand why you do the things you do better now, you have a brain disorder don't you?"

"Ha," He laughed. "My brain hasn't had any order in it for eons, there must be some kind of order in the first place, for any disorder to emerge."

With that said, Darius finally got off the ground, walking over to where Quigley stood.

"Alright, Let's go into your home away from home," Darius joked once more. "Not like I've haven't already seen it, but if you say there's something in there that can show me how my parents are doing, then I guess I have no choice, now do I?"

"Not really," Quigley said as he looked at the beautiful light purple colored sky of Nod. "I'll take you to the waterfall, show you what you want to see, then will you quit your whining?"

"Probably not, to be honest." Darius said as he patted him on the back. "I know how much you enjoy my whining, so why in the world would I ever stop now?"

"That's the spirit!" Quigley shouted with a huge grin on his face. "You're learning my boy, you're finally learning, I'm so proud of you, my little boy is growing up so fast, it brings tears to my eyes just thinking about it."

"Yeah, yeah, whatever old man," Darius laughed. "Just shut up and lead the way."

They entered into Nod, the door behind them closing as they did, with all of the vines that covered the wall moving slowly back into their natural spots, as the door came to a gentle thud, concealing the doorway slightly. The hill leading to the main path and to the path that would take them to the building they once slept in, where Quigley made his children, was their first obstacle. Quigley quickly headed straight down the hill, past the huge trees that intertwined at their tops, which made a natural arch, making their way slowly to the start of their path, turning to the left, instead of to the right like they did the last time they were in there.

The path was a long one, getting very narrow, to the point of them having to duck down a few times, even crawling under and over quite a few trees that had fallen across the path.

"Hey man," Darius asked loudly. "I thought you said you went to this place all the time, not much of a path here buddy."

"I do!" Quigley chuckled. "Who do you think made this remarkable little path? I find it more fun if it feels like you're lost in a jungle, you have to admit, this place has a jungle kind of feel to it."

"I'd say it's becoming more like a swamp," Darius replied, as his feet sank a few inches into the ground.

"I know," Quigley giggled. "I love this path, it's the nastiest one in Nod. It's such a fun one, it gets harder up here though, we'll have to climb to the middle of that cliff you see up ahead, tall huh? Well, the waterfalls inside of a crevice up there. It's pretty much an easy climb, but try not to fall. Although you can't die in this world, I still don't want you whinning, or freaking out about this little adventure. If you do fall, try to have a good time with it, you'll be in some severe pain after the landing, but hey, live life to its fullest I say."

"Oh great, you've got to be kidding me," Darius said as he moved the last few branches out of his way, entering the clearing, gazing at the three hundred foot cliff, which stood before him. It was pretty much straight up and down, but with many holes in the side of it to grab onto.

"Oh no, I'm not kidding," Quigley giggled as he pointed at it. "You've got to climb this thing to get to that crevice you can see it right there in the middle."

"What do you mean I've got to climb it?" Darius asked. "You're coming with me aren't you?"

"Of course I am," He replied with a huge grin. "I never said I'd climb up though. I'll just hover next to you while you climb, you know, give you someone to talk to while climbing, giving you all kinds of encouragement and moral support. I do have my powers you know, but if you heard me earlier, I already explained, I don't help people very often, so, sorry, you're on your own here."

"Oh, gee, thanks," Darius replied, as the two of them finally made their way to the cliff's wall. "Why don't you just go ahead and go to the crevice, I'll be up there in a little bit."

"Are you kidding?" Quigley stammered. "I wouldn't miss this for the world. I can tell you a story or two while you climb. This is going to be so much fun, it'll be our little bonding time."

"Fantastic," Darius said as he placed his hand into one of the holes on the cliff. "I so look forward to storytime."

Darius placed his left foot into a hole, moving his right foot forward and slowly, but surely, began to climb up the wall. After getting around fifteen feet up the wall, he bagan to find a much better climbing style, as he'd never scaled a wall like this before.

"How ya doing there Sport?" Quigley spoke out, as true to his word, he was hovering his way up the side. "You know, you're about thirty feet up now, you might want to slow down a tad, some of these hand holds are slippery."

"Oh," Darius said sarcastically as he rose even higher. "You don't say, I'll keep that in mind. I think I got this though, piece of cake."

With those words coming out of Darius's mouth, suddenly, without warning, Quigley grabbed hold of his shirt, pulling him slightly backwards, causing him to fall helplessly to the forest floor.

A loud thud could be heard as Darius slammed into the ground, it must've been a hard hit, as a large cloud of dust encircled his body.

"Ow, wow, ow," Darius said as he just laid there on the ground. "What the hell did you do that for? That really hurt you know, I think my back's broken, I can't feel my legs."

"Oh, man, that was classic," Quigley laughed out loud. "You should've seen the look on your face. So, did you have fun with it? I mean, come on, did you like the feelings that went through your head? Do you feel like a new man?"

"I don't know about feeling like a new man, a broke one maybe," He replied. "But as for the horrible pain I feel right now in my body, this I could do without it. Believe it or not, I did have fun with it, but you should fix my broken body now, I know you can do it."

"See, you're no fun," Quigley pouted. "I was going to see if you could climb the wall in your current condition, I think it would've really looked funny, I would've loved to watch it, but as you wish, I'll fix you up."

Instantly, all the broken bones, as well as any pain, disappeared, with Quigley still hovering about fifteen feet above him.

"Alright pokey," Quigley demanded. "Get a move on, we don't have all day, playtime is over."

"Ha, ha," Darius replied, as he got himself off the ground and started climbing the cliff again. "Playtime with you is not at all what it's cracked up to be, I think you're the one having the most fun with it. I know I'm not."

"Oh calm down Beavis," Quigley snickered. "Now how much fun would life be without me in it? I'm a part of not just the lives of us immortals, but I'm a part of the human world as well,

I'm the fun that everyone has, without me life would be boring and dull."

"You're more of a nightmare." Darius joked as he rose higher, closer to his goal.

"Oh come on," Quigley said in an offensive voice. "I'm the fun guy, I infect people's minds. I do believe I promised you a story though, so here's a good one. We all have what's called a conscience, well, I'm the voice in your head when your little, telling you to do the things you know you shouldn't do. I'm the reason so many awesome memories are made for kids. Who do you think talked you into sledding down the hill at Chigger Hollow when you were to afraid to do it? Come on, that place had a car hood ramp at the bottom of it, we flew farther than anyone else."

"Yeah, you're right, we did! Good times, huh?" Darius replied. "Then again, I had to get fourteen stitches in my chin and twenty in my arm for that stunt."

"I know!" He giggled. "I bet you'll always remember that day then huh? See, this is one of the things I do for people, I talk them into making some *real* memories, even if they may be painful ones. Like I said, I'm the fun guy."

"You sound more like the devil," Darius laughed. "Sitting on some unknown kids shoulder, talking them into smoking a cigarette, or beating up some other kid or something."

"Never tried sitting on someone's shoulder," Quigley spoke out, as he flipped a few small pebbles at Darius, striking him repeatedly in the face. "I usually just infect their mind, it doesn't take much effort though, most people want to be bad, they've just been told no repeatedly. If you convince them that whatever it is they're wanting to do is a good idea, then it's just a matter of time before they do what they want to do. I just help them figure out that they can do anything they want to do, all they have to do is try."

"I guess you got a point there," Darius spoke out as his hand reached the edge of where the crevice was. "I was pretty scared to climb this wall, that is until you taught me that falling wasn't going to kill me. I still don't like what you did, but by doing so, I got over my fear of falling really quick."

"See," Quigley said with a bright smile on his face. "I'm the fun guy after all, told you so."

Darius pulled himself to the top of the ledge to where the crevice in the cliff was, it was a very narrow ledge, around fifteen feet still from the crevice opening, but after quite a few carefully placed steps, firmly hugging the side of the cliff, he made his way inside of the crevice.

" Now that was fun," Quigley spoke out as he hovered his way into the crevice. "I don't know about you, but I think that ledge is a little on the scary side. Anyway, we need to go around the corner up ahead, the waterfall is right there."

"I don't hear any water falling," Darius snapped back quickly. "In fact, the only water I hear sounds like just a little drip."

They both just stood there for a few moments, the silence inside the crevice cave had an eerie feeling to it. The only sound you heard was that of water dripping in the distance, with it's echo ringing along with it. The water didn't drip fast, only a drop every five or six seconds or so, not exactly the rushing sounds you'd expect to hear.

"Trust me buddy," Quigley laughed. "You're going to love this, let's go."

Darius walked closely behind Quigley, as they made their way deeper into the cave. The walls became very narrow very quickly, with Darius barely being able to squeeze his way through. Quigley had no problem though, as his body seemed to mold with the walls, with him getting through the narrow pass quite a few moments before Darius finally made it to him.

"You're really slow, did you know that?" Quigley announced. "I was getting ready to take a small nap, about time you got through."

"I still don't hear any water," Darius spoke out as he looked over Quigley's shoulder to see what lay ahead. "You're not just messing with me are you?"

"Just follow me," Quigley snapped back. "I promised you a

waterfall and a waterfall you'll soon see."

They began walking once more, the floor's surface started changing a little bit, becoming slick feeling, as well as wet, the closer they got to the corner. Rounding the corner, the small tunnel they'd been walking in, opened up into an extremely large area, with it's own mini jungle flourishing everywhere. They walked on the path that lead out from the cave, many small animals to which Darius couldn't identify, ran around, scattering as they made their way through the soon dense thicket. Huge trees covered the area, the green canopy only letting in a little of the lavender sky light, which barely was able to touch the ground of this wonderous place.

After walking through some of the thickest brush Darius ever saw before, they finally broke through to an enormous open area. No water anywhere, just wet rocks everywhere. On the far side of the area, up by the wall of the cave, you could see a small puddle, which was still collecting drops every few seconds. They stood at a definite line in the ground, on one side, the side they stood on, the rocks were brown, but the area's where the puddle's rocks were didn't look normal. They were all very moist, what stood out the most was their color. After a few steps forward, Darius took his first steps on the coal black, terribly slick rock.

Darius walked carefully towards where the puddle was, slipping and sliding with every few steps. As Darius got closer to the puddle, he looked back at Quigley, who still stood on the brown colored rocks, just smiling away, like he was really enjoying something.

"Hey, are you coming or what?" Darius yelled out.

"Nope!" Quigley replied. "I promised you a waterfall right? Well, those drops are what's left of it. If you want to see the waterfall, as well as your parents, just think about them really hard while you stare at the droplets hitting the water. I promise the waterfall will turn on, then you'll know everything you want to know."

Without a second thought, Darius began thinking as hard as he could about his parents, concentrating only on them. Instantly, a loud rumble could be heard, with the loud laughter of Quigley quickly following.

Before Darius could even take one step, the water began flying up to him, from below his feet, quickly surging into a massive amount of water, which carried a choking, half drowned Darius to the top of the cave, with the water disappearing into the top as well. The sound of laughter could be heard even over the sound of the water crashing into him, until finally, Darius used his feet to push off the rocks, falling out of the water, with him crashing down on the rocks below, right at Quigley's feet.

"Now, you have to admit," Quigley giggled. "That was one crazy fun ride huh? I do it all the time, but you, oh man, you had no idea that was going to happen, the look on your face was even better than watching you fall, I'll forever cherish this moment."

"You're a real comedian huh?" Darius spoke out in an angry tone. "I'm kind of getting tired of these kinds of pranks, now would be a good time to stop doing it, at least if you want me to do that little task of yours."

"Ouch," Quigley said with a frown on his face. "Somebody's

butt hurt. No worries though, I'll stop for now. I bet you've never seen a waterfall that flows upwards before, huh? You have to admit, it's impressive."

"Yeah, that's cool," Darius replied. "So, how do you work this thing anyway?"

"I already told you," He said offended. "Weren't you listening to me?"

"You mean to just think of what I want to see?" Darius asked confused

"Yes, Einstein," Quigley laughed. "Now if you don't mind, I gave you the directions, you took almost over an hour to get in here, kind of wasted my free time, I have something I have to take care of, I'll be back really soon."

"What?" Darius replied. "You're leaving? Come on, I've never used this thing before, what if I can't do it right?"

"You already can," Quigley said as he looked at the still flowing water. "If you hadn't used it correctly, it wouldn't have turned on in the first place. Anyway, I'd love to stay, it would be fun to see what people are doing right now, but I'll watch

everything later, like I said, I have an important issue right now. I'll

be back soon."

Before Darius could say another word to him, Quigley

disappeared, leaving Darius with exactly what he asked for, the

waterfall. He stood there for a moment, looking around as if

Quigley was going to return, before turning around, once again

facing the falls. Without hesitation, Darius began thinking about

his parents, with the waterfall suddenly splitting into two separate

falls. On one side he could clearly see Jupiter, his father, the other

side had Maria, as well as Von and that Thomas guy in it. It

reminded him of a split screen television set. Darius gazed intently

at the images appearing before him in the waterfalls, watching

them like this, in a way felt like spying, but he was just glad to see

everyone was okay.

CHAPTER 9

"Well now Johnson," Jupiter spoke out as the wormhole closed. "Been a long time since you and I got to hangout with each other, we've had some pretty good times together huh?"

"That we have my friend, that we have." Johnson replied. "I remember the time you, Pierce and I went to Sweden. Now that was a real trip huh?"

"Oh man," Jupiter chuckled. "I forget all about that one. How heavy the snow was falling, reminded me of the blizzard of 1854, the non-stop blowing of the ice cold air, still sends chills up my spine. Of course, who can forget the hot water springs we ended up boiling those swedish vampires in, stew anyone?"

"That was an incrediable night my friend," Johnson replied with a grin. "Watching as you held them in the boiling water, I really thought you were going to let them up much quicker then you did. Then to see them emerge from the water all red looking, with no skin attached anymore, really burned into my brain. I'll never forget that night, plus, you know one thing for sure, I'll never piss you off."

"Well hey," Jupiter laughed. "I told them to leave us alone while we ate our icecream, they didn't want to listen. They even caused me to drop my cone into the hot water. I mean come on who does that? Icecream is the only human food we can even eat without having to throw it back up. Watching it melt away like that really upset me, what can I say, I may be a vampire, but I still have my sweet tooth. How was I supposed to know the water temp was just getting ready to increase dramatically? I didn't know that thing came to a boil every two hours, I don't think any of us knew that. Kind of a good thing they showed up when they did, we would've been scalded if they hadn't picked that fight with us."

"Very true, I'll never forget the look in your eyes," Johnson laughed loudly. "I'm sorry, I just can't help it, but the look in your eyes when your icecream fell into the water, it was just like the look a three year old gets on thier face when they do a doodie, it's the funniest face I've ever seen anyone make, I'd love to get you an icecream the next time we're in Sweden, so I can throw it in the water, see if I can get you to recreate that look."

"Ha, ha," Jupiter replied. "You're a funny guy, I'll have you know, that particular icecream was the flavor blue moon, it's really hard to find, it's also really yummy. That was the first time in years I'd been able to find that flavor and I only got to eat maybe a third of it."

"I'll have to get you some," Johnson said with a smirk on his face. "I actually serve that flavor at my restaurant, got hundreds of pounds of the stuff, it's our most popular specialty flavor, so I eat it anytime I want."

"Must be nice, I may just have to take you up on that offer," Jupiter spoke out as he looked towards the blood center. "For now though, I think we should quit our gabbing and get to work, I know many vampires that will be coming very soon for their nightly meal."

"Right," Johnson said as he looked at his watch. "We don't have but twenty minutes or so before they start arriving, we better head into the center. We've got really no time to spare either."

The two of them quickly made their way across the front garden area, through the white gazebo which had vines growing on the top of it. Soon finding their way to the huge front doors, which thankfully Johnson had a key for. Upon entering, the place was utterly silent, eerie in a way, yet it would be filled with the voices of many people in an extremely short timeframe.

Walking past the service desk, quickly rounding the corner, they boarded the elevator, making their way to the maintenance floor, which housed the one item they really needed to get their vile of the virus in. The blood in which the center bagged, had a very large processing unit, which also had a very small filtration unit attached to it. The ideal place to pour the virus into, thus, filtering the virus into every bag made.

"We'll need all the old bags Johnson," Jupiter spoke out, as he unscrewed the lid to the filtration unit, quickly pouring the vile into it. "Hurry, we'll get a couple of hundred bags filled really quick, hopefully being finished before people start arriving."

Johnson instantly transported himself to the bagged blood area, grabbing one of the large laundry sized carts, he started scooping the bags into the cart with his hands. After a few moments, he stopped for a second, smiled and finally began using his powers to have all the bags in the room fly into his cart.

"Just what are you doing to the processor?" A voice behind Jupiter rang out. "I don't remember anyone ever telling me that someone was going to be working on it. So just what do you think you're doing?"

Suddenly Johnson, who'd gathered all the bags in his cart, transported himself and the cart back to Jupiter. Appearing in between both of the men, but only looking in Jupiter's direction.

"I got all of it," Johnson rang out. "Every last bag. Let's hurry up and contaminate them, I'll keep a few bags for myself though."

The look on Jupiter's face was enough for Johnson to know they weren't alone, which he quickly looked behind him, seeing a vampire he didn't know.

"You guy's aren't contaminating anything," The man spoke out. "I don't know who you are, but, I sure do know you Jupiter. I'll rip you apart before I allow you to ruin my dinner. I wonder if Maria even knows your here right now, or is she close by? Not going to let her destroy me tonight, or any other night for that matter. I know what she's become, she's a monster now. So, come on big guy, don't just stand there looking all wierd at me, say something."

"Huh?" Jupiter stammered. "Who are you anyway? I don't know you. I never met you before in my life."

"That's awesome!" The man said excitingly. "I must be getting good, even the great Jupiter Anderson has no idea who I am. Hmm, if you'd like a hint, I'll give you one if you ask nicely."

"Alright," Jupiter answered. "A hint would be nice."

"Hmm, let's see hear," the man said as his voice began changing, sounding much more familiar to Jupiter. "Now that's a fire!"

Jupiter began thinking really hard, taking him a few moments to put two and two together.

"Tony?" He finally spoke out. "Is that you?"

"In the flesh, give that man a cigar," Tony replied. "I've been practicing my shapeshifting, I think I'm getting pretty good at it as well, even you couldn't tell it was me. Now listen, I don't want any trouble with either of you, but I do want a few of those bags from that cart. I don't want any part of whatever it is you two have planned, but I do want to eat tonight, just not anything contaminated. So if you don't mind, I'll just take a few bags and be on my way. What are you guys going to do to the blood anyway?"

"Well, Jupiter said with a grin." "Now if I told you, then I'd have to kill you."

"Yeah," Tony laughed. "Fat chance at that one buddy, I've mastered my powers. I can assume any form I want."

Suddenly, and to Jupiter and Johnson's amazement, Tony transformed himself into a Rhino, snorting at them, as he stared intensly at them. He waved his head back and forth a few times, before placing his eyes back onto them once more.

"Yeah," Tony said in a growl of a voice. "Like I said, I've been practicing, want to see what this new body of mine can do?"

"I'll pass on that," Jupiter said as his eyes grew red. "Now, as for what we're doing to the blood, well we're putting in a flesh eating virus that actually eats you in twelve hours. It'll be a horrible, but rather quick death, we've added a little extra to make sure things fully effect everyone, would you like a bag? I'm sure it'll be a better death than what Maria will do to you. She's coming to get you, she has to do it, she has no choice in the matter, you really want her to rip you apart? You guys were close friends, don't force her to kill you. You should drink a bag, at least it'll all be over with your approval."

"I don't think so Jupiter," Tony snorted, as he sprang forward, running full force at the two of them, smashing head on into Johnson, knocking him down as he still ran straight towards Jupiter. "I think I'll just be going now."

"Oh no you don't," Jupiter said, as he disappeared, reappearing on top of Tony's Rhino back, grabbing both of his ears immediately, pulling them as hard as he could back towards him, causing Tony to come crashing nose first to the ground. "The fun's just started, no need to leave quite yet."

Tony tried to get back to his feet, but Jupiter began pounding relentlessly at his head. Rhino head or not, Jupiter's punches were rock hard, with the force of a shotgun blast. He lost control of his Rhino form, but formed into an even more formidable foe, as a giant Grizzley bear suddenly formed facing Jupiter, biting him on the shoulder, That is as quickly as his new body form became solid.

This infuriated Jupiter, as he screamed out in pain, with him having to mentally force his hand to move up to the bottom of the bears jaw, grabbing it with his injured arm, as he quickly grabbed his top jaw with his other hand. Pulling the bottom jaw down, he pushed up on the upper jaw at the same time, until an unnatural popping sound was made, with Tony quickly changing back into his human form as this happened. He reached his hands to his lower jaw, with a horrible sound, his jaw was now back in place.

Jupiter began pounding away on his back as Tony quickly melted his body, until he was facing Jupiter, fighting his way to his feet once more. Two hard uppercuts rocked Jupiter for a moment, which was all Tony needed. He began to transport himself to some place other than where he was at, but Johnson quickly jumped in, grabbing hold of Tony so he couldn't disappear.

"Let me go you idiot!" Tony screamed out. "You don't want a part of me!"

Tony once again melted, this time into a temporary puddle of goo, which instantly transformed back into Tony. A devastating punch followed his re-emergence, which caused Johnson to fly back at least thirty feet, sliding across the hallways floor upon landing. Tony quickly turned to Jupiter, hitting him full force with the hardest blast he could muster.

Jupiter, still standing back up, threw his arms up across his face and chest, with the blast hitting him immediately. Tony stood there in amazement, as Jupiter took the blow as if it were nothing, not even causing him to stumble.

"My turn!" Jupiter said as he dropped his arms, exposing his hidden evil looking grin.

The blast that followed was just under what Jupiter knew would be a fatal blow, hitting Tony with what looked like the force of a train slamming into a semi. He walked slowly over to where Tony stood, circling around him a few times, looking at him like he was waiting for him to die.

"That wasn't even a challenge, I'm really disappointed now, I expected much more out of you than this. I've wanted to beat you like this for years, I really thought you'd be much more than you are." Jupiter suddenly said. "You've been a friend of Maria's for a long time, I'll stop now, before I do what I was going to do. I'll just make this as painless as I can, for Maria's sake at least, but as my way of saying thank you for being a friend."

"You're no friend of mine," Tony replied as he spat in Jupiter's direction. "I hate you, I always have."

"Yeah, I figured you'd say something like that," Jupiter replied as an angry face began to appear on him. "Did you know I can hear your thoughts? I've always heard them, in fact, I know how you truly feel about Maria, you've always been in love with her. I've known this from day one, why do you think you got turned into that weird little dog like creature in the first place? It was my idea. Now remember Tony, I did say, if I told you what our plans were I'd have to kill you, well, I've pretty much said all I'm going to say here, by the way I wasn't joking. Always remember this, Maria is now, as well as forever, mine."

Suddenly, and without any warning, Jupiter bent down beside Tony, grabbing his head on both sides with his hands. He began twisting and turning his head violently, wiggling it from side to side, in what looked to be an excruciating experience. Putting a little more effort into it, Jupiter suddenly pulled Tony's head right off of his body, an eerie look still on his detached head. Standing up quickly, he dropped the head towards his foot, kicking it down the hallway.

"HOLY HELL!" Johnson screamed out. "WHAT IN THE WORLD WAS THAT?"

"It's cool," Jupiter said as he turned around displaying a huge grin on his face. "I've been wanting to kill that little shit for a long time now, how dare he try to plot amd plan against me, with his only intentions being to try and take Maria away from me. Let's keep this a little secret between us though, I don't know how Maria will feel about this one, so mums the word, alright?"

"No problem," Johnson laughed. "Just promise me you'll never do anything like that to me, I've got a slight attachment to my head, I'd like to keep it. I'll never discuss with anyone what really happened here tonight, in fact, was Tony even here?"

"Never saw him," Jupiter said as he used his powers to dump the cart of blood bags into the processors recycle compactor. "Now, I turned on the processor before our little encounter, so it should be good and warmed up by now, turn it up to high, make it pump out bags for everyone coming here tonight. Give them all plenty, I can't stay, I must go to the Eiffel Tower, I'm meeting up with Maria at your restaurant."

"I'll take care of everything," Johnson announced. "You can count on me, I bid you a safe journey and farewell my friend, it's been a real pleasure to have had you as a friend, I do hope to be able to see you again before my time here is over, if not, so long brother."

"Like wise and take care my brother," Jupiter spoke out as he prepared to transport to the tower. "It was a pleasure to be your friend as well, see you on the other side."

With those words spoken, Jupiter disappeared, no more

would Johnson ever see his friend alive again. Johnson felt alone for the first time ever, as he looked at the tainted bags of blood filling the cart. Knowing that he'd have to destroy himself wasn't such a bad thing to him, at least he had control of something in his life finally, his own death. A smile suddenly crossed his face as he began wheeling the cart to the elevator.

CHAPTER 10

As we left Paris, I concentrated on my old suite back at DEP, with the wormhole instantly pulling us in it, almost spitting us out on the other side just as quickly. A really warm feeling came through my body each time I went through the wormhole, as did a queasy feeling in my stomach.

My suite hadn't changed one bit, it had been a few years since I'd last been in it, but everything was maintained very well, not a speck of dust could be seen anywhere. I walked over to my refrigerator, grabbing a bottle of some vintage unicorn bloodwine I'd left behind from my last trip here.

"Anyone else want a glass?" I asked as I fumbled with the glasses in the cabinet above the kitchens countertop. "I don't know about you guy's, but I'm famished."

"I'm good thank you," Von spoke out. "I'll take a glass later, only after all of this is over with, said and done."

"I'm Game!" Thomas rang out happily. "That stuff's the bomb!"

"Actually," I laughed as I poured his glass, handing it too him. "The virus we have is the bomb, even has it's own timer."

"True," Thomas laughed, as he took a sip of his glass, trying not to just gulp it down. "Now will I still get to have a glass of this stuff like Von said, when everything's over with? You know, before I have to like die and everything?"

"I tell you what my friend," I replied. "You do a good job for me, I won't have a choice but to celebrate our victory with you, please don't fail me though, I'm really depending on you quite a bit. You're going to be the one to decide when everyone gets to finally drink our tainted mixture. It takes twelve hours for the virus to kick in, I don't know how soon it will kill people fom there though, so you might want to wait an hour or two before you start letting people get any drinks."

"I'll make sure there's quite a few people already there before I serve any of them," Thomas reassured me. "I promise I'll do my best Maria, I can't say I've ever been entrusted to do anything important like this before, I'll try to not let you down."

"You know," I laughed. "That's exactly why I promised you a human to hunt, you're such a good boy. I already know you'll do your best. I only wish you could've had more time with our little troop here, we could've had so much fun together."

"Well, we still can," Thomas spoke out loudly. "You could decide to just not kill me, you know, go out and have some adventures together, stalking people, or whatever you guys do for fun."

"Sorry," I said sarcastically. "Not that you're not a good dude or anything, but what you don't know is, I can hear your voice growing louder in my head as well, if it's not actually a little bit louder than the others, at least I think it's yours, probably just because you're here with me."

Without warning, once again a surge of energy entered me, this time I recognized exactly who it was, it was my best friend for life, Tony had just been killed. I momentarily just stood there, staring at Von, as if not knowing what to do next. Just knowing he was gone, broke my heart into a thousand pieces. A friend like him only comes once in a lifetime and now his time here was over.

"Well hey guys," Von belted out. "I know we're all having a

good little bonding session here, but can we get back to the business at hand?"

"Sorry about that," I said as I realized how long we'd actually been standing there talking. Handing a vile out to Von, who quickly grabbed it. "You might want this huh?"

"Might be a good idea," Von spoke cheerfully as he handed my blood to me. "You better take this as well. Well, we'd better get this show on the road. I think I'll be able to get this done pretty quick to be honest, I have a plan in mind."

"Good!" I said smiling, as I put out my hand for Thomas to grab onto. "I'll meet you right here in this suite. Of course that is once I get Thomas his lunch for his island hunt."

"I'll be waiting right here for you then," Von replied as he opened the suites door, stepping out of the room. "See you soon."

Once again, I opened up my wormhole, with Thomas and I being swallowed up in it.

Making his way slowly towards the elevator, Von reached into his pocket, feeling around, but didn't feel his keycard. Quickly realizing it must've fallen out of his pocket when he was in that fight earlier with the Elders. Placing his fingers on his temple, Von concentrated, before speaking out.

"Nora?" He spoke out loudly. "Could you please come down here, I've forgotten my keycard once more, I've had a bizarre evening, let me tell you all about it."

Von stared at the elevator, which showed it wasn't moving yet, finally, after enough time for him to just begin to get upset, he could see the numbers changing, growing lower, as he stared intently, letting him know Nora was on her way.

The doors finally opened up to a smiling Nora, who had a new keycard in her hand, just for him.

"For some reason, I just knew you'd be here today," She said as a small sigh of relief escaped her. "Nice to see you finally made it back home. I figured you'd forget your keycard like always, so I had this one made a few minutes ago."

"Odd," Von replied. "How did you know I'd be here today? I mean thank you for coming to get me and for bringing me my new keycard, but how did you know?"

"Jasmine was just here," Nora replied. "She let everyone know she wanted them all to go to the island for a large party she's having. A few of the lower ranking vampires didn't want to stop working on their projects in their labs, so Jasmine ripped the essence straight out of them. Little blue orbs came out of their bodies, but these orbs were soon absorbed into her, trapping the people inside Jasmine. I assume Maria has become the destroyer by now, she has just enough power for me to feel her, but her power level got a boost when Jasmine took those orbs. I figured you'd be the one sent here, with whatever diabolical plans Maria had come up with, I was correct. You can count me in as well, Jasmine told me to stay here and direct people to the island, I've sent all kinds of messages out, she's planning on absorbing them all, even let me know I'd be one of the last ones to enter her body. I'd rather take my chances with Maria, then Jasmine, at least if Maria kills me, I'll be free to enter a nice peaceful death, where as Jasmine would trap me within her for all eternity."

"Jasmine was here?" Von quickly asked. "Is she gone? I mean I take it she is, but how long ago did she leave, where did she go?"

"She's gone, don't worry," Nora replied in a reassuring voice. "She said something about a girls night out, I'm not really sure what that means, but I did hear her tell JC and Julian that Michigan was going to be so much fun, that they'll never want the night to end."

"Well, not sure what they're doing there," Von said confused. "At least that lets us know we have time to do what I need to do here. We have around maybe thirty minutes before our nightly regulars come here to feed. I have a vile with me, it's special, we're going to put a drop in each bottle, or bag of blood we have, so we'll need to hurry with this one."

"A special liquid huh?" Nora said as she looked at the vile Von still had in his hand. "Just what's so special about it?"

"Well," Von began. "Given the fact that I've always told you everything, then you know death is coming for you soon in the form of Maria. The stuff in this vile will actually make a lot of peoples deaths happen. It has a flesh eating virus in it, so carefull not to get any on your skin, unless you'd just like to completely bypass Maria killing you in the first place."

"Oh my word, how horrible," Nora said with a terrified look on her face. "Am I going to be expected to drink this stuff as well? I really find nothing very appealing about being eaten alive from the inside out."

"No worries," Von reassured her. "If you wish, Maria herself will destroy us once her mission is completed. To be honest, it could take us years to kill everyone that has to die, so by helping us, you're in turn prolonging your life."

"Well, that will work for me," Nora said happily. "I'd much rather have to deal with Maria anyway."

"Let's get everything taken care of," Von spoke out. "We don't have much time, so let's do what needs to be done."

Without another words said, Von entered the elevator, with Nora pressing the button which would take them to the blood storage floor. The elevator seemed like it ran a little slower than normal, but finally, after listening to some really boring elevator music, it came to a stop, opening it's doors for them.

They walked down the short hallway, making their way to a blue door. Upon Von opening it, he could see that his shipment of Unicorn blood he'd long ago ordered from Maria, was still untouched.

"Two hundred pounds of fresh unicorn blood," Von said proudly, as he looked across the room to the machine that bagged the human blood . "Let's mix and match Nora, let's pour the unicorn blood into our vat, there's still human blood in it as well. We'll have enough to fill every empty bag in all ten of those boxes this way, let's just make it something they want to drink plenty of. You'll want to bag us a couple of clean ones first though."

"You got it boss," Nora spoke out cheerfully. "I've ran this machine many times, so it's all gravy."

Von used his powers to lift the unicorn blood up to the feeding area on the machine, as Nora, started flipping switches.

Von floated up to the top, pouring his little vile of virus into the batch. With a thunderous roar, the machine fired up, spitting out bag after bag of now tainted blood, as Von and Nora looked at each other, with her smiling brightly at him.

Nora used her powers to cause all the bags that had so far been filled to suddenly fly into a cart on the other side of the machine, probably left there by the last person that had blood bagging duty

With the cart now filled, Nora instantly transported it to the actual feeding station, which to her happiness, only had six untainted bags to which, she removed from the shelve. She made the bags in the cart rise into the air, with them quickly lining up all in place on the side of the wall. Once they were all in a long row, she looked at the wall to which there was a laundry chute opening nestled in the wall.

The bags made their way to the chute, which Nora quickly had all the bags fall into. Once there wasn't anymore room for any bags to fit, she knew she'd put more than enough out for everyone that feeds nightly. The chute went straight down the building, ending in the alley behind DEP. A fake window hung over it's dispensary, which had a spot for keycards. This was to make sure their little dispensary wasn't discovered by any humans, there was no access to it without a keycard and only vampires had those. Von cleaned up any evidence of their tampering with the blood, with Nora returning just about a minute later.

"All done!" She said happily. "With five minutes to spare. There's around four hundred bags in the chute, I filled it all the way to the top, couldn't get another bag in there if you're life depended on it."

"Awesome," Von replied. "I should get back to Maria's suite now, she'll be picking me up pretty soon."

"Wait!" Nora yelled out. "What about me? I thought I was going to help you guys, I thought you were going to get me out of here."

"You are helping us," Von replied. "Unfortunately, you're expected to help Jasmine right now as well, so you'll have to stay here, directing people to the island like she asked. I'd direct anyone contaminated straight to her party, maybe they'll be able to put a damper on Jasmine's night."

"I'd really rather just come with you," Nora spoke out. "I do understand though, you want everything to appear normal, well just don't forget about me, make sure you come back for me once this is all over."

"I can't say things will be alright with us once everything's over," Von replied. "But I'll make sure to come back for you, after all, what kind of boss do you take me for?"

"One that loved me at one time," Nora replied. "Maybe I've never changed, maybe I still feel the same way you did before that Joan woman came into the picture, guess you'll never know how I really feel, nothings ever easy, especially me, but then again, what kind of secretary do you think I am? Surely not an easy one?"

"Hey," Von said softly, as he leaned in, gently kissing Nora's lips." I think you're an awesome secretary, but you forget one thing though."

"Oh really what's that?" She asked curiously.

"Everything comes easy to me," He said as he once again kissed her, this time with much more passionately. "I do love you Nora, very much to be honest, but there's no sense in us falling for each other once more, when we already know we're going to be dying soon."

"That's all the more reason for us to get back together now," Nora spoke out nervously. "We can at least spend our last days together. Some time will be better than no time at all, please, give us a little time."

"I guess I can see your point," Von replied with a sexy smile. "Let's see how tonight turns out, we could have longer together than I think we'll have, guess it depends on how many vampires get their free nightly feedings from here on out. I hope we actually have a small turnout for awhile."

"Me to," Nora said as she leaned into Von, kissing him as passionately as he'd kissed her. "You should get back to her suite now, no telling when she'll return, she might already be in there by now."

"I don't feel her to be nearby," Von replied, as he hugged her tightly. "You're right though, I'd better get back downstairs."

With that, Von leaned into Nora one last time, kissing her, as his body faded into the air, with him materializing back in Maria's suite, all safe, sound, but above all, with the knowledge that his long lost love, Nora, forgave him for his unforgivable mistake. The knowledge of knowing she still loved him made his head swoon.

CHAPTER 11

The sun was setting over the island, a beautiful reddish glow, with yellow highlights covered the forest floor, it's light twinkling off of the green leaves on the trees. An eerie silence soon came over the area, as suddenly the air opened up, a wormhole suddenly appearing, with Maria and Thomas stepping out of it.

"You're getting better at this wormhole thing," Thomas spoke out surprisingly. "I'm not as sick feeling this time."

"Me either," I replied proudly. "I think I understand how to do it better now that I've had a little more practice."

"So!" Thomas quickly belted out. "When do we eat? You were going to hunt with me right? I feel how weak you are right now, a little snack might be a good idea, I don't mind sharing."

"Actually Thomas," I replied. "I already have a little snack in my pocket. Which thinking about that, I guess I should go ahead and drink it now. When I was fighting my brother Quinton, I heard something inside of his head that I need to find out for myself. If what I heard is true, I can't be a good person anymore, so I'll go ahead and drink it. This way I'll be able to do what I have to do. In my current state, I just can't find it in me to hurt anyone, or bring harm to them in any way shape or form. Anyway, if I change for the worse, please remember that I'm actually a good hearted person inside. I'm very sorry for anything I'll say or do in the future."

I pulled out the bag I'd put inside of my bra, squishing it in my hand a few times, before I began just staring at it. How young and nieve of a girl this blood came out of, if someone would've said that years later I'd be drinking my own blood, I wouldn't have believed it. Here I am though, staring at it, thirsting for it, needing it.

I raised the bag to my mouth, placing my teeth through the bags plastic. The instant my teeth even touched the blood inside of the bag, the voices in my head momentarily ceased to exist.

"About time you drank that stuff," Quigley's voice rang out. "It's once again time for the Quigley Express to arrive, you my dear are going to be the locomotive pulling the train, just watch your caboose. This is going to be an extra fun ride, I'm not looking forward to seeing the end of it, just knowing it'll soon be over is bad enough. Once this rides finished, the cycle will once again be completed. Enjoy your new found self, I think you'll be pleased with the powers bestowed to you now. Oh yeah, just so you know, this is getting ready to turn into an extremely explosive night, enjoy your evening."

I continued to drink my blood, acting as if nothing happened, as Thomas had a scared look on his face, not taking his eye's off of me. I could feel the power growing in my body with each swallow, making me feel powerful once more, yet, I was totally unprepared for what happened next.

I was still trying to stand steady as if nothing unusual was going on. Upon finishing my bag, I stood there for a moment, looking at Thomas as the look of relief fell upon his face.

Suddenly, like an atomic explosion, a blast wave surged throughout my entire body, bursting out from within me. Thomas flew immediately backwards hundreds of feet, as the trees themselves were blasted away, crumbling like dust in the blasts wind. A huge clearing had been made, with at least two hundred feet of lifeless barren land, in the circle made around where I stood.

"Are you alright Maria?" Thomas asked as he got back to his feet. "That was freaking awesome, how'd you do that? I can't do anything like that, do you feel a difference now?"

"I feel something alright," I spoke out, without a care in the world. "I feel like a new girl, a fun one at that! Sorry about the little explosion there, I just don't know what came over me. Now didn't you just ask if I'd hunt with you tonight? Well if I wind up deciding a certain person has been a bad boy, I'll at least watch the game, maybe even toss the ball a time or two, never know, maybe I'll even join you."

"Cool," Thomas said in a shocked, yet excited voice. "I'll have to try to come up with a good scary idea like you guys did to me, I'll make it worth watching, I promise."

"Oh Thomas," I replied. "I have total faith in you. I know this will be an amazing night now. I should really get going though, you need to gather every bottle of bloodwine we have at the bar area in the mansion, take it to the room behind the bar, there's more bottle's in there as well. Pour every single one of those bottles into the big barrel in the room. It has a hose attached to the bottom of it, which goes straight into the underground tank we used for our tapped bloodwine. I want all the blood in the bar, that is, except the few bottles you hide for yourself, only available from the bar's tap. Of course, I want this vile poured into the barrel first, that will help it mix up a little better. By the time you finish doing all that, I should be back with dinner."

"Got it, I'll get right on it," Thomas replied with a little laugh. "You know, you're not quite what I expected, not that I'm complaining, but to be honest, I thought you were going to be a little more like that old bitchy version of you."

Without another word said, I threw my hand up, causing the earth around him to explode out of the ground, wrapping around him, imprisoning him with nothing but the dirt around him.

"Oh I can still be a bitch when I want," I said as I held my grasp, with Thomas squirming in his cocoon. "I just choose not to be. Did you know as each person dies, entering me such as they do, I get whatever their special power was as well? I just thought that you'd like to know that, now little boy, are you sorry for your comment?"

"I'm sorry, I'm sorry," Thomas shouted, as I made his prison squeeze a little bit tighter around him. "I wasn't trying to offend you."

I dropped my hand, releasing the ground which entrapped him, the dirt fell immediately off of him into a loose pile that came up to his knee's.

"Thanks!" He said as he stepped out from the pile, quickly taking off his shoes one by one, pouring the dirt out of them, before he suddenly began bouncing around all over the place as he tried getting them back on without getting his feet dirty again. "You know, that was terrifying, I felt like you could just crush me at any moment, I feel sorry for the vampires you have to hunt down, they're in for a big surprise."

"You know," I said with a grin. "I think you're right."

Thomas and I just stood there for a few moments, looking at the devastation I'd caused to the beautiful forest that once stood around us. The dust had settled now, the area looked like a bomb had been set off, a perfect circle, with me standing at ground zero. The usual sounds of the woods were completely absent now, as if everything were in hiding from me, terrified.

"Wow, you really did a number on this place," Thomas said as he dusted off the rest of his shirt. "That was a lot of power that went through you."

"Yeah, I know," I replied as I lowered my head, looking down at my now hovering feet. "I can't believe I destroyed this area like I did, I really didn't mean to do it, it just kind of happened. I really hope everything grows back quickly though. I love this forest, it's always so pretty, and you have to admit, this spot just became pretty nasty looking."

"You're right!" He chuckled. "But Thomas to the rescue, I'll get a bag of grass seed for the place next time I go to town."

"Ha, ha," I said as I held back my own laughter. "I don't think a bag of grass seed will quite fix things like they once were, only time will, but good looking out."

"You know Maria," Thomas suddenly said. "If you weren't already married to Jupiter, I think we'd make a perfect couple. I really like the person you just changed into, are you guys like together forever? Or do you think I might have a chance?"

"Sorry Thomas," I replied. "My heart belongs to someone already, that will never change. Maybe if I'd never met Jupiter I might see that comical self of yours in a different light, but I've already met him. I've been with him for years, I never plan on not being with him, he's my everything."

"See now," Thomas said with a frown. "I always wanted that in my life, but no, not me. I was always cast aside, thrown to the back. Even now I can't catch a break, I mean, I do understand that you guys have been together for a long time, but, to be honest, this new you is really turning me on."

"Hey now," I spoke out quickly. "There will be no more talk like that, I'm glad you like the new me, but this girl is a one guy chick."

"Never hurts to ask," Thomas laughed. "Sorry, I don't know what it is about you now, it's like your very scent attracts me to you, hard to explain. I guess now would be a good time for me to leave, go do that little job you asked me to do for you. Please bring dinner back quickly though, I'm really starving, but I'm saving myself for the hunt, so I won't be drinking any bloodwine or anything like that, I'll just be waiting with a gurgling belly."

"Yeah, you're right, I think now would be a good time for you to go," I replied. "Thanks for hitting on me though, even though I'd never leave Jupiter. It's still nice to know people find me sexy."

With that said, Thomas began zip speeding his way in the direction of the islands mansion, the dust that he kicked up when he first started running made me look at the ground around me once more in disgust. Yet, as bad as it now looked, I was very happy with my decision to hold the other half of the blast inside of me. It was an extremely good thing I did that, as the devastation would've been at least double this. I did like one thing though, I really liked how much stronger I'd become, and now was the time for me to become an even stronger one, as I had a person to see.

I concentrated really hard on this person, suddenly opening up the wormhole, this time walking into it slowly, just standing there, controlling the hole, keeping it open. I stepped through it, yet kept it open like a doorway, testing to see what limitations, if any, my new powers had. Upon stepping through, I was in the back of an alley, somewhere in Wisconsin.

I stood in this alley for a few moments, playing with my wormhole, shrinking it, making it grow large, making it take different shapes, there wasn't much I couldn't do with it, with nothing but a thought. I finally closed the wormhole, realizing it was now time for me to do what I came here for. In a way, I knew I'd be leaving with this man, but I really hoped I'd be wrong. So making sure to not hover, I walked out of the alley, to which, a bar stood waiting for me just around the corner. Rounding the corner, I stared at the door of the bar for a minute, walking up to it, looking in the little window the door had at eyes heighth, making sure he was in there, finally grabbing the handle.

CHAPTER 12

The area was dark, dirty, as if it weren't cleaned for many months. The smell of tobacco was heavy in the dim smokey air. The heavy aroma of alcohol drifted through the room even over the smell of smoke.

I scanned my eyes across the bar area, only two really old men sat up there, talking to the bartendar. Looking at empty tables everywhere, I finally noticed a table in the back corner, with a single gentleman sitting there, drinking beer.

Making my way through the bar, the bartendar behind the counter, as well as the two older gentlemen, turned in my direction, all three smiling at me like they'd never seen a woman in here before.

"Hello miss," The bartendar blurted out. "My names Mike, can I get you anything and I really stress the anything?"

Mike, a skinny middle aged man around forty five to fifty, with his odd shaped half bald head, with long blondish hair, reminded me of a weird version of Macaulay Culkin.

"Actually," I replied. "I'd like a nice red wine, I'll be sitting over there with the gentleman in the corner, you can bring my glass to me over there, also, go ahead and get him another beer and keep them coming."

That perked up the man in the corner, who'd overheard me. Standing up quickly, he went to the other side of the table, pulling a chair out for me.

"By all means pretty lady," He announced. "I'd love for you to join me."

"You don't mean Casey do you?" Mike the bartendar replied. "You don't want to sit with that loser, he beats women you know. I'd hate to see what he'd do to a pretty face like yours."

"Don't you worry about me," I said with a wink and a smile,as I started walking the rest of the way over to my brother. "I can take care of myself."

I went to the chair he pulled out for me, sitting down in an area which was even darker than the rest of the bar. He couldn't completely see my face, which I could tell bothered him, but welcomed me at his table all the same.

"Did I hear something about a beer?" Casey asked as he sat back more comfortably, taking a drink from his bottle. "I'm about do for a refill."

"Well then," I replied. "You won't have a very long wait, as your buddies bringing our drinks to us now."

"Maria! Is that you?" Casey spoke out in a shocked voice, as he grabbed his lighter from the table, striking it several times before finally a flame emerged. "This isn't possible, you're dead! I went to your funeral, I watched them put your casket in the ground. You don't look like you've aged a day since I last saw you. How can this be?"

"Do I look dead Casey?" I laughed. "I mean I know I've had a bad day today, but do I look that bad?"

"This is just to unreal," Casey replied. "I must be drunk, this isn't possible, get out of here lady, I'm having some kind of nervous breakdown. My nightmare of a sister has returned from the dead to haunt me."

"Nightmare of a sister!" I said, surprised with his remark. "Why in the world would you say such a thing? I figured after twenty five years you'd be a little happier to see me."

"Happy to see you?" He laughed. "Now why would I be happy to see *you*, of all people?"

"What's your problem with me Casey?" I asked curiously. "What have I *ever* done to you?"

"Oh," Casey laughed as he tipped his bottle to his lips, finishing off the last of his beer. "Gee sis, where do you want me to start? Maybe a good example would be college! You my little princess, went straight out of highschool, where as I had to wait until you were finished until I could go. Do you know how ackward it was being a twenty four year old freshman? Rumors began to spread around about me, like I was some kind of idiot. I was treated like I'd failed college so much, that I was still a freshman six years after highschool ended, people avoided me. Needless to say that because of this rejection, I never even graduated college. I stayed for the first year, part of the second, but just couldn't take the rejection and ridicule anymore. After quiting college like I did, I ended up bouncing from job to job, place to place. Broke, hungry, no place to live half the time, oh yeah, you've done plenty to me."

"I had no idea what even happened to you," I replied as I waved Mike over to us. "Why didn't you call any of us for help? I have more money than I know what to do with, I would've helped you no questions asked."

"Yeah, I'm sure you would've." Casey said sarcastically. "So you could rub that in my face as well. Thanks, but no thanks, I've had to live in the shadows of the great Maria all of my life. Quinton was the first born, as well as a son, you were the only girl born, I was just the unwanted child. I wasn't special like you guys, I saw the way mom and dad treated you two, I would've loved to have had just one day with that kind of attention. Everything you have in life was just handed to you, same with Quinton. I have no respect for you guys at all."

"I'm sorry you feel that way," I replied sympathetically. "Can I at least buy you another beer?"

"How about this you stupid bitch," He said as he stared at me intensly. "How about you go over to that bar, turn a stool upside down and go fuck yourself. I can buy my own beer. Unlike you, I've worked hard for my money, which I have just enough to get trashed on tonight. So take your pity somewhere else, just what the hell did you come here for anyway? I'm sure it wasn't to catch up on old memories."

"Actually, you're right," I replied with a slight grin. "I came here to hear something with my own ears. Oh, by the way, you don't have to worry about Quinton anymore, he died about twenty four years ago, if you ever would've called mom, or dad, you'd already know this. Mom and dad are dead as well now, they died a few days ago, so I guess it's just you and me."

Mike walked over to us, carrying a tray with four beers and two red wines on it. He carefully placed them on our table, you could tell he could feel the tension in the air, as he didn't say a word to us.

"Thanks Mike!" Casey said as Mike made his way back behind the bar. "You can always tell when I'm having a bad night and this night beats them all."

I picked up my glass of wine, tipping it gently to my lips. It had been a long time since I'd drank wine without it being all doctored up with blood, I'd forgotten how good it really could taste. Casey sat there staring at me hard, as he slammed down three of his beers, one after the other. Only sitting back in his chair after he picked up the fourth beer bottle.

"You know Maria," He laughed as you could see the alcohol beginning to take effect on him. "Thanks to living in your shadows, I can't even keep a relationship. I've been married three different times, to three horrible women. I have ten nasty little girls who's only ambition in life are to become whores, every last one of them want to become an adult film star. Thanks to you, I wasn't much of a father to them, just look how you affected my kids. I feel like you're my curse, I ended up with children just like the one person I hated more than life itself, you. After all, you whored yourself out for a job, you're a star yourself, look how many riches you have now, all paid for by that nasty twat of yours. I couldn't even have a son, just little clones of you. What a slap in the face, even as an adult, you managed to find a way to torment me."

I waved Mike back over too us, he held five of his fingers up in the air, to which I nodded at him. As Casey sat there trying to mellow out some, you could tell he was about to blow his top, as he finished drinking his beer.

Mike came walking to us quickly, just in time to, as Casey'd just set his bottle on the table.

"Just what the doctor ordered," Casey said as Mike placed a new bottle in his empty hand. "You're a good man."

Mike smiled at us nervously, looking at me very weirdly all the while. As he stepped away from the table slightly, he asked a question I guess he shouldn't have.

"Hey, uh, Casey," Mike stammered. "I'll need your lady friend here to pay for all the beer you've drank tonight, also, if you don't mind, I'm going to go ahead and cut you off."

"IF I DON'T MIND?" Casey shouted as he stood up from the table, grabbing an empty beer bottle, throwing it hard at his bar area, the bottle hitting the corner of the bar, ricocheting off of it, smashing hard into the large mirror behind it, shattering the glass. "OF COURSE I MIND, I'M NOT DONE DRINKING YET!"

"Sounds like someone's had too much to drink already," I laughed. "This is becoming an interesting night after all."

"Screw you sis!" Casey said as the hate echoed in his voice. "You think something's funny do you? You think it's funny that I've ended up becoming nothing but a drunk? You think it's funny that I'm so damn poor I live in my car? Let me tell you miss goody goody, all of my money goes to child support, so I might be a piece of poor crap, but at least I live up to my responsibilites. What have you ever done for the greater good? I'll tell you, nothing, you know why? Because you only think of yourself. I may not want to see my kids, but at least I get money to them when I can."

"I have a question for you Casey," I said calmly. "If you've hated me all of your life, then why did we always hangout together as children?"

"Well," He said as he slammed down three more bottles of beer, making me sit there and wait as he did. "You know what they say, keep your friends close, your enemies closer. How else could I make sure to get you and Quinton fighting again? Do you remember when all of your dolls had their heads ripped off of them? I'm so very proud to say, I did that, of course Quinton got the blame, it was fun to see you guys throwing those punches at each other though. I loved getting you two into fights, seemed only right, since everyone acted like the world itself was already yours. I only wish I wouldn't have saved you two that day when dad was fixing the tractor, I've never figured out why I did, I always wanted you guys to die. I could tell it wasn't on that stand very well, the tires barely even got off the ground. I just knew it was going to fall off like it did. To this day, I kick myself in the teeth for pushing you guys out of the way, I could've completely changed my life, if only I could go back in time, believe me, I'd change everything. Then I wouldn't have to be sitting here talking to you like I am now."

"You know," I said sadly. "I always knew Quinton had a driving force behind his attacks on me," I spoke out harshly. "Now I know the truth, you actually caused our problems with each other didn't you?"

"It only took you fifty years to figure it out?" Casey laughed. "I guess you're smarter than I gave you credit for. I didn't think your brain could even comprehend what all I've actually done. I'm glad to hear of our family being all dead though, you know what would've been even better? If I could've kept on believing you were as well."

Drinking down his last two beers, Casey stood up from the table which he immediately stumbled, catching himself on the table.

"I got to take a piss," He announced as his speech began to slur. "You could make my evening a really good one though, just don't be out here when I get back."

As Casey disappeared into the bathroom, I knew one thing, I knew I'd heard what I kind of already knew he'd say. This solidified my decision, Casey would die tonight, after all, maybe it was finally time to show him *why* I was treated so special. I noticed his car keys on the table, I couldn't help but put them into my pocket.

"Hey Mike," I said as I walked to the door, "Let my brother know I have his keys, he shouldn't be driving anyway, make sure you let him know that I hope he *fully* enjoys his walk home. I'll be in the alley if he'd like to continue our conversation, maybe I'll even drive him home if he can act like an adult, you know, show me the respect I deserve."

CHAPTER 13

The old brown bathroom door at the back of the bar began opening, at least ten minutes had passed by, but finally Casey emerged from within the bars bathroom. Walking back to his favorite table, he noticed his three buddies just staring at him. He knew he was drunk, but wondered if he stumbled showing everyone else he was, as they didn't take their eye's off him.

He moved his chair, sitting in it with a thud, as he was clearly getting as trashed as he planned on getting tonight. Grabbing Maria's half drank glasses of wine, he slugged them all down. As he was placing the last glass back on the table, that's when he finally noticed his keys were gone.

"Hey Mike!" Casey shouted across the bar at him. "I'd like my keys back please, I'm not *that* drunk dude."

"Oh, you will be!" Mike laughed. "I mean, sorry about this, but I didn't know that was your sister, but you know how I can be sometimes. I put a little something extra in there for her, I planned on having a really good time tonight, that chick just screams out for me to do her. I'm actually glad she's your sister though, let's me know for cetain that you're not interested. Funny though, I put quite a bit in there, it didn't seem to effect her much, let me know if you start feeling anything. By the way, I didn't take your keys this time, your sister did. She wanted to talk to you in the alley, but she's probably passed out by now. I can go out there and check on her while you wait, you know, make sure she's alright, not cold or anything, I'll make sure she's good to go, *I guarantee*! Might be best if you just have a seat for a few minutes, you know, make sure you're good to go."

"Mike, you sick fuck," Casey spoke out as he got to his feet, heading in his direction. "I tell you what, if she's passed out, she's all yours I promise, lets go guys."

"Cool, cool," Mike said as he rubbed his hands together, a huge perverted smile stamped across his face. "We'll, get your keys bro, I'm just ready to get this party started, I know Joe and Paul are ready, we're all three going to have a blast with her."

"You're awesome bro!" Joe spoke out. "Love you man."

The four of them walked out of the bar, with Casey leading the way. As they turned the corner to the alley, just as Mike had hoped, they quickly saw what appeared to be a passed out Maria lying in the middle of the ally, my pretty dress pulled up high, almost exposing a truly wonderful site, which Jupiter calls his snack shack.

"Oh, hell yeah guys!" Mike shouted merrily, as he unzipped his pants. "Just look at that site, baby, I'm going to make you shake."

"Well I get first dibbs," Paul blurted out pushing him aside. "You guys need to show a little respect to your elders."

Paul, who looked as if he hadn't ever bathed in the seventy six years he'd been on earth, suddenly looked at his equally filthy buddy Joe, who still stank of the fish he cleaned in the factory earlier that day. Fish scales still clinging to Joe's clothing, as did very small pieces of guts.

"Hey Joe?" Paul suddenly spoke out. "You know, I'm seventy six years old, your what, like seventy right? So we've both been around the block a time or two. In all of your years have you ever wanted to bang a chick more than this one?"

"Sixty nine," Joe replied with a dirty grin. "The magic

number, don't forget it. I'm not old like you yet, but yeah, I've been around. I've never wanted a girl like this before, I'm going to really enjoy this, you really should let me go first though, I buy a lot of beer for you man".

"Alright you perves," Casey spoke out. "Will you shut your pie holes for a minute, let me at least get my keys before you wip out your junk in front of me."

Casey walked over to her, starting to feel a little light headed as well. Carefully bending over, picking up his keys, stumbling a little as he stood back up.

"Alright guy's, she's all yours," Casey spoke out as he started heading back to the bar. "I'll be inside, enjoy!"

Casey walked around the corner, the three of them all surrounding their treasure. As they heard they door of the bar make it's loud normal thud it always did when it closed, they knew Casey was gone.

Suddenly, all three of them bent down, with Paul and Joe grabbing at my breasts, as well as Mike placing his hand up high on my inner thigh.

"I take it he's gone?" "I suddenly said as I opened my eyes, staring right at Mike. "Good! It's about time."

"Yeah baby," Joe butted in. "He's all gone, your a dirty girl aren't you? Coming to this bar all dressed up in your pretty little dress, just asking for it. You wanted us to come out here and ball the shit out of you, admit it."

Suddenly with Joe's one hand on my breast, his other hand went up my dress, grabbing hold of something he shouldn't have touched. I sent out a nice little blast wave from all over my body, with the three of them flying back away from me, slamming into the alley walls on both side of it.

"That was really a big mistake Joe!" I spoke out as I rose from the ground by my heals, hovering above it once I was fully erect. "I've delt with sicko's like you before."

"Holy shit man!" Mike yelled out as he grabbed Paul, dragging him down the alley as the old man finally got to his own feet. "I'm sorry lady."

"No your not, not yet at least," I said as I suddenly disappeared, quickly reappearing at the end of the alleyway. "Come on boys, I thought you said you wanted me, come and get it."

"Nope, I've changed my mind!" Mike rang out as he farted loudly. "You're not even pretty to me anymore, I mistook you for someone else. I'll just be going now, nice to meet you lady."

"Oh no, not yet baby, the funs just starting," I said as I raised my hand, pushing the men back into the alley around thirty feet. "You guys are some real sicko's, I can't let you do this to anyone else. The law may have never found you guys, probably would've been better for the three of you if they had found out what you do to women. I'll admit it though, it's an extremely unlucky night for all of you, because I just did."

Without another word spoken, I evaporated into my fog, creating a thick shield of myself, filling up the alley completely. I'd never been able to form myself into such a perfect form of this fog before, so pure, so thick, I could feel every little emotion that went through each man's head, as they quickly dropped to the ground feeling around frantically, all of them trying to find their way out of the alley.

I waited, took my time if you will, making sure I knew they were all three at their full peak of adrenaline from the fear I was causing them.

Slowly, I began filling myself into their noses, with just a breath of me going in at a time. The men, still on their hands and knee's, started noticing that the fog was lifting. Mike stood back up, with Joe following his lead, helping Paul up as well. They just stood there, breathing heavy, as if they'd all just ran marathon's, breathing my fog in all the while.

The air in the alley cleared up more and more with every breath taken in, as the men finally began trying to walk down the alley. Every two or three steps, they all had to stop to catch their breaths, breathing in the last of the fog that was me.

"Man," Mike spoke out. "I just can't breath, I need to catch my breath, hold on guys."

"Not a chance, sorry," Joe replied as he let go of Paul's hand. "I'm doing good just getting myself out of here, I don't know what that crazy bitch did, but if I ever see her again, I'll choke the shit out of her."

"I'm still a little bummed out," Paul spoke out heavily winded. "I was just getting ready to rip her dress off of her, I really wanted to see that naked body of hers."

"You know, we've all been drinking," Mike pointed out. "I think our imaginations might've got the best of us, maybe she put something in *our* drinks as well, can't say she didn't. She's Casey's sister, so she might've, but hey, never fear, we'll get her the next time she comes here."

The three guys finally made their way to the edge of the alley, within feet of escaping it. Suddenly, without any warning, I came exploding out of the first of the them. Joe was the first to feel his death, I made sure he could feel everything as well, with Paul quickly following his lead, as I exploded out of him next. Mike just stood there, frozen in fear, as I couldn't help but let him watch his friends explode in front of him. I think what got him the most was the simple fact that there were now two of me standing next to him.

Pieces of flesh dripped off our skin, but the both of me's smiling at him at the same time, as suddenly we each flicked a piece of flesh off our shoulders with Mike standing there in the middle of us, getting hit in the face with each piece as they were launched.

"WHAT ARE YOU?" He screamed out in terror. "OH GOD!"

"I'm the Destroyer," I replied inside of his own head,

Immediately I began melting my body into the very cells that made him. He tried to run, but soon found he had no control over his motor functions anymore.

"By the way, I've had a lovely evening, you're such the gentleman, so much it's making me hot, can you feel it?" I said as I turned up the heat so to speak, quickly bringing the inside of his body to a boil.

He stood there unable to move, shaking violently, foamy spit coming out of his mouth, as I turned the heat up the rest of the way, turning myself into pure heat, bursting out of him in flames, standing there as the ash flew off of me.

I stood there for a moment, looking at the other two me's, our dresses were exact copies of each other, I hadn't realized what a real mess I was now, Jupiter was going to be mad about this one. I put my hands out, with my other me's coming right to them, grabbing ahold of me. I pulled them in towards me, hugging them firmly. As I hugged them harder, we began merging back together into one again, until once more, I was the only woman standing there, except now I had all the junk they had on them on me now.

I used my powers to clean myself up, quickly making my way back into the bar. As soon as I got in there, I quickly noticed Casey was passed out on the floor, next to a couple of turned over chairs. Guess he got more trashed tonight than he anticipated, I quietly thought to myself. I walked over to where he lay, concentrated on where I wanted to go, with my wormhole appearing right on schedule, sending us immediately to the island. To be exact, I transported us straight to the prison area, depositing Casey in my favorite cell.

The stench from the cells past inhabitants rang through my nostrils, as I laid Casey on the hard rock floor. I stared at him for a few moments, as he lay there on his back, thinking about all the things he actually caused to happen. The constant fighting with Quinton, set us up for the fight we eventually had, a fight in which I was given no choice but to kill him. This fight was also the reason Darius had to be born that night, which Quigley took advantage of, invading my unborn child's very soul, which I felt turned him against me.

Casey may not have directly caused our fight, but he was the reason we never got along in the first place. We might've never fought that night in the Castle, that is, if Casey hadn't played us against each other all our lives.

He was totally passed out, the aroma of alcohol seemed to ooze out from every pore. What a total disgrace my brother had become, his IQ was just as high as mine and Quinton's, yet, he seemed to forget who he was, not really applying himself. The years had not been very nice to him either, as his salt and pepper colored hair seemed to have a area of extreme thinning around the top of the back of his head.

His mouth hung halfway open, I could see where three of his teeth were missing, many of the others brown in color. I wasn't even sure if he even knew what a razor was, as his facial hair had been grown wildly long. The biggest thing I noticed about him was his weight. As kids, he was always so scrawny, not an ounce of fat to him. To look at him now, five foot eight, three hundred pounds or so, was just unbelievable. I never would've imagined he'd ever get so large.

His extra weight was going to make this little hunting party an extra good time, I couldn't help but get that feeling you get right before you right a wrong, even though the way I was righting this wrong, was wrong in itself, but oh well. I'd let Thomas play with him for a spell, but only one person was killing my brother and I've decided that will be me.

I quickly felt for Thomas, he was still in the bar area, the mansion was empty besides us. Transporting myself straight to him, I arrived directly behind him, using his sudden terror as a way to practice for some of the other vampires I'd be running into.

"HOLY SHIT!" Thomas rang out as he dropped the glasses he was polishing up, dropping his almost finished cup to the ground. "Oh man, you're really going to have to not do that to me, I mean, after the other night, when I got to be your hunted prey, going through all that, come on, don't just appear behind me like that, it's freaking scary man."

"Sorry about that," I laughed. "I wasn't thinking, then again, maybe I was."

"I had enough of that the other night when I was terrorized," Thomas said nervously. "Did you get my dinner?"

"Kind of," I replied." I mean, you'll get to have your fun with the guy, but only I will kill this one. I'll have to find another person for you."

"Oh man, really?" Thomas replied in a very disappointed voice. "I was really looking forward to your returning, this sucks! Why can't I have the one person you brought back? Did I do something wrong? Are you mad at me or something?"

"Not at all," I giggled. "I'm not mad in any way shape or form, maybe mad in a different way, but that's yet to be determined."

"So why can't I have this person then?" Thomas asked confused. "Who is it? Do I know them?"

"No," I replied. "You don't know them, but I do! It's no matter *who* they are, though, it should never matter *who* your prey for the evening is anyway. We are but creatures of the night my friend, ment to drink from the vines swinging and pulsating on the human neck, all humans are our prey, *who* they are makes no difference for the vampire."

"To be honest," Thomas spoke out, interrupting me. "I think it makes a *huge* difference *who* your prey is. I plan on finding a few old highschool assholes once you let me know I can leave this island, especially Butch McCalister, he'll be on the top of my list. He wanted to be this big bad bully of me, well, wait until he gets a load of me now, I doubt he'll want to flush my head in anymore toilets. So I think it matters quite a bit just *who* your prey is, I'm singling out all the people that treated me like Butch did."

"You got me on that one I guess," I joked. "You really hold grudges huh? It's alright though, I do know what you mean, I've just never gone after specific humans, they were all delicious to me."

"You never did answer me though," He quickly replied. "Who'd you bring?"

I sat there for a moment, wondering if he'd think I was a bad person for bringing my own brother here, let alone knowing that I myself wanted to kill him. Picking up one of the untainted bottles of unicorn bloodwine off the floor, which Thomas sat aside, I turned to the bar, walking to it without saying a word. I picked up a couple of glasses he'd just polished, I uncorked the bottle, placing the cork into the wooded oak trash can, which was built into the solid oak bar. I began pouring us both a glass, when Thomas once again asked his question, which, just thinking of my own answer, actually made me cringe a little.

"Who are they Maria?" He pried. "I really want to know why they're so important to you that I can't eat them?"

"Alright, alright!" I said sternly. "His name's Casey Myers, my name wasn't always just Maria you know, I do have a last name, it's Myers as well, he's my brother."

"YOUR BROTHER!" He said as he choked. "Are you joking me? Your freaking brother? Out of all the people in the world, you picked your own brother to bring here too hunt? I tell you, I didn't think you were completely like the other Maria I remember, yet I think I might've been wrong. Wow, all I can say about you bringing your brother here is, that's really wacked out, it's just wrong."

"Look, I really don't know why I even picked him," I said harshly. "He was just the only person I could think of to bring here. I don't even know why, I've never singled anyone out before today, like I said, I was more of the random type. For some reason my mind could only focus on him, sorry to disappoint you. Now tell me more of this Butch guy, do you know where he lives, or what he would be doing right now? If so, let me see inside of your mind, so I know what he looks like, I'll bring him to you instead."

"Actually, I know exactly where he'd be right now," Thomas said with excitement in his voice. "I'll be one happy camper if you bring him to me, like I said, he's at the top of my list. I'll do whatever it is you want me to do, that is, as long as you promise to bring him to me *and* let me hunt and kill him. Where'd you put your brother at anyway? I don't see him anywhere in the bar area."

"Oh," I laughed. "He's in a safe spot, I'm sure he feels right at home, he'll be asleep for at least a couple of hours anyway."

"A couple of hours?" he said excited. "Are you and I going to hunt our dinner together after all?"

"Of course we are," I said happily. "We'll have just enough people for a wonderful dinner party, might as well enjoy the evening together with our awesome friends and family huh?"

I reached my hand out, placing it on the side of Thomas's head, instantly, all of his thoughts filled my head. I could see the factory Butch McCalister worked at, as well as exactly what he looked like. If Thomas was correct, Butch would be getting off work very, very soon.

Looking at Thomas as I dropped my hand from the side of his head, I suddenly winked at him, smiled brightly, instantly summoning my wormhole, which I placed directly behind me.

"Be back in a jiffy," I said merrily. "Meet me in the dungeon area, make sure you grab your bottles as well, you might want those later."

Thomas nodded as I finally stepped back into the wormhole, instantly disappearing from his site.

I was surprised at how close to the back of the factory I was when I arrived, the wormhole opened up right in between two loading areas for semis. Three men sat with their backs to me on the docks, they were all eating their lunches.

I immediately recognized one of the men, it was Thomas's

favorite person in the whole wide world, it was Butch. He was smoking a cigarette while he ate his sandwich, bragging about what he did on the the weekend.

"Yeah, I beat the shit out of the guy," Butch spoke out as he took another bite of his sandwich. "Teach him to come to my house looking for his ole lady. If he'd bang her right in the first place, she wouldn't be calling me in the middle of the night, begging to come over."

"I don't blame you bro," One of his two younger companions spoke out. "If he don't know how to make her happy, what's wrong with you doing something he just can't seem to do."

"You said she's married to the guy right?" The other guy spoke out. "They have kids dude, that kind of makes you a home wrecker."

"Watch yourself buddy," Butch spoke out as he grabbed the red headed young man by his shirt's collar, shoving him back slightly. "I've stomped people's asses for less than what you just said, would you like a demonstration?"

"Excuse me boys!" I suddenly blurted out from behind them, with all three of them instantly turning in my direction. "I was wondering if any of you know a man by the name of Butch McCalister, I heard he's like the biggest stud around here, I stress the biggest part."

"You're in luck lady," Butch rang out, as he stumbled to his feet. "I just so happen to be Butch, so what would a fine ass woman like you, like for *me*, to do to you first?"

"Oh wow," The younger guy spoke out. "You're absolutley beautiful, take me instead lady."

"No," the other guy quickly followed. "You don't want Butch, I'll treat you the way you *really* want to be treated, that's for sure, come sit by me."

"Well boys," I laughed. "I don't think I'll be able to handle you two, that is once I'm finished with Butch here, I'll take a raincheck though."

"Oh man," The younger guy replied. "I'd do anything to trade spots with you Butch, have fun bro. I'll go ahead and go back to work early, I'll make sure your boxes don't get to far backed up, but don't take all night man, we don't have but an hour left on our shift."

"Well," The other guy said as I stared intently at Butch. "I can tell when I'm not wanted, my better late then never lunchtime is about over anyway, I want details bro, so don't forget me."

"Oh, I'll give you plenty of 'em," Butch laughed as he placed his arm around my shoulders, copping himself a feel as his hand settled directly over my breast. "You came to the right place baby, I promise you that, I'm going to give you a night full of screams of delight."

As Butch was talking, I watched as his companions went back into the building, upon his finishing his sentence and with the sudden locking click sound of the door, I did what only came naturally, as I formed my wormhole behind him. The wormhole made no sound, it never does. The blue and white stripes made a coloration which illuminated around the back of him, swirling none stop in a counterclockwise direction.

"Oh, they'll be screams all right, but I'll bet they'll be all yours," I said with a huge smile on my face, as I suddenly slammed my elbow into his chest area. The force of the blast causing him to fall backwards into the wormhole. His hand still clutching my breast all the while, as I fell into it with him.

CHAPTER 14

The wormhole opened, with Jasmine, Julian and JC stepping out from it. They stood in an office, which just happened to be Von's. Jasmine immediately sat down at Von's majestic oak desk. Opening up the top drawer, retrieving a laptop from it, quickly setting it on the desks top.

"What are you looking for?" JC suddenly asked as she knelt down next to her, trying to get a good spot to watch whatever it was she was doing."

"Addresses," Jasmine announced. "I have a few addresses I need, this is where they hid them."

"Addresses for who?" Julian quickly asked. "Why would you need addresses, can't you just feel everyone anyway?"

"Of course I can feel everyone," Jasmine replied harshly. "These people aren't magical though, they're just human. I don't feel humans the same as I feel vampires, so I need their addresses, we're going to show them all a good time, make them talk."

Jasmine turned her attention back to the laptop, which was now up and running. Scanning through files like a mad woman, suddenly she found just what she'd hoped to find, the addresses to all ten of Casey's children.

"Bingo!" Jasmine spoke out happily. "I guess we got ourselves a winner here. I know exactley where this place is, they all live in the same area as well, how lucky for us. This shall be an interesting night after all."

Suddenly the office door opened up, with three security guards standing there with what looked like flamethrowers. Before any of them were able to pull their triggers, Jasmine instantly froze them in place.

Standing up slowly, she made her way over to her would be assailants. Their eyes were the only thing they were able to move, giving Jasmine a little something to giggle at as she ambled over.

"I'm sorry," She spoke out. "I shouldn't laugh. I was just so pleased to see you guys, I was wondering how long it would be before the silent alarm brought me more food for my baby."

She raised her hands, one in front of each man, as the third man stood there frozen, forced to watch what would soon be happening to him.

Jasmine closed her eyes, both men began screaming, just a little at first, before they're screams soon became deafening, echoing all throughout the floors of DEP. Suddenly, two blue orbs came popping out of their chests, with their screams instantly silenced, as their bodies dropped to the floor.

"Hang on baby, "Jasmine said as she placed both orbs in one hand, freeing up her hand for one more orb. The man's eyes almost popped out of his head in terror, as she placed her hand in front of his chest. Jasmine smiled at him, with another giggle escaping her lips. "Mama's getting you something yummy to eat."

Suddenly screams filled the area once more and with another popping sound, she finally had what she'd came for.

"We'll get you all fixed up and full, mama loves you." She spoke out in baby styled talk.

Cupping all three orbs into her hands, she began pushing them slowly into her, with a sudden popping sound, not unlike when the orbs come out, the orbs were now inside of her

"Come with me guys," She suddenly said as the orbs left her hands. "We need to hurry things up here, we have some unsuspecting girls waiting for us and one lucky boy. The lakes name at the moment is Gull Lake, but after tonight, it'll be known as Skull Lake."

Jasmine walked to the doorway, stepping over the bodies carefully. As she came through it, Nora of course was sitting at her desk, just like Jasmine knew she'd be. Jasmine knew how Nora truly felt about Von, but the guy was just so obsessed with Joan, Maria's mother, he didn't give her the time of day, hardly even a thank you for the coffee she brings him. Yet she always sits there, just waiting for a chance to get a glimpse of him, if only brief.

"Oh Nora!" Jasmine rang out happily. "Would you be a dear and get ahold of every single vampire you know? Find out if they'll be available for an all you can drink fiasco on the island. The party starts in just a couple of hours from now, I expect to see a huge turnout, after all, it's not everyday I throw my victory party."

"Victory Party?" Nora asked inquisitively. "What were you victorious in? Did I miss something?"

"No need to worry about what I'm celebrating," Jasmine replied. "All you need to know is I'm having a party, I expect everyone to be there. Now, unless you'd like to join your friends that are lying on Von's office floor, I suggest you do as I say."

"I'll start informing people immediately," Nora spoke out in a professional secretarial voice. "Is there anything else I can help you with tonight, or is that all?"

"That will be all Nora, thank you." Jasmine spoke out in a cocky professional voice. "I have some other pressing issues to tend to at this time, I'll expect to see you at this party as well. Don't worry, you can arrive later than the others, but you *will* come."

With that said, Jasmine opened her wormhole, waving her hand for Julian and JC to enter, looking at Nora with an evil grin, before stepping into it herself.

Instantly, they arrived at Gull Lake, arriving inside the thicket right by a general store. As the worm hole closed, they all three began peering out from the bushes, Jasmine smiled as she looked at the address on the store.

"I tell you," She laughed. "I'm better than any GPS."

"What are we going to be doing here?" JC quickly asked. "You said we needed to make people talk, who are they? Why are these humans of any interest to you?"

"Because my dear girl," Jasmine replied in a motherly tone. "These particular children are Maria's nieces and nephew. The only one we'll not kill yet will be the boy, the girls can all be disposed of now, but not until after we have the boy."

A young woman suddenly walked out of the store, heading in their direction. She was looking down at her cell phone, not noticing them at all, that is until Julian slightly moved, rustling the branches.

"Hey, what are you doing in there," She yelled out suddenly. "I ain't gonna have no creepers hanging out my bedroom window without paying me first. I'd suggest you guys go creep on some other house, ain't gonna be no free show tonight."

"I'm sorry," Jasmine said as she exited the bushes, coming into the clearing with the young lady. "I didn't catch your name, by chance you wouldn't know the whereabouts of a Casey Myers would you? We work for Publishers Clearing House, he's won the main prize. I'll need his signature, if he's not available, then I'll need the signature from another male family member, is your brother home?"

"Sorry lady, I ain't seen dad for months," She replied. "I never had no brothers either, hang on, let me get my sisters, they might know something I don't, plus, I'm sure they'd like to hear all about this."

The girl quickly ran to the door of the old looking dirty store, Jasmine could not help but overhear her, as the young girl was pretty excited.

"Candice, Danielle, where are our sisters at right now?" She asked curiously. "We got some lady out here saying dad won the Publishers Clearing House top prize, do you guys have any brothers I don't know about? She asked for him as well. They ain't harvesting yet are they?"

"Cut your shit Tabitha," Danielle quickly shouted. "I'm getting tired of your bullshit, always got some new drama going on. If I look outside, there better be a lady out there, or I'm beating your slutty little ass."

"Bring it on bitch," Tabitha said as she motioned Danielle to the window. "Take a look for yourself and choke on it, I hear you like choking on things anyway."

Danielle pushed Tabitha aside, quickly looking out the window. Sure enough a woman stood by the store's Jeep, just as her half sister had just claimed.

"Is there anyone there?" Candice suddenly asked. "Or was she just lying again?"

"Oh there's someone there alright," Danielle replied. "It don't mean she's no lottery woman, actually, she looks pretty scary if you ask me. How do we know she's not some kind of undercover cop trying to find our growing operation?"

"True!" Candice agreed. "What if she's DEA or something even worse?"

"Well," Tabitha joined in. "If you want, I'll go out and talk to her while you guys see what everyone wants to do about this. I think the lady's legit, but not my call, see what Stephanie says, call her cell phone real quick, even if she put it down somewhere, one of the girls will pick it up, after all, there's seven people in there right now, someone will hear your call. I hope this doesn't ruin our harvest though, I was looking forward to us getting out of this place and getting to California. It needs me there you know, I'm meant to be a star, so it just won't be the same without me."

"Alright," Candice spoke out. "You go ahead and go back out there, keep her busy, I don't know, show her the lake or something, just stall her while I call Stephanie."

Tabitha handed over her cell phone to Candice, with Danielle looking at them as if she should've been given the phone instead. With Tabitha quickly making her way back through the small maze of the stores shelves and out the front door.

"So!" Jasmine spoke out as Tabitha walked back over to her. "Any luck finding your father?"

"Uh, well, I'm kinda working on that right now." Tabitha replied as she tried to come up with a good excuse. "See, we got really bad reception here, my sisters gotta walk like a mile to use the phone, so it could be a minute before they get back. So just hang on lady, don't go no where, it ain't gonna take too long, we'll

get dad here as soon as we can."

"Well you know," Jasmine spoke with a soft tone in her

voice. "If you can't find your dad, your brother can sign as well, do

you not have his phone number? Or were your sisters calling him

as well?"

"Oh, him?" Tabitha stumbled. "Yeah, we got his digits,

they'll call him if they can't get ahold of dad."

"I thought you said you didn't have a brother?" Jasmine

replied with a grin. "Now all of the sudden you do? Did you loose

him or something?"

"Well he ain't my brother," She said nervously. "He's my half

brother, I have ten siblings, three real sisters, and six half ones. I've

only met him like once, I just forgot that he was my bro, sorry."

"No need to apologize," Jasmine replied politely. "So there's

eleven of you guys then? I was under the impression there were

only ten."

"Would you like to come in lady?" Tabitha blurted out. "We

got beer in there, we're allowed to sell it now, my mom even just got a liquor license for the place. Ain't got nothing more than just beer though, but we have like eight different brands."

"Now you don't seem old enough to be able to sell alcohol," Jasmine said in a motherly tone. "How old are you anyway?"

"I'll be eighteen in two weeks," Tabitha replied proudly. "My birthday also marks the new start for me and my sisters lives as well. What it means the most is that I can leave this depressing place, California here I come! I'm gonna be an actress you know."

"Oh really?" Jasmine replied surprised. "And just what all have you acted in? Anything mainstream?"

"Oh, well, not yet," She replied as she looked at the ground kicking her foot back and forth in the dirt. "Once I get to Hollywood though, you'll see, I'll be a star, even if I have to start out doing porn, that'll be cool, I'm no stranger to men's desires."

"So you plan on doing porn then?" Jasmine said in a stern voice. "What do your sisters think about this idea of yours?"

"Oh, they're all cool with it," Tabitha said proudly. "We all plan on being stars, believe me, in this little vacation area we live in, we've all had our fair share of so called auditions, so if we end up on a casting couch, so be it, that's how people get discovered in Hollywood now anyway. People don't get discovered by their acting talent anymore, but by their secret hidden talents, which, if you're good at it like I am, it could be your launch into instant stardom."

"Well," Jasmine laughed. "I wish you guys luck with your career choices, not sure I'd quite agree with you, but we all have our opionions, such as talents, which I have a few you'd never believe, or even want to know about, as that would more than likely be a bad thing."

"I like your outfit by the way," Tabitha spoke out suddenly, as she reached out her hand, touching Jasmine's shirt, gently rubbing it over the fabric. "I bet it was expensive. I hope you're for real lady, cause if you are, then I might not even go to California. I'd just stay right here, but then again I'll do just about anything to be rich and famous, but rich is all I really want to be. I really can handle being here if I had money, it's nice and quiet around this place. Plus, we have very handsome vacationers that come here all the time, I don't want to like sleep with all kinds of guys, I really just want to be a star for the money."

"Yes, It actually was expensive," Jasmine replied as she slightly moved back from Tabitha, causing her hand to drop away. "Sorry, I'd prefer if you didn't touch me though. How soon before your sisters get back, I do have other awards I have to disburse, I can't be here all night you know."

"Hang on, let me see if they've made it back to the store yet," She replied cautiously. "Sometimes they just go inside through the back door, not letting me know when they're back, so give me a minute, I'll be right back."

Tabitha once again ran back inside of the store, as soon as she did, Jasmine waved back at Julian and JC, who were still in the bushes, to come to her.

"I don't like this!" JC whispered into Julian's ear. "She's going to absorb us just like the others, I know it. If not right now, she will eventually, I wish Maria were here."

"I do too!" Julian whispered back into her ear. "At least we're on the same page, I'm afraid to talk at all, when the time comes, we help Maria, agreed?"

"Agreed!" JC spoke as the two of them moved the bushes out of the way, stepping out into the clearing."

"What a lovely evening we're having tonight," Jasmine spoke out in a bubbly voice. "I just love family reunions don't you?"

"I have no idea what you're talking about," Julian said as he lowered his face towards the ground. "This isn't what I'd call a reunion."

"More like a massacre," JC whispered softly as she put her hand up to her face, as if she were wiping something off of it.

"Oh come on guys, perk up," Jasmine laughed. "The fun is just getting ready to begin, don't you like to have fun? This is going to be more fun than you've ever had before, so don't loose your head in the matter."

Suddenly Tabitha, who was only in the store for about a

minute or so, emerged with two other women. She lead them straight to Jasmine, stopping around three feet away from her.

"Alright lady," Danielle spoke out harshly. "Just who are you? Our dad never sent any of those Clearing House things in, our sisters are on their way here right now to tell you the same thing. So cut the crap bitch, who are you and what do you want?"

"Mellow out Danielle!" Candice said softly as she bumped into her. "Let Stephanie handle this."

"Alright, you caught me," Jasmine replied with a smile. "I heard you girls grew the best weed around, I wanted to buy it all from you, you're right Tabitha, my clothing *is* extremely expensive, just where do you think I get all the money from? I was told your dad was in charge, but I figured he'd be too busy getting drunk right about now? Who's that scumbag bartending buddy of his, oh yeah, Mike, he's probably ringing up a good bill for him, I have cash, hope your dad does. If you girls don't want my business, I can take my money elsewhere."

"Hang on a minute," A deep sounding voice rang out from

behind the store, as seven girls quickly came tearing around the corner, half running. "We got here as quick as we could, did I hear you say you got cash? You also got ID lady?"

Jasmine turned her head, looking behind her, towards the bushes. As she swiped her hand across the air, she looked at Julian and JC, motioning them to the bushes, which they walked over to, quickly picking up the two suitcases full of money she'd created. They walked back over to Jasmine, with each of them standing on a side of her, suitcases still in their hands.

"This is the only ID I need," Jasmine said as she motioned for Julian, then JC to show the contents of the suitcases. Both of them bent down, unlocking and opening them up, Julian's face lighting up slightly as he opened his, such as JC's face did, as neither one of them had ever seen so much money before. "Need I say more? Or like I said, do I need to take my business elsewhere?"

"Who told you about us?" The manly woman spoke out. "Who are you anyway? Does anyone here even know this lady's name?"

"Look, Casey Myers said he could get me a huge amount of weed," Jasmine said sternly. "My name's Jasmine, and just who do I have the pleasure of speaking with? I gave you my name, I think it's your turn now."

"Casey Myers huh?" She spoke out as she stared at Jasmine in the eyes. "Well I'm Stephanie Myers, Casey's oldest daughter, no relation to the author unfortunetly, like to have her money though."

"Stephanie huh?" Jasmine laughed. "I figured your name would've been Dave, or Mike or something more manly. God, I mean look at you, long brown hair pulled back in a pony tail, six foot two, pushing two fifty or so and so buff. Is that a mustach you got going on there? Maybe *you're* the son your dad spoke of."

"Hey, fuck you and your money!" Stephanie yelled out. "You come here just to piss me off? I'll beat the bricks out of you lady."

"I'm sure you would," Jasmine said calmly as she smiled, looking at Tabitha. "This sister is going to be a porn star huh? I really need to see how they cast this one, will it be a guy, or a girl role you'll be playing. I see you have all of your sisters to back you up here, too bad your brother isn't here to help."

"Man, lady, we ain't got no brother," Tabitha suddenly yelled out, as she came from behind everyone, holding a shotgun. "You ain't leaving with that money either."

Without another word spoken, Tabitha suddenly pointed the gun straight at Jasmine's face, pulling the trigger. A huge puff of smoke hung in the air, with Jasmine's half slunk over body still where she'd been standing.

Jasmine slowly began to stand back up, bringing instant terror into the girls that stood there watching in disbelief. Her face missing chunks of flesh, skin dangling off her half gone chin.

"Now now, Tabitha! That wasn't very nice of you now was it?" Jasmine asked as her face began reconstructing itself, as thousands of tiny pieces of her flesh flew from the ground, reattaching to her. "I guess I'll have to teach you ladies a lesson after all. Just so you all know, I really only came here for your brother, seems you don't have one yet, I guess your magic will do."

Using her powers, Jasmine suddenly froze all the girls in place, so none of them could run away.

"Oh god lady, I'm sorry," Tabitha shouted out as she watched the pieces of flesh flying through the air, molding her face quickly into a healed one. "My finger slipped, I, I, I was only trying to point it at you, please don't hurt me, I'm sorry, I'm sorry."

"I thought you said you wanted to be a star," Jasmine replied, as the last of the pieces landed in place, with her injuries now healed. "Don't you still want to be famous?"

"Huh?" Tabitha replied all confused. "What's that got to do with anything?"

"My dear, you wanted to be a star," Jasmine spoke out wickedly. "Well then you'll be happy to know all of you will be on TV tonight, but not the way you quite wanted though."

Before any of the girls could say anything else, or move out of the way, Jasmine swiped her hand through the air, instantly the sky above the girls seemed to condence, into more of a sword of air, with her sending the blade of wind across the necks of all the girls at the same time.

Stephanie was the first to realize what had just happened to her, as she grabbed at her throat, immediately looking at her hand, showing her what she feared, it was blood covered. The look on her face suddenly became more of a cross eyed look, as her head suddenly fell off her body, onto the gravel.

Some of the other girls freaked out when this happened, trying to run away, which the sudden movement caused their own heads to fall to the ground as well, followed by their bodies

One by one they all began to fall, until only one girl still stood standing, it was Tabitha, she'd just got done taking off her shirt and wrapped it around her neck, standing there, almost frozen with fear as Jasmine walked over to her.

"Why?" Tabitha managed to say in a raspy voice.

"You wanted to be a star right?" Jasmine said sarcastically. "How often does such a mass murder like what I just did take place around here? You'll be famous for years now, maybe even forever.

Immortallity comes in different shapes, sizes and ways, you my dear are immortal now, at least in a sense. California is over-rated anyway!"

A tear slowly fell down Tabitha's face, as suddenly, she took a step away from Jasmine, untying her shirt. She stood there for a moment before finally the empty look in her eyes said it all, with her body dropping to the gravel, head falling on the ground, rolling towards Jasmine's feet. Jasmine stood at the feet of all the girls bodies, suddenly putting her hands out to her sides. Within moments, ten very small yellow orbs came out of each girls body. They floated straight to Jasmine, who placed them all inside of her, one by one, as each one entered her body, she giggled from all the excitement, as she could feel the baby moving inside of her.

"Well now," Jasmine spoke out as she kicked Tabitha's head out of her way. "Would you guys like to play a game of kickball, or would you rather go get a drink or two at the island, after all, we have a party to host."

Julian and Jc dropped the suitcases to the ground, with the

suitcases instantly disappearing, grabbing hold of Jasmine's arm quickly.

"You two are just no fun, huh?" Jasmine said with diasappoitment in her voice. "I didn't think I'd ever say this, but I miss my Quigley, now *he* knew how to have fun, too bad I killed him, he was created by Nod, only fitting that he died there as well."

With that said, Jasmine commanded her wormhole to open up once more, with Jasmine falling backwards, with her companions in tow into the abyss, a huge wicked smile across her face all the while.

(HAPTER 15

The water flowed constantly, as Darius watched the images on it intensly, learning all there was to know about his mother. How she'd been changed, every little aspect of it, all being shown to him like one long movie.

Watching as Quigley went inside of his body during the last

part of the show, reminded him that Quigley had given him a task to do. Curiousity set in as his mind began to think of what lay ahead for him in a few hours.

Suddenly, the images in the water began changing, forming into two men He'd never met before. It looked like a fight was about to take place, with an already beaten up man sitting down against a tree and he was all bloody and looked exhausted. Heavy breaths stopped the man from saying anything, with the other one hovering over him. For some reason there was no sound, but he could tell the man hovering over the other one was getting ready to kill the guy.

Before Darius could even blink, Quigley's face appeared in front of everything, blocking all view.

"Now, now," He spoke out grinning from ear to ear. "No peaking."

Instantly the water's image faded into his mother, she was holding some guys face under water, with him gagging and choking up water at her.

"Oops," Quigley's voice rang out with a little giggle at the end. "We're sorry folks, but tonight's programming has been canceled."

Once again the images faded away, with his father in view this time, he was just sitting in a chair in what looked like a restaurant, waiting on his mother to return. Nothing special, but still nice to see his father being a normal guy for once. His head had always been shoved so far up his mothers butt, that he never really acted normal, no matter what memory Darius tried to think of, his dad was always a pushover, not even man enough to stand up to his own wife.

"Hey Quigley!" Darius spoke out very loudly. "I know you can hear me, who were those two men fighting? I take it one of them was the person you need me to help."

"Now we'll have none of that!" Quigley's voice surprisingly rang out from inside of the water. "I don't remember you ever being that kid that opened his Christmas presents before Christmas. So why do you think I'd spoil the surprise now?"

"Just tell me!" Darius demanded. "I have a right to know who I'll be helping, at least let me know which guy it is, the one on the ground, or the one hovering over the guy on the ground?"

"That's for me to know!" Qugiley's giggles echoed throughout the cave. "Trust me, you'll find out, I think your choice will be the right one, I have faith in you. All you have to do is help the one that you feel needs your help the most. I do hope you make the right choice, as this man is of utmost importance."

"So I need to help the guy on the ground then, alright," Darius quickly replied. "I can do that."

"I never said that now did I?" Quigley laughed. "Now like I said, you'll only know for sure once you're actually there. You'll have to make haste with your choice though, I'll be cutting things pretty close now because of Jasmine."

"Jasmine!" Darius said shocked. "Have you seen her? If so, why didn't you stop her from doing what she's doing? I just got finished watching her absorb these little blue orbs into herself, I'm not for sure, but I think she's taking the souls of people, as her victims hit the floor pretty fast once these orbs came out. It sounded really nasty by the way, this big, ear screeching popping sound rang out everywhere when the orbs actually came of those people."

"Nope haven't seen her." Quigley said, as his voice suddenly for the first time Darius could remember, became serious. "Don't want to either to be honest, especially after what she just finished doing moments ago."

"Why?" Darius asked. "What did she do just now?"

"Let's just say she just ruined your mother's plans, not really mine," Quigley said in a disappointed voice. "Your mother had such a wonderful evening all planned out, it's almost a shame I have to intervene, so much for family reunions. I guess I have to save this piece of crap after all, this will change the events for my pets though. I guess I can always go for a new war, so vicious our my puppies. Hmm, this is a twist indeed, I shall have to use plan B now, good thing I took precautions, I guess as they say, let the games begin."

"What are you talking about?" Dairus asked confused. "What plans? You mentioned family reunions, who does my mom have with her right now? I thought you said you never intervene with anything."

"Shut up boy!" Quigley snapped. "My brain's thinking right now, it happens sometimes, I actually have a new thought from time to time. Never question the Quigmiester, he knows all, designs the rest. I've designed many things in this world, you'd be surprised at what all I've done."

"I'm sure I would," Darius replied. "You still didn't tell me *who* she has, I take it their a relative of mine?"

"Alright, alright," Quigley spoke impatiently. "Don't keep drilling me over this, I didn't choose him, she did, she's hanging out with your Uncle Casey right now on the island. She's leading him towards the beach area right now. Well hanging out is much too mellow of a word for what she's doing to him at this moment, she's tormenting him, your mom is back to more of her old self finally, I'm so proud of her!"

"My Uncle Casey?" Darius replied, totally shocked. "Nobody knows where he even is, how could she ever find him in such a short timeframe?"

"My boy," Quigley giggled. "What runs in his viens is like a magnet to your mom, she could feel that tiny bit of magic I gave him anywhere. Plus, all those voices she's been hearing in her head, well they're all Casey's. I made her drawn to him, just as you'll see how everyone is now drawn to her. I did this in the event I had to go to plan B, so no worries, good thing I planned ahead huh?"

"Drawn to her?" Darius said completely confused. "Why would you have people drawn to her? What does that do? Why would you have Casey's voice's rattling all over her head like that? You know, sometimes even I don't get you. I thought you had more important issues than messing with people."

"My boy," Quigley said as he laughed uncontrolably. "Messing with people *is* my job, it's what I do. I love it so much, I set things up, sometimes thousands of years in advance, getting to watch everything play out brings much joy to me."

"You're a sick man my friend," Darius laughed. "I guess if I was going to be on this earth forever, I'd cause my own drama as well, your own personnel TV show, just add your ideas, then watch everything playing out. See I do get you, I just don't agree with your choice of violent programming."

"You don't understand me at all then," Quigley said in a serious tone once again. "You don't even know what land your actually in right now, you think you're in Nod, but before Nod was created, a much greater land sat where you are. Do you know the name of this place I speak of? I bet you've heard of it a time or two."

"What are you talking about?" Darius asked as his confusion grew out of control. "I Don't even see why where I'm at, whether in Nod, or on the moon, has to do with anything."

"It has everything to do with what you just asked," Quigley giggled as his words came to a slight pause. "My brother, welcome home, welcome to Eden."

"WHAT?" He shouted in disbelief. "You mean like The *Garden* of Eden, Eden?"

"Yes sir," Quigley replied happily. "You're where it all began, life itself, created by the disobediance of our mother and willing participation of our father."

"I don't believe you," Darius replied. "I'm in a cave, I doubt this is Eden."

"You know Darius," Quigley spoke out as he contained his laughter. "I think I should really give you a few more brains the next time around, you're almost impossible to have a descent conversation with. Now, as I was saying, no, the cave you're in isn't Eden, but all of Nod is. You don't understand, so how about I telll you a quick story, as I'll have to save your uncle very soon, so it can't be a long one this time."

"You never did say why you're going to intervene," Darius quickly spoke out. "As for my brains, hmm, didn't you say that genetically you and I are like brothers? Well my friend, just remember, the apple doesn't fall far from the tree."

"Wow, you're right, it didn't fall far at all," Quigley giggled. "Well, I'm not quite talking about what you think I am, I'm talking about more than you could comprehend. So, speaking of apples, I guess it's storytime again. See, many many years ago there were these two people, a man and a woman. They were placed in a paradise with only one thing they were not allowed to do. A huge tree grew out of this paradise, with many many glorious looking apples on it. The creator of such a good place knew that without evil, there would be no such thing as good, so in one of the apples, he placed all of the evil the universe had ever known inside of the delicious fruit. Now the two people had no idea why they weren't allowed to eat any apples, as there wasn't anything such as good or evil in the world, it didn't exist. Because of these apples, one thing did exist though, it was called temptation, but as the tree grew more apples on it, the tempation grew to great for them to endure, with the end result being they picked an apple from the tree of life itself. Upon picking one of the apples, the woman accidentally picked the apple that contained all of the evil which the creator had safely placed inside of it. She took a bite of it, giving it to her male counterpart, to which, he did the same, tossing the apple on the ground after taking his bite. Upon the earth feeling evil touch it's dirt for the first time, the creator suddenly pushed the two people miles back. Solid earth flew out of the ground in a huge circle, entrapping the evil inside of the magical mountain which sprang out of the ground. The man had taken a bite as well, so unbeknownst to them, the woman was already pregnant, but the child inside her had done no harm. So they'd cursed the next child to be an evil thinking one instead, a child that would some day kill his own brother. The mountain you're in right now is the mountain I speak of, so like I said, welcome home!"

"You mean this is Eden?" Darius spoke out as he looked around the cave again. "I knew this was beautiful, I never would've guessed it was because this was Eden, why is the sky color lavendar, instead of blue though?"

"In case you haven't noticed," Quigley laughed. "Nod is kind of the opposite of Earth, it has to be, it's just one of the differences between good and evil. What I *can* do is finish my story, that is, if you'll shut up for a minute, I really have to go soon you know. Now, where was I? Oh yeah, the mountain. See now once the mountain contained the evil inside of it, the apple which had been eaten, had five seeds in it. As the apple rotted away slowly, these seeds began sinking into the ground, until they were completely submerged in perfections dirty fertile ground. Upon being fully covered in the dirt of life, an apple quickly began transforming into the shape of a baby, within just a few minutes, a newborn child was suddenly spit onto the ground by the tree the apple had been taken from. This child was a child of magic, growing into a full grown woman within just a few minutes after touching the ground. Upon her transformation ending, she walked over to the stream next to the great tree. Scooping up water in her hands, she walked over to where the five seeds lay, already fully encased in the dirt. She sprinkled this water drop, by drop, onto each seed, until all the water from her hands had fallen upon them. Within minutes, the seeds reacted to their drink, with each one pushing through to the surface. A massive vine grew from each seed, as only a single flower bulb emerged slowly on each one of them, with all of them not showing the contents of their bulbs for days. Finally, after the seventh day, each bulb burst open, with them all spitting their own newborns onto the dirt, newborns which were cared for by the woman from the great tree. The babies, all girls, were magical as well, yet grew much slower than the woman that came out of the great tree. She cared for them for many years before giving any of them names, she named them for who they were. Which in the end, her girls all named her, just like she'd done for them, they named her by who she was, so her name became Life."

"OH WOW!" Darius replied as he just stood there dumbfounded. "How do you know all of this?"

"You're looking at it," Quigley laughed as he pointed all around him, referring to the waterfall in which Darius was looking at. "I told you, you can see anything you want, you could even watch me kill you that day so many years ago if you choose too. I wanted to see a little farther back than that, the first time I came to the falls, I wanted to know where everyone in Nod came from, to which, now I know. In a really weird kind of way, the women of Nod would be like our sisters. Mom and dad did create them didn't they? They created us as well, so itso facto, flippity flop, deal with it, or the story will stop. It's a lot to take in all at once, you can turn that brain off now, because storytime is over. Still I figured you might want to know just *who* that sexy girlfriend of yours is. But hey, for real, I have a choking issue to attend to, I have to get your mom all wet."

With that said, his image disappeared from the falls, with a huge image of Life taking his place. Darius tried to get the falls working for him again, but only her image appeared, no matter how hard he tried. Quigley had shut the thing off with Darius's final thought in his mind the moment he disappeared.

Not being able to get any other image to show up, Darius walked away from the falls, looking back at it as the water immediately ceased it's flow. Thousands of drops rained down from the ceiling, with only one drop remaining steady, immediatley after the rain effect from above, of course, the only drop that remained was the drop that suckered him in.

"Figures!" Darius said out loud as he began heading away from the falls, back towards the caves entrance. "Just when the guy lets me know exactly how cool these falls are, he messes up the reception, I was going to watch Quigley's creation, I think that would've been interesting to say the least."

CHAPTER 16

The wormhole opened in the dungeon area, followed by the loud thud Butch and I made as we landed on our backs on the ground. Thomas was standing with his back to us, over by a still sleeping Casey.

"HOLY SHIT MAN!" Butch yelled out terrified. "WHAT THE HELL JUST HAPPENED? WHERE ARE WE?"

"Calm down Butchy," I said as I got to my feet, dusting off my dress. "You're where people like you need to go."

"Where's that?" Butch replied as he looked around the dungeons surroundings. "Prison?"

"NO! With me," Thomas suddenly yelled out as he spun around, exposing his true self to Butch. "Now get in my belly! It's dinner time."

"OH MY GOD!" Butch screamed out. "What the hell are you? A Demon?"

"You only wish," Thomas replied as suddenly he leaped at Butch, flying right past me, almost knocking me down with the blast of air the followed him. "I'm something much cooler and you're making me hungry, guess what I am."

With that said, Thomas grabbed Butch by his throat, picking

him up off the ground, tossing him with ease at the bars of the cell that Casey was in. Butch slammed hard against them, a slight cracking sound echoed throughout the dungeon area.

"Oh, man, wait," Butch spoke out slowly as he quickly grabbed at his back. "I think you broke my ribs."

"Good!" Thomas replied with a huge grin on his face as he picked him up off the ground, Butch's feet dangling below him. "I hope it feels awesome. Maybe even as awesome as the time you broke my back in the gym at school. You broke a lot of bones on me, you know, man, to think, you're actually complaining about your back. Butch, just so you know, I've just begun to break bones on you."

With that said, once more, Thomas flung Butch across the dungeon area, this time throwing him as far as he could, with Butch screaming like a little girl. He landed just a few feet from the doorway leading outside into the forest, sliding twenty feet across the stone floor to it, before coming to a crashing halt up against the wall by the doorway.

Butch was all torn up, scratches and gashes covered his body, with what appeared to be a large rugburn covering his entire arm. He just laid there on the ground for a few moments before letting out a moan, followed by another one. Staring blankly at the ceiling.

"Hey Butch, are you having a good time yet?" I suddenly asked. "Probably not quite what you expected, huh stud? You were right about the screaming, there seems to be plenty of that going on."

"You crazy bitch," Butch said as he opened his eyes, slowly getting to his feet. "Come on over here, I'll show you a good time, oh yeah."

"Still the defiant bully," Thomas belted out. "Even in your last hour you still have no manors. Nobody speaks to the master of vampires, the mother of all, the destroyer of many, such as you just did."

Thomas zipped straight at Butch, slamming into him with such force they broke through the wooden door, landing out in the clearing. Solid thuds could be heard echoing across the island, as

Thomas slammed his fists repeatedly into Butch. A bloody mess of a face was the only thing I really noticed on Butch as I made my way outside to watch the show.

"YEARS! YEARS MAN!" Thomas screamed out as he continued to beat him. "You tormented me for years, terrorizing my life to the point I tried to kill myself because of you, I was in a hospital for six months from that crash. All the pain I felt during those days are nothing compared to the pain I'm going to put you through tonight."

"Alright Thomas, stop." I suddenly said as I just couldn't stand to see him hit the guy anymore. "I don't think he's going anywhere anytime soon, so let's go wake up my brother. It's time for him and I to play our game. Butch can just tag along with us, this way he can watch what's going to soon happen to him as well. So, if you want to carry him during this little hunt, that'll be fine."

"Carry him?" Thomas laughed. "He doesn't deserve that much repect from me, I'll just take the guy on a nice long drag if you don't mind. His ponytail will make a good handle, if you know what I mean. Seems only fitting since the guy drug me on the ground through our cafateria by the hair when we were kids."

"You're a vindictive little man aren't you?" I laughed back at him. "Well drag your toy if you want, I'll be right back, I'm waking up Casey."

With that said, I walked briskly back into the dungeon, straight up to where Casey lay in the cell. Opening the medicine cabinet next to the keyring holding the cell keys, I grabbed a syringe out of it with one hand and a bottle of adrenaline with the other. I opened the package holding the new syringe in it, sticking it's sharp tip into the bottle's top. I made sure to fill the syringe as full as possible, I wasn't really worried about giving the guy a heart attack or anything, if he died from the injection, then I guess at least he's dead.

I grabbed the keys, walking the rest of the way over to the cell door, unlocking it, as that familiar clicking sound confirmed. Stepping through, trying not to kick Casey as I came in.

Bending down next to him, I quickly injected the adrenaline

into the vein in the bend of his arm, blood trickled down his skin upon my removing the needle. Suddenly, without warning, he opened his eyes and began screaming like a mad man.

"WANAMATERHOE," He screamed out in his still medicated state with nothing but babble. "AKFOMOR."

"Oh shut up!" I replied as I slapped him, waking him up more. "Don't think I couldn't figure out what you just called me. Back for more huh? Real tuff guy you are there little brother. I could always show you a bitch if you'd like, call me a Hoe again, you've yet to see how much of a real nasty girl I can really become. You can rest easy knowing this though, I hate you just as much as you hate me."

I walked out of the cell and towards the door leading outside, using my powers to drag him just a few feet behind me on the floor. He was still groggy, yet I could tell the adrenaline was really starting to kick in for him, as he started looking around more and more as he was drug across the ground.

"Wha, what's going on here?" Casey slurred. "What are you

doing to me? Stop it!"

"Oh, hang on," I spoke out impatiently. "We're almost there".

I drug him over next to Butch, letting go of my magical grip on him. I enjoyed very much watching his eyes almost pop out of his head once Thomas turned towards him, showing him his true self.

"Whoa! whoa! Holy shit!" "He stammered in terror, as he tried to crawl away from us. Get the fuck away from me!"

"Oh man, this is awesome," I laughed. "The look on your face right now, it's classic, I'll remember this moment forever. To see you cower on the ground like that, makes me feel better than I ever have in my life. You stole my brother from me, because of you I never really had a brother in Quinton. Fooling me all my life, making me believe you were the good brother, the one I could count on."

"Well count on this Maria," Casey spoke out suddenly, as he came too a bit more. "Count on going to Hell, you filthy demon. You've always deserved such a fate, I can die a happy man knowing I'm going where you'll never be."

I couldn't help what I did next, I threw my hand up, using my powers, I picked him up off the ground and began choking him.

"DO IT! DO IT!" He gagged. "GET IT OVER WITH!"

I squeezed his throat only a few moments longer, before releasing my grip on him, with Casey landing on his feet, stumbling for a brief second, quickly steadying himself. He just stood there, staring at me, rubbing his hand across his neck a few times before smiling at me.

"What? Couldn't do it?" Casey spoke out. "Or just not done playing with me yet? If you think I'm going to start running from you or anything, you're wrong. I'm not afraid of you, you're still that stupid little girl that helped me convince our parents that Quinton killed all those farm animals. I don't care what kind of monster you've become, you'll never be more of a monster than I already am, after all, I killed every last one of them, all by myself."

"Oh trust me," I replied with an evil look, as I changed into my own true self. "I'm by far more of a monster than you could even fathom."

"You think that scares me?" Casey laughed, *even though his face told a different story*, as I completed my transformation. "You don't frighten me, in fact quite the opposite, I think you look funny, hideously funny to be exact. So what if you kill me! That's all you can really do, so *you* trying to scare *me* is about the most ridiculus idea you could've come up with, almost as ridiculus as you look."

"So you want me to scare you?" I asked as I grabbed hold of his arm. "How about this?"

Instantly I flew straight up into the sky, bringing Casey with me. Soaring high above the tree's below, which all looked like small bushes now, I picked Casey the rest of the way up to my face and smiled at him, as I let go of his arm. He immediately began plummeting towards the ground. Casey's screams of terror were music to my ears with what only could be described as a beautiful melody. I wasn't done with him yet though, there were many more screams I wanted to hear and so many different tunes I wanted to play.

"Oh god!" Casey spoke out as he could see the ground approaching very quickly. "Here we go!"

Suddenly, just as Casey was about to crash into the ground, a wormhole appeared, with him falling straight into it. The wormhole opened up right next to me, as I quickly caught Casey by his foot, as he was spit out it, with him dangling head first towards the ground.

"Alright, alright, you scared me, happy now?" Casey replied. "No need for anymore of that, I get it, you hate me, that's cool, the feelings are mutual."

"You know, I just can't believe you," I spoke out. "Even in your final moments, you have to be this way to me, what have I ever done to you to deserve this treatment?"

"I'll tell you what you did," He replied with hate filling his vocal cords. "You were born, that's what you did. Quinton was the first born son, dumb as an ox, but still the first born, so he got plenty of attention, you were the only girl, so you got the rest of it. I got nothing, I always got shafted. You even got to be this vampire that's getting ready to drop me, what did I get? Ten horrible kids and three even worse ex wives? So do what you brought me here for, get it over with already, I'm ready for whatever you feel like you need to dish out."

"You know, you could've apologized to me," I said as I let go of his foot. "So I'll just dish things out to you instead."

Screams echoed throughout the forest, as wormhole after wormhole could be seen opening up all over the place, with Casey falling uncontrollably through them. Placing wormholes at the bottom of tree branches seemed to be what he liked the best, so I made sure he fell through many of them, over, and over again, getting beat to hell by the trees in the process.

Finally I grew tired of hearing his constant screaming, having the last wormhole open up on the beach, with him rolling through the sand, until coming to an abrupt stop up against a sailboat I had delivered a few years back. I'd never found the time to go sailing in it, actually, it had been beached since the day it got here. It sure was fun to watch him slam into it like that though, made me feel like the boats purchase had just paid for itself.

As I lowered myself down to Casey, hands out to my sides, I placed myself gently on the sand directly next to him. He didn't say a word, all he did was look at me, with that sickening smile of his on his face once more.

"You know," I suddenly spoke out, as I grabbed him once more, this time tossing him into ankle deep ocean water. "I planned on killing you, but everyone has to die to become a vampire. I was going to change you, bring you into my world so I could punish you for eternity, or at least until you said you were sorry and actually meant it. I see now that would've been a big mistake, as your contempt for me knows no bounds. I wanted to have at least one family member of mine enjoy the spoils this world has to offer, I think I'll just kill you though, you're a true scumbag through and through, I know this now, there's nothing that could ever make you into a good person, there's no helping you."

I walked out in the water where he was now trying to stand

up. Using my powers, I had the water itself grab hold of him, with him crashing down straight on his back, a huge water ring splashing up in the air.

"Can't fight me with your hands huh?" Casey said as he gasped for air. "Come on Maria, fight me with your hands you piece of shit, I'd better die tonight, if not, I'll kill you, I promise."

"Oh you will, will you? I asked as suddenly I plopped on my knees, placing my hand on his face, submerging it under the water. "Then I'd better make sure you die then, never make a promise you can't keep."

Casey fought with all his might, shaking his head around in a violent manor. The water splashed around everywhere, including all over me, even soaking my hair. Finally, I gave him a little break, you could hear his gasp, which quickly refilled his lungs. Pressing down even harder now, I moved my hand just enough to be able to look him into his eyes as the life was soon to leave his body. I wanted to make sure I'd be the last thing he'd ever see.

He struggled for what seemed like hours, as time itself

appeared to slow down for this event. I watched as he finally took his first breath of the salty water, terror took over in his eyes unlike anything I'd ever seen before. He fought me even harder at this point, but I was just too strong for him, smiling at him, all the while blowing kisses his way. I could tell his life would finally be over within just a few more moments, a great feeling of accomplishment came all over me, like I just made something that was wrongfully done to me right, even though death was the answer. His eyes began fading, the excitement inside of me was almost too intense to endure.

"Like always, my timing is impecable," Quigley suddenly spoke out, as he suddenly appeared standing in the water just behind me. "Can't let you do that this time, sorry!"

With not even a wave of his hand, I suddenly flew fifty feet back, landing on the beaches sand with a rolling thud. By the time I even looked back at him, Quigley already had a now bent over and gasping Casey, on his knees and out of the water, right next to him on the beach.

"This doesn't concern you," I said as I suddenly threw a massive fireball straight at Casey, with Quigley suddenly breathing in extremely hard, sucking the fireball into his own lungs.

"BLURBGT," Quigley belched out loudly, his hand covering his burping mouth. "Lovely, just lovely, I'll take more please, your powers taste is exquisite, once you're finished wasting your time, I'll be more than happy to explain what's going on here. You don't have to stop throwing fireballs though, I love a hot meal! We really would've had a problem if you would've thrown a cold bowl of oatmeal at me though, I don't think I could've brought myself to get in the middle of an oatmeal blast."

"Stay out of this Quigley," I demanded as I stood there getting madder with each passing moment. "I've had a bad enough life the way it is, this man caused a great deal of my misery. Plotting, planning, doing things way out of the ordinary to make sure his schemes worked out, he's a real sicko."

"Hmm," Quigley said as a grin appeared on his face. "Sounds more like a chip off the old block, I'm so proud of you my boy. I'm kind of like, I guess you could say, not quite, but almost your daddy. Good job son, way to go."

"Alright, I agree," I replied as I cringed. "You're the original sicko, guess there's no topping you with that one, but you sure aren't our daddy. Now if you don't mind, I'd like to finish this wonderful evening I've been spending with my brother alone."

"Ahh," Quigley giggled. "To be honest, I do mind, in fact I mind quite a bit, that is if I were ever to be honest. Hang on a second, let me even the players in this little game you and your brother are playing just a tad bit more."

Quigley reached out his finger, his nail began to grow out from it, quickly becoming a sharp jagged looking claw. He looked at Casey who was still bent over coughing, jabbing this claw deep into the back of his neck, with Casey's head instantly looking up with his mouth opening as if to scream, yet as his eyes quickly began changing into a dark maroon color, the look of total peace fell upon his face. Pulling his hand away from Casey, Quigley began walking away from us, turning around about twenty five feet or so away from Casey.

Suddenly Casey, who had been in like a frozen state for quite a few moments, suddenly screamed out, but not with his normal voice, this was by far a deeper voice, if not a growl.

"I CAN FEEL IT!" He shouted, as he suddenly looked up at our moon, which was but just a slight sliver of the nights skyline, the rest of it being the cloud cover remnants of a storm that must've been on the island earlier that day. "NOOOOOOO, IT'S TOO HOT, I'M BURNING UP!"

Suddenly he began tearing at his clothing, ripping it all off of him. Becoming completely naked seemed to be the only thing he could think about, as he flung his items about the beach.

"MARIA," He screamed out in a demonically low sounding voice, as his face began elongating, making a nasty popping sound. "I'M COMING FOR YOU!"

Casey's fingers as well as his arms and legs began popping and cracking, as they quickly grew, his face still taking form. His legs became very odd looking, yet extremely muscular, with almost dog styled looking feet. Long scraggly hair began growing in an extremely odd fashion all over his body, quickly covering any skin that still showed. He fell to the ground in agony, rolling and squirming around wildly as a loud popping sound could be heard coming from his hip area. He just laid there for a minute breathing heavy, all curled up in a ball of hair, shaking as if cold.

Suddenly, a bolt of brownish fur flew off the ground right at me, slamming into me, causing me to fly back a few feet, but I managed to still have control of my landing though, as I landed on my feet, hitting Casey immediately with a nice fireball blast. The blast hit him with the force of a comet, entering our atmosphere, pushing him back several feet as well, his fur now all singed. The stench of burnt hair in the air, almost made me sick.

"Ready for round two Maria?" Casey spoke out as he dusted himself off. "I think this will be a much better fight than our last don't you?"

"I'm ready whenever you are," I replied. "As you said earlier little brother, just do it."

Casey lunged, as did I, but a split second before colliding, Quigley once again intervened, freezing us in the air.

"Now now children, we don't have time for this at the moment," Quigley spoke out as he looked at both of us and began lightly slapping our faces. "I promise we'll do this again sometime, but a twist of tonight's events have given me no choice but to do a change up. Would you guys like to hear a story? I have a good one."

Quigley looked at us like we were going to answer his question, but it wasn't possible in the frozen state he had us in.

"Well now," He giggled. "I'll take your silence as a yes. So let's see here, where to begin? Hmm, I know, see there once was these special children born, there were three of them. They've since been born many times over, but the first time they were ever created, something wonderful happened. During their first time being alive since their creation, they were all capable of having children, to which they did. Unknown to anyone was that because the original children were created by magic, the children that they had took different magical forms as they grew older. One of the three siblings fathered people with magical powers, these people have had many names throughout history, but powerful they all become. The second of the three siblings fathered children of a wild and fierce nature, who could blend in perfectly with ordinary people, as well as animals. While the third sibling gave birth to the terror that lives in the night, giving people a reason to leave a light on. Unfortunately once all three siblings died and were recreated, they couldn't make magical children anymore once the magic awoke in them. Only after years and years of developing these siblings are they able to have children now. Usually though, they are programmed to have a certain amount. Such as you Maria, you always have one child, to which you chase him across the world, always entering our favorite cave, loosing your powers. Once exiting the cave, your true genetics take hold, with you in the end being not only the Destroyer, but the mother of all vampires, you'll see what I mean soon enough. Casey, normally you just live out a life of plotting, planning and drinking, you never know what you're trying to plot out, your plans never workout the way you want them to, then you always drown your yourself until you die. Thankfully you're the family whore, always giving me eleven new little scumbags. Ten sluts, and one awesome son, a boy that's extremely devoted to the people he loves. You're boy always becomes sterile upon the magic entering his body, so he never fathers any children, at least in the normal sense. He's more of the opposite of you this time though, luckily for me, you just never know when it comes to werewolves. As for your brother Quinton, he always has four children to which he never learns about, such as he had no clue they'd all been born on the same night you gave birth to Darius. They're all just beginning to learn of their true selves as we speak right now, everyone's turning twenty four, just like Darius has and Casey's son just did. Everyone has the same birthday, such as the three of you guys do. These young adults are going to bring about a new age for magic once more. They will be the ancestors of all that is magical, with their teachings to remain within each childs group. A true rebirth is upon us, the rebirth of all that is magical once more! Now if you two will mellow out for a minute, I'll let you guys go."

I was dumbfounded, the story he just told was of my own, actually, of all three of us. I didn't know what this all meant, but I knew I'd better listen to Quigley and calm down, at least a tad bit.

He released both of us at the same time, with us landing face first in the water, drenching my dress completely, as well as suddenly tasting a pretty salty flavor in my mouth, as I got some of the sea water in it.

"You two need to cool down," Quigley laughed wickedly. "I hope that helps a little bit."

I picked myself up off the ground, as Casey stood up next to me. A sudden blast of high winds began drying both of us off at a phenomenal rate, just as I instructed it to do.

"I always knew you wanted to blow me," Casey snarled, his singed hair atrocious, now that it was all wet. "From what I hear, you're pretty good at it!"

"That's enough Casey!" Quigley said as his voice echoed in

my head. "Don't make me rub your nose in any doodie, mind me, or you'll be a bad boy. I won't take you on any car rides, or stroke your hair if you don't mind me, my puppy, I promise. Now, be a good doggie and shut up before I get the flea soap out, you really stink, a bath might be a good idea anyway! Don't make me put a collar on you."

"You're a funny guy, but you're wrong about one thing!" Casey spoke out nicely. "I only have ten kids, you're right about how they are though, they're all whores! Sorry, never had a son, would've been cool if I had, then I could've trained him to be just like me."

"Which is why you never knew about him," Quigley laughed histerically. "You never get to meet the son you always have, well, not normally anyway. As for those ten wonderful wannabe virgins of yours, I hate to tell you, but this is the real reason I've come here and saved you tonight."

"What do you mean," Casey spoke out as he turned human, exposing his naked self to the world. "What about my girls? Are they in some kind of trouble? I'll do anything for them, well except for living with their mothers again. Are they okay?"

"Unfortunately," Quigley spoke out as he bowed his head. "A tragic event I hoped wouldn't happen did happen, claiming all ten of your daughters lives, which is why I intervened between you and your sister tonight."

"What," Casey said as he dropped to his knees. "My babies, all gone? NO!"

"Yeah, sorry to tell you, I know how you're father of the year and all," He continued. "Anyway, with their deaths, there won't be anyone to continue the bloodline, as your son will become sterile upon being changed into what you are. The only way for him to create new life, is for him to stop the beast inside of him, at least long enough for the person to fully change, that is, without killing them while waiting. It takes twelve hours for the venom to consume a person enough for them to change. You changed instantly only because of the DNA I implanted inside of all of you when I created you three. So he'll have twelve hours to figure out if he wants to keep the person in his troup, or just eat them instead. *You* my man, are going to scratch him, changing your son into what his destiny is, which you'll do in about thirty minutes. I'm keeping you alive so you may continue breeding, as the magic doesn't effect one that wasn't supposed to have it. I know your upset about your daughters, but you can father as many children as you wish and yes, they're all going to be daddies little girls. "

"Who is this guy?" Casey yelled out at me. "Does he have some kind of mental illness? Can he just shut up? Really dude, first you tell me my children are dead all nice and calm like, then in the next breath you expect me to help you change a son I've never had? Are you crazy? Is there something wrong with you? I don't want to do anything but go back to Michigan and see my kids."

"I think you should listen to him Casey," I suddenly spoke out, as I noticed Thomas finally arriving at the beach, with his half dead friend. "Quigley might be insane, but he seems to plan out everything about our world, like some kind of designer."

"You're way smarter than your son is!" Quigley giggled.

"Now Casey, as I was saying, if you don't do as I ask of you, I'll imprison you inside of a mountain for all of eternity, you think your ex wives drove you nuts, I got six surprises for you."

"Alright, well if I had this son, then who with?" Casey asked all cocky. "I've only been with a few chicks."

"Does the name Tabitha ring a bell?" Quigley laughed. "It should, you even named one of your girls after her."

"No way!" Casey spouted out. "You mean that waitress from Indiana? That was like twenty five years ago, we only hooked up once, the next time I went back there, she'd moved away, that was the only woman I'd ever truely felt like I could've ever really loved. I just can't believe it, I gave her my phone number, I just know it, she never called, kept our baby a secret, what a bitch!"

"Such is life," Quigley sighed. "Now, as I was saying, you have a son, I can only take you so close to him, it's for his own safety, because I know someone that'll be feeling for me to use my powers when I normally turn him, then for the next twelve hours his life will be in jeapordy as she'll know his location, or at least the vicinity of him. You'll have to find him with your new sense of smell, when you find your own scent in the air, you'll know you found him. As for you Maria, Jasmine has taken a turn for the worse, I need you to gather up all the ladies of Nod, making sure not to forget any babies they might already have. Get them all back to the cave safe and sound, let them know Jasmine's trying to absorb magic, they'll know what you mean by it. This is a priority, don't fail me on this!"

"Now Casey, I think you have a job to do," Quigley spoke out real calm as he threw clothing at him, which appeared from nowhere. "You ready to go for a ride boy? I'd let you hang your head out the window, that is if we had one."

"Here Maria, you may need this," Quigley spoke out as he touched my temple area. "Now listen, once you touch Jupiter or Von, they'll feel my lovely women like you now do, bring them home Maria."

Casey struggled to put his cloths on, but upon finishing, and with a slight wink from Quigley directed right at me, they just vanished. No sound, no nothing, nothing like my wormhole, only a maroon twinkle was seen with it disappearing into itself.

"I have a question for you Maria," Thomas suddenly spoke out with a disturbed look on his face. "Why in the world was your brother naked in the first place? I mean you brought him to the beach for what? A late night swim? Skinny dipping if you will? A far cry from eating him, or, uh, did you?"

"Watch your mouth there Thomas!" I spoke out harshly. "I know you're just joking around, but that's not anything to joke about. My brother is a werwolf, at least he is now, he wasn't when you first met him, Quigley changed him, wants him to breed the bloodline so to speak, after turning his own son into a monster like him".

"Well I guess that explains why he was naked," He laughed. "Sorry that you lost your dinner though, if you'd like, you can share mine with me."

"NO!" Butch who was lying there motionless on the ground, groaned out. "Let me go, I'll be good I swear."

"I'd really like that Thomas," I replied, ignoring Butch completely. "Are you sure you won't mind sharing?"

"Ahh, come on man," Butch pleaded as he looked up at Thomas with his blood covered face. "You don't have to do this bro, I'm sorry okay? I'm sorry for everything I ever put you through, please, just please, let me go home."

"I don't mind sharing at all Maria," Thomas said as he ignored Butch's pleads as well. "In fact, I'd be honored to share my meal with you."

Both of our faces suddenly turned in Butch's direction, the look of terror soon began filling his face, as we both transformed into our true selves, moving around until we stood on both sides of him.

"Noohohohoh," He cried as he grabbed at his neck. "Please no."

With a sudden forward motion, Thomas followed my lead, as I struck. Pinning his arms to the ground with my hands, Thomas and I sank our teeth into his neck at the same time, me on one side,

Thomas on the other. It only took about three seconds before the guy stopped screaming, which is when I finally noticed I no longer heard voices in my head anymore.

The taste of human blood hadn't crossed my lips for some time now, it's bitter sweet flavor completely engulfing my mouth, as I drank down more than my fair share of Butch.

Without any warning, the power inside of me tripled, with another explosion coming out of me. Blasting Thomas completely off the beach and out of site. I got to my feet, with a new feeling inside of me, a powerful one at that, I was unbeatable, there would be nobody to stop me from any task I decided to do.

I looked towards the woods, finally seeing that Thomas was starting to move around, I couldn't waste anymore time though, Quigley needed me, I wouldn't fail him I had women to retrieve for him. I opened my wormhole and began to walk into it, I paused for a moment, as I suddenly smelled the scent of Jasmine in the air. No way, I thought to myself as I entered into the twirling light.

CHAPTER 17

Thomas had just gotten to his feet, when suddenly and surprisingly, right next to where Maria's wormhole had just closed, a new wormhole appeared, with Jasmine, Julian and JC stepping out of it. Jasmine looking around the beach area frantically.

"Where are they?" Jasmine suddenly asked. "I just felt them, both of them. At least I know for sure I felt Maria, but I could've sworn I felt Quigley. We're too late, their gone."

"Oh great!" Thomas who was behind them out of sight suddenly spoke out. "Not you!"

"Oh yes!" Jasmine spoke out happily as she spun around now facing him. "It's me, aren't you happy to see me? I thought you said you were with me, where you not suppose to stay right at Maria's side? How do you expect me to know what she's doing now? Did you just help out Maria, Thomas? I hope not, yet I feel as if your answer will not be a truthful one though. So tell me, did you just betray me Thomas?"

"Well that depends," Thomas replied reluctantly. "Are you going to let me go if I tell you? If so, then I'll be happy to fill you in on what happened here."

"Let you go, hmm," Jasmine said as she rubbed her chin with her hand. "I tell you what, tell me what just happened here a few minutes ago and I'll think about it. Tell me what I *really* want to hear and you'll get an unusual reward."

"That's cool, what all do you want to know?" Thomas asked quickly. "I really didn't get to see what all happened here, I was a little late arriving."

"Well," Jasmine replied in a soft tone. "Just who all was here when you got here? Where did they go?"

"Well Maria was here," Thomas started slowly. "Not sure who the other guy was, probably some vampire. They fought on the beach, with them both just disappearing, I have no idea where they went. All I know is once she kills that one, she'll be going after more of us, I just got lucky that she didn't decide to kill me first, I fear I wouldn't be here telling you this now."

"Oh how I just love liars," Jasmine said as a smile suddenly crossed her face. "Do you not think I can feel what happens in our world? Besides that, I can hear inside of your mind. There are no vampires under attack at this time are there Thomas?"

"Oh, well, she must've killed the guy then." Thomas said as he looked around the beach. "I hope she's not on her way back here now or anything, she's pretty powerful now, especially after drinking her own blood."

"Just how do you know she did that?" Jasmine said as her smile grew brighter. "I thought you missed the events."

"Well, I saw her drink it right before she began fighting that guy," Thomas replied. "She's even much stronger than what I feel you are."

"Really?" Jasmine spoke out as a slight giggle escaped from her lips. "You know why you can't feel how strong I truly am?

Because I wasn't mad yet. Now tell me, was Quigley here, I felt him, don't lie to me, don't you want your reward?"

"Never met the guy!" Thomas replied. "I've heard of him, but sorry, he wasn't here."

"See now," Jasmine replied as she slowly rubbed Thomas's shoulder. "I can hear things, things you wouldn't believe, things that are coming out of your own mind right now, as we speak. Quigley was here, as was Maria and her brother Casey. We have a regular family reunion going on here, huh? Oh wow, Quigley changed Casey into a werewolf? So that's how he plans on bringing his most powerful pet back to life, get good old daddy to do it, so I won't feel Quigley's energy. Hmm, I didn't think of that one, good plan sexy, as always, you're one step ahead of me, I doubt you can keep up though, I walk fast."

"So, now you know everything," Thomas said as a lump went down his throat. "Can I go now? You said I'd be rewarded."

"That I did," Jasmine said as she slid her hand off his shoulder, down his chest. "I always make good on my promises, your reward is spending eternity inside of me, that is once your essence powers up my child. Remember, last time I saw you, I told you I'd kill you next time we met? Well consider yourself lucky."

Suddenly, without anytime for Thomas to do anything, Jasmine began using her powers, slowly removing his essence, as his screams filled the empty sounding night air. Thomas looked straight at Julian and JC, as he could feel his insides being ripped out, with both of them bowing their heads in shame as they refused to watch the life leave his eyes.

"POP!" Jasmine spoke out, just as the popping sound erupted from Thomas, his eyes fading into a blank gaze. "Got ya', don't be sad, be glad, you're going to a better place now."

With a sudden hard push into her stomach, once again that awful popping sound echoed around her. With Jasmine suddenly grabbing at her belly in pain.

"Are you okay Jasmine?" JC suddenly asked. "You don't look so good."

"JC's right," Julian agreed. "You should probably feed on

some blood, or for that matter, bloodwine, we're on the island, so hey, lets drink, after all, Maria has plenty of the stuff here, even a bar area for you to sit down for a bit, collect yourself."

"You may be right," Jasmine replied. "A little time off my feet might be exactly what the doctor ordered. I guess being pregnant isn't such the easy task I thought it'd be. It seems to take a lot out of me, everytime I place another orb inside of me, I feel even more drained. I'm starting to think that maybe I'm absorbing the wrong orbs, I mean, I know of six other orbs I can get, the only problem is finding them."

"What do you mean?" JC asked nervously. "You're not talking about us are you?"

"I'll kill you in due time JC," Jasmine laughed. "Just not tonight, as I don't think the baby wants anymore blue orbs anyway. I think it'd like some different tasting ones, what can I say, some people like variety. I do know of six perfect people, with six tiny orbs for me, all I have to do is find them and take them. Thomas just let me know that Maria has the ability to find these women for me, so I think Maria and I will have a conflict she just can't win, I'll use her to get what I want."

"Well in that case," JC replied as she looked at Julian. "You should get some rest, you look like you're about to collapse."

"I think you're right," Jasmine replied as she suddenly opened up the wormhole directly in front of everyone, half collapsing as she did, to which Julian and JC caught her as she fell, helping her into it, carrying her, Jasmine's feet dragging all the while. "I could use a little rest and a quick refill, right now I feel like I need all the energy I can get."

Making their way through the wormhole, they found themselves instantly in the island mansion's bar area, with Julian and JC setting Jasmine down at the closest table to them they could find, just a few feet away from the bar. Julian instantly made his way up to the bar, grabbing three highly polished glasses, filling them very full, with the bloodwine from the bar's tap.

"Here Jasmine, drink this," Julian said as he handed her glass to JC, who handed it to her. JC took a glass for herself as well as

Julian, as they all three enjoyed the wonderful flavor of the bloodwine, drinking down every last drop.

The power Jasmine felt she'd been lacking quickly re-emerged, with her being able to once more get back to her feet. She walked over to the bar, handing her empty glass to Julian.

"I think I'll have another," Jasmine said as she smiled. "I'm glad to see you guys feel free to join me."

Julian filled her glass back up, handing it back to her as he re-filled both his own, as well as JC's glasses. They stood there for a few moments just sipping, Jasmine looked normal now. It was as if all of her energy hadn't been drained from her after her experience with the last orb, yet, all was now well with her.

"I can feel that Maria has picked up her loverboy now," Jasmine spoke out. "They'll be getting Von next. We'll need to be ready to go to them once they make a move to any of the women of Nod. Thomas told me way too much, this is a good thing though, we'll be able to find the women I need much easier now, that's Maria's new goal in life you know, to save these women from me. My dear Quigley, you may live, but you have no life. I plan on spicing things up for you a tad bit, I do wonder, did your waterfall show you just exactly what I'm going to do to your precious babies. I know you can hear me, no need to hide anymore, I know you're not just lying there all dead on the ground anymore, I saw you in Thomas's vision he shared with me."

Jasmine stood there looking up at the ceiling, silence suddenly covered the bars area, as the time passed by tick by tock, no reply ever given. For about three minutes not a noise could be heard, finally, Jasmine looked back down at the ground, a sad face on her usually smiling one.

"I know you're upset with me," She said softly. "I'll be a good mother, I'll show you, I'll show everyone, nobody is dying in vain, our child lives! I can feel it moving around. Look how big I'm starting to get already. I'm sorry I'm taking this route, you left me no choice, but remember, everything I do, I do because I love you."

Aa eerie silence fell upon the place, as once again, no reply came from Quigley. Jasmine sat down, placing her head in her hands, and in a surprising twist, began crying uncontrollably, with Julian and JC just looking at each other as if they didn't know what to do. Both of them patting her on her back, which felt very uncomfortable and unnatural to them, as she wept, her body shaking with each breath she took in.

CHAPTER 18

"Well, that was cool!" Casey spoke out as he instantly found himself in the woods, about thirty miles outside of a little town called Ketchikan. The air was extremely cool, yet it felt fantastic to him, as the coolness of it seemed to help his body temperature finally feel more normal. "Can I do that instant transmission thing, you know, like you just did? I'd love to pop in on a few people you know?"

"I know the feeling," Quigley spoke quietly. "Unfortunetly though, you really just have the power to transform into the beast, but you'll be the strongest one of them all, well beside's your son that is."

"Well what's his name? What's he like? Is he like me?" Casey spoke loudly. "What's he doing all the way in Alaska? I thought he was in Indiana?"

"So many questions, awe, how sweet, such a concerned father you are," Quigley laughed. "Now keep your voice down and listen. You need to transform into the beast and run as fast as your feet can carry you. You're a little over thirty miles from where you'll need to be, so speed is everything. You only have twenty six minutes and thirty seconds before you'll need to accidentally bump into your son in the bar he's walking into as we speak. Make sure you scratch him just enough to draw blood and make sure it's before he goes outside."

"So I have to run to this place, enter the bar, walk up to him and scratch him?" Casey asked. "Then what? What's in this for me? I don't even know his name, or what he looks like for that matter."

"If you'd be so kind as to transform," Quigley giggled. "I'll show you everything you need to know. As for what's in it for you, I'll let you decide that once you've finished doing as I ask. I think I know what Casey Myers wants out of life, but be careful what you wish for, it just might tear you apart in the end."

Instantly, Casey tore out of his clothes, with the fur emerging, standing straight out on him, as he transformed into the beast from within. He looked at Quigley with his new and terrifying grizzly face, hair still burnt. The foul odor of burnt hair emanating from him. Quigley waved him over to the side of him, to which Casey did reluctantly, kneeling down at his feet.

"My poor puppy," Quigley spoke out as he suddenly began

stroking Casey's head like a dog, all soft like, filling his head with images of his son. "You really need a bath! You might need to run even faster, maybe find an abandoned cabin, I don't know, with a shower maybe, or I like I said earlier, I can get some flea soap and we can kill two birds with one stone. Try not to draw any attention to yourself, you're son isn't a werewolf yet, but all the people that'll be outside of the bar when he leaves will be. Make sure you scratch him before he makes it outside, timing is everything with this, so you should do it as soon as you go in the bar and locate him. Don't be hanging out in any bathrooms either, just get the job done and go."

"Well now," Casey spoke out with pride. "Now that's a good looking boy, you just showed me in my head, you sure he's mine? He's got way better muscle tone than I ever did. I bet he gets lots of girls, he's probably the town stud. So, I now know what he looks like, do I get to know his name? I mean come on, he is my son, I think I have a right to know what he's called."

"Hmm, seems like it's storytime," Quigley giggled. "I love

storytime, but I'll have to make this a quick one, you really need to get going. See there was this woman, she loved a guy, he loved her, they were made for each other, in the end they were only just supposed to have a kid together, as the woman was a rare kind of woman indeed. She was in fact one in a million, as she herself was already a werewolf, but what made her special is the fact that she could actually have a child, she was allowed just one, as two becomes a problem. Only the correct bloodline entering her would cause a baby to delevope, to which the woman believed she was infertile, not taking many precautions. Unknown to her, a drunk college kid, which whom she slept with, was the match her body needed. Upon finding out of her pregnancy, she feared the other werewolves would hunt her down, in an effect to stop the cycle their ancient scrolls told them of. A cycle which ends with the dethrowning of the current leader, with the chosen child to re-establish the true nature of the werewolf once more. Well the woman feared for her child's life, so she moved deep into the Canadian bush in an effort to not be found. She raised this child never knowing his father's full name, all she could remember was the father's first name, which was Casey. The only other thing that came to mind when she thought of him was the coffee stain on his white tee-shirt he left behind that night. She gave the only name she could for the child, still naming him after his father. The first thing she noticed about him was the coffee stain, to which she named him Stain. His last name was an easy one, to which it became Casey. A person isn't quite a person without a middle name, to which she thought long and hard. In the end, she couldn't think of anything else that represented who his father was, with no middle name given to him. So, an answer to your question, your son's name is Stain Casey."

"So now, why do you need me to change my son anyway?" Casey spoke out confused, drool dripping from the corner of his beastly mouth. "You changed me, seems like you could've done the same for him."

"Well, I normally do," Quigley spoke out sternly. "This time though, I have someone feeling for my powers to arrive, her name's Jasmine, you might want to stay clear of her, she's not very fond of my doggies. She didn't feel me use my powers yet, because of that little fight between you and your sister. With Maria using her powers such as she did, I was able to sneak in under the radar. Jasmine probably felt Maria's powers, but even if she did feel mine, she'll think it was Maria she felt, she'll never find us now."

"Why do you care about this woman?" Casey quickly asked. "You seem to be pretty powerful yourself, is she more powerful than you or something?"

"Oh, oh, man, that's ripe! I think I like you after all," Quigley laughed out loud uncontrollably. "Actually, I created her! Not going to go into details, just understand that your ten dead children's soul's are all trapped inside of her now, she would like to make that number eleven instead of ten though. If she feels me use my powers, that'll help her zero in on your son's location, this is why I changed you, so you can change him. That's your only goal in life right now, sorry to make you run so far, but oh well, just pretend someone threw a stick. Just don't make me have to rip you apart, as I promise you I will if you fail in scratching him in time. I think you might want to get going now. Run boy, run, go get the stick!"

With a sudden loud roar, Casey rose to his hind quarters, momentarily howling at the moon before dashing off down the roadway, running on the center line.

"I'll be watching you," Quigley yelled out, his voice echoing down the road. "Before he steps outside understand? If you want to have some fun, then get er' done!"

Instantly Quigley disappeared in the same fashion, just a maroon twinkle of light left as he made his way to his destination. He did as he did with Casey, using minimal magic which Jasmine couldn't feel. Folding space and time together, instead of just stepping through a wormhole, leaving no residue of his travel for her to feel.

Running seemed to bring out the beast even more in Casey now, as he tore down the road, trees were more of a blur than anything else, as he swept by them, causing a slight breeze to move them just moments after him passing by.

The cool night air aided him in his little run, keeping a fresh clean feeling in his lungs, with him not running out of breath at all. As he ran down the road, he could see the faint cast of headlights getting ready to come around the corner. Baring down as hard as he could, he increased his speed. In his effort to try and take the curve straight by running through the woods in between, his front foot suddenly fell into a huge pothole he hadn't seen, causing him to tumble out of control, just as the car came around the corner, with Casey slamming into the rear end of it, sending the car spinning out of control, to a sudden stop.

"Holy shit Donovan, something ran into us!" The man yelled out in excitement to the driver. "Are you alright? Dobs is gonna be pissed about his car man, I'm glad I wasn't driving it. And just what the hell is that smell? Did you drop your cigarette into a pile of hair or something?"

"Hey Walker, I wasn't even smoking, I have no idea where that smell's coming from," Donovan replied as he sat there looking out of the windows all around the outside of the car. "Forget the car though, I'm more worried about what the hell hit us? Felt like a moose, or a bear, if it was, we get a free snack, I'm up for a quick bite to eat, how about you?"

"Don't mind if I do boys," Casey suddenly spoke out as he lunged in through the window, ripping and tearing his way back out again. Growling, crunches and screams rumbling throughout the secluded area, as he finally tore through. "Thanks guys, I needed a quick lunch, mind if I borrow your car?"

Casey opened the driver door, with Donovan's disfigured corpse immediatley falling to the ground. Quickly, he grabbed the arm of Walker, pulling his lifeless body over the gear shift and out the door next to his buddy.

"Thanks guys," Casey laughed as he began changing back into his human form, stripping them of their clothing as well as boots as he transformed. "Redwings! Oh Walker, how'd you know, I love these boots, you're to kind my man, just my size."

"Oh, don't worry Donovan," Casey spoke out to his dead

body. "I've always wanted a nice leather jacket, a little water and yours will be good as new, thanks again guys. By the way, I don't think I smell that bad, that comment was a little rude you know, you really hurt my feelings."

Sitting down inside the car, Casey turned the key, with the engine firing right up. He placed the gearshift into gear and with a loud pop, the back tire on his side pushed the bent metal out of its way, with the rear end sliding in a burnout, quickly following the sound, as he sped off down the road. The rear end slid over from all the power, with two thumps being felt underneath the car, as he ran over the bodies.

"Sorry about that guys!" Casey hollered out the window, as he slammed the gearshift into second, with another chirp coming from the tires as he did. "Hope I didn't hurt you much, thanks for the Mustang, I love these cars!"

Shifting the car a couple of more times, Casey found himself a cd from the console, quickly putting it in the cd player. It had no name on the cd, and he soon found himself listening to the familiar sounds of Vanilla Ice, as Ice, Ice, Baby began booming loudly from the trunk, as the car had a complete audio system in the back of it. Casey's seat rumbled and vibrated as he drove incredibly fast down the road, half sliding around several sharp curves, with him singing happily along, bouncing his body all around as if he were dancing inside of it.

Looking at the speedometer, he knew ninety miles an hour was much faster than he could've been running, which meant he'd actually get to the bar before Quigley even claimed he would, guess he was proving the guy wrong already, he wondered what else could be different as well.

It didn't take long before he got to the outskirts of the city, quickly turning down the radio, as well as pulling over in a small wooded path of a driveway. He shut the motor off, opening the door. As he got out, he could smell his own scent over his own burnt aroma.

Following the scent, as he walked into the town on the partially gravel road, Casey soon found himself standing just outside of the bar his son was in. It was a small bar, nothing special, nothing fancy, but a bar just the same. He walked up the six steps leading to the door, turning his head, looking on the deck like porch to his right which was just round the corner. No sign of his son, just a group of seven guys which gave him the death stare, they probably wondered who this new stranger was..

He grabbed the door handle, making his way inside of the bar, looking around as he stood by the open door. There was only about ten or so people in there, which made it very easy for him to pinpoint his son, especially since he sat at the bar with a gorgeous woman. Looking around a little bit more, he found where the bathroom was, which is where he immediately headed to

"Wow!" Stain whispered to his female companion. "Did you smell that guy when he walked by? Nasty!"

"Yeah, I did unfortunately," She replied loudly, as she tipped her glass up to her mouth, taking a drink of her Bloody Mary. "Smells like someone here cooked an animal without skinning it first. I agree with you though, nasty!"

"Shh, Corie, he'll hear you!" Stain whispered again. "I have more important things to think about right now. If what all you just told me is true, then I'm in real trouble here."

"Look, all I know is we're going to have to go outside eventually," Corie replied as she watched Casey go into the bathroom, the door closing behind him. "I don't know what you're waiting for, those guys aren't going to go away, you know what they are and they sent me a long way to get you."

"I know they did, but like I've told everyone, my last name's Casey, not Myers." Stain said as he looked Corie in her eyes. "I don't want them to hurt you either, Dobs said you'd pay for turning sides on him like you did a few minutes ago."

"Look, don't you worry about me. I take my orders from a much higher power than Dobs," Corie announced. "What I did for you, I'd do even if I hadn't been instructed to protect you, well maybe not when we first met, but you know what I mean."

"What will you do if this Quigley guy doesn't show up?" Stain quickly asked. "Then what?

"Don't worry sweetie," Corie spoke out softly. "I'm sure we'll see him soon."

Casey, who could hear everything they just said, looked out the bathroom window. A huge burly beast of a man immediately looked up at him, smiling a wicked smile.

"Alright boys!" The big man said as he stood up and began walking to the door, reaching out his hand towards the knob. "I'm tired of this already! Now that we know she'll fight over this guy, I guess Corie can just ring the bell for food from now on, just like the other traitors. That is once we capture her and her little boyfriend. I thought he was supposed to become this great lord of us all, if this is true, he should be able to fight us off by now, this guys been twenty four for almost a full day now, if he's not changed by now, then I don't think the stories we've been told are true, or he's not our guy, after all, you guys already have a great leader right here, me!"

"Now, now Eugene, a great leader you may be, but a lord you are not!" Quigley's voice suddenly spoke out from the air around them. "You won't open that door if you're as bright as you think you are, if you do, you'll never make it inside, I promise. Twelve hours Mr. Dobson, you can try to destroy him all you want then, but you *will* give him the required timeframe, understand me? Twelve hours from the moment he opens the front door and steps on the porch, not a moment sooner, do not make me have to intervene, I want to watch things play out realistically, so don't do what your already thinking, or your death will soon follow your choice."

Dobs let go of the doorknob, turning around, walking back to the table he was just sitting on. His stares becoming even more intense as he sat down facing the door.

"Twelve hours, fine!" Dobs replied. "Then I'll kill him!"

"If you can Eugene," Quigley's voice echoed as he laughed, "if you can, I look forward to the show. I've enjoyed the programming so far!"

Casey could hear Quigley just as much as the men outside, he knew he'd better get out there and do his job, these other guys seemed to fear and respect Quigley, he figured he might want to do the same thing.

Upon opening the bathroom door, Casey immediately noticed Stain and Corie headed towards the door. He was a good twenty feet behind them, with no way of getting to them before they exited the building. Elongating one of his fingernails, and stepping up his pace, as they exited. Casey came barreling behind them, first pushing Corie out of his way, as he pretended to stumble and fall, grabbing the back of Stain's shirt in the process, pulling him down with him. As the two of them crashed onto the porch, rolling down the stairs, ever so swiftly Casey scratched the back of his son's calf with his now elongated fingernail, but just leaving a very slight wound, hardly even noticable.

"Sorry son," Casey spoke out as he got back to his feet, suddenly walking away from the bar as he wiped himself off. "I think I had too much to drink. Take care my boy, maybe I'll see you later and even buy you a drink or two."

"Whatever!" Stain replied as he stood back up, dusting off

his clothes. "Maybe if you took a bath first, I'd take you up on that offer, but really man, you reek."

Casey made his way down the road, out of everyone's site, but decided he'd stay for awhile and watch how things played out. He turned off the road, walking into the forest, suddenly crouching down so as to stay out of site.

CHAPTER 19

As my wormhole opened up, I was very happy to see a smiling Jupiter, just sitting there at the same table we once ate at, just waiting patiently on me. As I stepped onto the carpet, once again without warning, a sudden surge of power entered my body. I quickly had to grab at the closest table to me, holding on to it to keep me balanced. I was saddened to feel that it was Thomas's energy, I knew his energy well, you couldn't mistake it, no doubt it was him.

"We need to get a move on hunny," I spoke out as I stood back up, casually strolling over to him. "We kind of have an emergencey, we can't waste any time either."

"Whoa Maria!" Jupiter spoke out as he stood up, looking at me up and down, checking me out all the while, like I were a piece of meat to him. "I take it you drank your blood? I figured that was what I felt earlier. You look sexy baby, you have those bad girl eyes I like again, come here, we're all alone in here, it'll be our little secret, we have a little time I'm sure."

"Oh Jupiter," I giggled as he playfully grabbed at me. "What's gotten into you? Now cut it out, we don't have time right now."

"Oh baby," He replied with a slight laugh. "We could always

make time you know."

"Well I'll have to ask for a rain check this time," I laughed. "Why are you being so silly about this anyway, you don't normally get so handsy with me, I mean not like this."

"I have no idea," Jupiter replied, as he grabbed my hand, kissing it gently. "I must say though, not that I don't like the nice you, but seeing the evil you inside of the nice you is like a real turn on for me right now. You look even more beautiful than I remember you already being."

"I'm glad you like the combo," I replied as I opened up my wormhole. "Let's see what Von thinks about it."

Jupiter looked at me for a moment, before grabbing me tightly against him, falling backwards into the wormhole with me right in tow, kissing me all the while. He landed with a loud thud as our wormhole opened up inside of my suite at DEP. We couldn't help but laugh as this happened. Von standing there watching the show, all shocked and surprised, the look on his face was just too funny for us to contain our laughter any longer, with it exploding out of us.

"I'd say to get a room, but I'm afraid I'm currently in it," Von spoke out, turning his head and looking away quickly, as I rolled slightly on top of Jupiter. "Man, Maria, I'd say you've changed a little since the last time I saw you. I see that you've started throwing out a heavy dose of theremones as well, so I guess you've become the Destroyer after all huh? I myself am even feeling the attraction to you, but I already knew this would happen, it's part of you becoming your destiny. See, the way it was explained to me is like this. Once you fully become the Destroyer, you'll eminate a powerful theremone, one that attracts men as well as women, but attracts vampires around the world the most, of course they have to be within a certain distance from you, but it works for miles. I'm sure you have some already heading straight for you right now, probably even people that are at work right here. It won't take to long before the first ones seek you out and find you here in the suite. We should probably go before anyone shows up, Quigley spoke to me in my head, told me to tell you to use Jupiter's plan, he said your plans always fail, that you needed to listen to him for once. What's going on here Maria? Quigley didn't explain anything to me, do you mind cluing me in?"

"Jasmine is trying to find the women of Nod," I replied. "She plans on absorbing their babies! We have to find these women first and get them all back to the safety of Nod. No matter what happens, we have to do this task first and foremost."

"Great!" Von spoke out in disgust. "Plan B it is, just great."

"You're kidding me?" Jupiter replied. "You mean Maria's like a big sexual x marks the spot for people?"

"Hey!" Von yelled out to him. "Are you paying attention to what she just said? This is what Lars told you could happen, why he was afraid of this particular rebirth. I'm not sure if you're aware of this or not, but Lars is my father, if he's not born, I won't be either, we need to hear this plan Quigley says you have, I really don't want plan B right now."

"I don't really know what plan B is and I have no idea what plan he's talking about." Jupiter said confused as he tried to concentrate on Von instead of my chest. "This is pretty awkward though, how does he expect me to come up with an idea when all I can think about is cool new sexual things? I mean how about this one Maria? I come up from behind you, then poof, in front of you, another poof and I'm below you, with of course my last poof ending with me on top of you? See, my mind is stuck in the gutter right now. Even though we could just do a little poof, here and a little poof there, grabbing the women, poofing them back to to Nod. If we did this a few times, being as speedy as possible, to avoid a run in with Jasmine, I guess it could work for us. It's just a stupid idea though, it's just the only idea I have right now. Then again, I guess it takes Jasmine a few moments to locate someones energy and transport too them. We can use your wormhole to our advantage, opening it as near to each woman as possible, maybe even just grabbing them, pulling them in with us, all while just being there but a moment. This way she'll never be able to find us. That's about the only idea I really have right now, not sure if it's the idea Quigley spoke of, so I guess this is more everyone's call on this one."

"Actually, no!" I replied. "If this is what you say we should do, then that's exactly what we'll do. I remember first hand how bad *my* plans seem to turn out, maybe it's time I listen to *yours* a little bit more."

"To be honest, I've been meaning to say something about that," Jupiter surprisingly responded. "I've lived a long time being what most would call a pushover, well, being in that cave opened my eyes to many things, with that being one of them. I want you to understand that I really love you with all my heart and soul. I will tell you that if you ever treat me like some kind of obsolete, childish person again, who's feelings, or opinion doesn't matter to you, instead of the loving faithful husband that I am, our love affair will be over with. Also, after twenty five years together, I think it's about time you changed your last name officially to Anderson, instead of Myers, this to me is a completely disrespectful thing to begin with, I expect that to be what you go by from now on, understand?"

"I, I," I stuttered, never expecting for Jupiter to stand up to me like he just did. "I'm sorry Jupiter, I never meant to disrespect you, I had no idea you felt that way, of course I'll change my name immediately. Maria Anderson kind of has a ring to it. I actually think your plan could work, I think I feel one of them now, we could try this out whenever everyone's ready."

Suddenly, the door to the suite burst open, with two unknown men, lower ranking vampires, swiftly making their way inside.

"She's mine," One of the men yelled out to the other. "I smelled her first."

The second man pushed him to the ground as he tried to pass him, with him looking around the room, weighing out his odds.

"I think I'll go first if you don't mind," The second man replied to the first one, yet staring directly at Jupiter and Von, who were now standing in front of me. "Step aside gentlemen, nobodies getting in my way, come here lady, I got something to give you."

"I got this!" Jupiter spoke out as he transformed into an even more frightening version of his true self, one I'd never seen before.

"You got something to give do you? Come here buddy, let me see it."

The man dashed in almost a total blur straight at Jupiter, with Jupiter just standing there, doing nothing. Suddenly as the man began to almost make contact, Jupiter hit the man straight in the middle of his face, I never even saw his hand move. Jupiter's hand exploded out the back of the mans head, with Jupiter suddenly picking his lifeless body off the ground, laughing histerically, with his hand still through his head, as he brought his body towards him, slamming his teeth deep into the guy's chest. He drank fast, only taking about five seconds or so before draining him dry, tossing the dead lifeless body onto the ground.

"I take it you're next!" Jupiter spoke out to the second man, with his hand still dripping blood on the floor.

"Nope!" The man blurted out. "I'm good. I'll just let you all get back to whatever it was you're doing, sorry to interupt, have a good day now."

"Not so fast!" Von suddenly spoke out. "I think you'll fit

right in with our festivities."

Without even a chance for the man to reply, Von instantly appeared behind the guy, grabbing both of his arms, placing them behind his head, in what I guess you'd call a full nelson. Von bashed the guys head several times really hard against the corner of the doorway, with laughter actually escaping his lips after the first couple of slams. He tossed the guy to the ground, right at my feet, looking up at me with the most evil smile I've ever seen (and I'd seen a lot of those), before speaking.

"My Queen," He began. "Oooh that was fun! Sorry, just couldn't contain myself anymore. Anyway, I know how much you enjoy a good vintage vampire, I hope you're not filled up yet, this one was born in a marvelous year."

"Ha, ha, very funny," I replied. "Funny though, even after just feeding, I do still feel empty inside. So you say a good year huh? I guess I can check it out."

The man didn't say another word, the look on his face said it all, as he quickly tried to scramble away, with me grabbing his foot just as he almost made it out the doorway. Pulling him back towards me, sliding on his belly, with him just screaming away. I climbed on top of the man, sitting all straddled across his lower back, pinning his hands down to the ground. Bending my head towards the back of his head, I growled in his ear, before sinking my teeth straight into it, I even giggled slightly as I heard the popping sound of his eardrum as my fang penetrated it.

He tried to fight, but it didn't last but a moment or two before he just started shaking violently, with nothing but a bunch of babble coming from his mouth, not really words, more like sounds. It took everything in me to keep doing what I was doing, not stopping once to bust out laughing at his funny noises. Finally he barked a couple of times like a dog and just like that, his ending was over, with me using the back of his shirt as a napkin, wiping my face off with it.

As I was trying to stand back up, it hit me like a ton of bricks, an energy level I wouldn't even have thought possible surged throughout my body, I screamed out in pain as I felt as if I were going to burn up from the extreme heat that seemed to come with the power I was receiving. Falling back to the ground, I looked at both Jupiter and Von, who were both looking at me in disbelief, as I suddenly burst into flames.

The heat was so intense, there was no escape from it either, I was the fire itself. Flares flew off me, with Jupiter and Von running quickly to the fire extinguishers, as many little fires began popping up all over the suite. As the energy inside of me settled in my body, the fire began going out slowly, until finally all of the fire, including the flares flying off me, seemed to go back inside of me.

"Holy shit Maria!" Jupiter spoke out as he hurried to me. "Are you alright? I've never seen anything like that before."

"I wondered what would happen once you drank from a vampire," Von spoke out as he put out the last fire. "I must admit, that was pretty cool looking. I think you're more than ready to show everyone who the destroyer is."

"Oh no, what have I done," I spoke out in horror, as I looked around my once beautiful suite. "I don't understand what just happened, I didn't mean to do anything like this. I don't even know *how* I did it."

"It's alright Maria," Von spoke out in a reassuring voice. "This place needed redecorating anyway."

"Thanks Von," I replied with a sigh. "I still don't feel any better about it though, I loved this suite."

"We should probably be leaving it pretty soon don't you think?" Jupiter joined in. "I guess we could just stay here to see who all shows up next, but I think we'd better get these women first."

"I agree," Von replied. "I know I'm ready to do this."

"So," I asked as I looked at each one of them in the eyes. "Which woman shall we get first?"

"Hang on a second Maria," Jupiter suddenly said. "If we go straight to any woman, Jasmine might feel us, do you think we should do a test run first? You know, go somewhere not even close to anything, or anyone, then see if Jasmine shows up once we do?"

"That's actually a good idea," I replied as I smiled at him. "Let's go to Indiana, we can go to my parents old lake house, it's secluded, not a house for almost a half mile. Jasmine knows there's a lake house there, after all, she's already been there once. She'll think one of the woman of Nod might be hidden there by doing this, that is, if she's feeling for us to make a move."

"Sounds like a plan," Von chuckled as he grabbed my arm. "I'll be in that hot tub of yours though, you two have a history when it comes to those things, we're going there on business you know."

"Right on bro," Jupiter laughed. "There's a whole lake out there as well, we could always break it in the right way."

"I think I have a say in this," I joked. "We need to stick to the plan though, breaking that lake in can be done some other time."

Jupiter grabbed hold of my arm, so with both of them ready to go, I opened up the wormhole, once again stepping into the twirling void.

CHAPTER 20

The wormhole opened exposing an unexpected site, it was my parents old cabin on the lake, except it was trashed. It'd been such a long time since I'd last been here, the place looked like hell itself hit it. The roof had a large tree which had fallen on it, by the look of it, some time ago. The cabin supported the tree's weight fairly well, but the tree wasn't quite dead either. Branches grew directly into the roof, out of it as well, as if the woods were swallowing up the place.

Ivy grew all along the sides of the place, covering up almost all of the wood, with only a few strips still showing. Just looking at the place, thinking of all my childhood memories, plus the memories of the last time I was here, almost made me cry.

I always loved coming here when I was a kid, it may not have been as fancy as it later became, but it was cozy all the same. I'd stay up all night, sitting on the old dock, waiting for a fish, any fish, but usually a catfish, to take my bait so I could catch them. I wasn't really a girly girl, I was a little more of a Tomboy most of the time, after all, I did have two mean brothers to tend with toughening me up some.

"Oh, wow!" Jupiter spoke out sadly, as he glared at the place. "I never would've imagined the place would look like this, this is terrible, we must fix this immediatley once we're done finding the women. I don't even want to hunt anyone until we're finished remodeling, this is unacceptable."

"I agree," Von replied. "I've always loved this place, if I would've known it would end up this way, I don't think I would've sold it to your dad all those years ago. This place used to be my home, it was actually built for the first time back around seventeen twenty five or so. A fire here, a tornado there, over the years this place has taken a beating. It's been rebuilt countless times, yet it's still as disturburbing a site to me as the first time I saw it demolished like this, only it was a fire which was started by the native Indians in the local area, they feared me, but they had reason to, I fed on their families, eventually even the ones that set my home ablaze."

"I just can't believe it looks like this," I said sadly as I held back my tears with all my might. "I want it fixed as well, I love it here, we'll make it even better than it already was."

We walked off the forest floor, up the stairs leading onto the deck, none of the steps broke thankfully, but about all of them sounded like they couldn't take much more weight than we'd just gave them, as they made their own distinct cracking or popping sound.

Reaching the top of the stairs, I looked over to my left, straight at the hot tub. Miraculously, there wasn't any damage or wear for that matter, it still looked brand new, filled to the brim with bubbling water. Everything else around it looked as if it had been hit by an aging time warp, even the bench was missing a leg on it.

"Alright, now this is getting a little on the weird side," I spoke out as I made my way over to it. "How come everytime we go anywhere that we've had sex in the hot tubs, they seem to be in perfect working order, no matter how terrible the conditions of the rest of the place has fallen into, the hot tubs always look brand new, like we just used them yesterday."

"I have no idea," Jupiter replied. "You're right though, it's a little on the strange side if you ask me as well."

"You know guys," Von suddenly spoke out half laughing, as he sank into the steamy water, clothes and all, quickly placing his hands behind his head. "It is strange, yet, very relaxing. Never look a gift horse in the mouth they say, so I think a nice hot bath would be a good idea for all of us anyway. Keep your clothes on though, that's what really needs clean. I mean come on, I think this is a pretty big hint, we stink!"

Without warning, Von, using his powers, waved his hand under water, pulling us both in with an invisible hand. Water rushed up my nose, giving me an immediate burning sensation in my sinuses.

I sat up in the tub, wiping the water from my eyes, Jupiter sat up as well, except he did with a huge grin on his face, as he suddenly began laughing.

"Alright, you got me," Jupiter said still laughing all the while. "Do you remember that time I talked you into that Amazon jungle trip? The look on your face as those Piranaha's tore you up like they did, is nothing compared to the look Maria just had on hers."

"I know," Von burst out, almost bringing himself to tears laughing. "That was amazing wasn't it?

"Ha, ha, guys, very funny," I replied trying not to laugh, quickly grabbing Von by his foot, suddenly pulling him under.

"Alright, I guess I deserved that," Von spoke out as he resurfaced above the water. "I forgot to wash behind my ears anyway."

We all began rinsing all the grim off of us, it didn't take but a few minutes before the water was almost black in color. Once our clothes were descent looking again, well at least cleaner than they were, we all climbed out of the tub.

I once again used my powers for a large breeze to start blowing, whirl after whirl of air gusts surrounding us all the while. Doing it much slower than usual, trying to make sure Jasmine could feel me, as she still hadn't arrived. After a good few minutes of drying time, once again we were all good to go. We sure didn't look like we came from any laundrymat, but at least we didn't have blood stains on us anymore.

"So, where is she?" I asked as I looked around everywhere. "Where's Jasmine? We've been here for at least an hour, she should've showed up by now."

"I don't think she's coming," Jupiter replied. "She might not be looking for you Maria, she could be doing just about anything right now. I think we're good to go here, I mean of course I could be wrong, she could just be waiting for us to travel again."

"I think it's safe to say she's not coming here," Von spoke out. "Just as Jupiter says though, she could be waiting for us to travel again, there's only one way we can find that out for sure though, we'll need to be very quick about things if she does show up though, get the woman into your wormhole as quickly as possible."

"Well, as they say, you never know until you try," I said nervously. "I just hope we don't run into Jasmine though, I'm not in any mood for a fight right now, at least not with her. She's tricky, but at least if we do run into her, I'll at least be somewhat more of a match against her. I can feel her power right now, as we speak, she's a lot stronger than I am, but I'm stronger than she remembers now."

I concentrated on an energy, a much different one, one which I'd never felt, that is, before Quigley allowed me to feel it. I zeroed in on this power, pin pointing exactly where it was located. Concentrating a little harder, I suddenly sent my astro self there, opening my eyes up to a huge waterfall, falling from an extreme height. Behind this waterfall was a small cave in which I entered. A beautiful woman with very pretty long blonde hair and her infant were deep inside of this cave, with the infant getting a drink from it's mother. Upon seeing this, I began to return to my body, as I went backwards, surprisingly, the woman looked straight in my direction, as if she knew I'd been there.

"I found one of the women", I spoke out as I returned to my body. "She has a baby with her, they're in a cave behind a waterfall, I can transport us just outside of the cave. I don't think I can get us any closer, I don't want us to open the wormhole inside of a mountain's cave, what if I was just a little off with where the wormhole opened for us? Opening up in solid rock, not sure if that's anything I want to checkout."

"Just get us close to her, get her out of there even if you have to leave me behind," Von replied. "I'll make sure to take care of Jasmine if she does show up."

I opened my wormhole, with both Jupiter and Von grabbing my arm tightly, as we all looked at each other for a moment, with a smile and nod from Von, being our cue to step into the twirling void.

Water fell slightly on us, as we all came out of the other side of the wormhole. Splatter's of water coming off the rocks soon covered our faces, with Jupiter soon wiping his hand across his face.

"Follow me guys," I spoke out as I headed around the side of the falls, stepping carefully over the rocks. "As I entered the cave, I could hear the distant sound of a babies cry. "She's this way!"

Suddenly, a wormhole I didn't open appeared directly in front of me, with Julian and JC being flung out of it. Jasmine, looking at least four months pregnant immediately appeared behind them, stepping out of it.

"Which way did you say?" Jasmine spoke out as she exited the twirling blue and white light. "Did you find something? Do tell!"

Before I could even say anything, or move out of the way, she used her powers to divert the waterfalls directly upon us, sweeping us off our feet. We slipped and slid for at least fifty feet, watching as Jasmine swiftly turned, disappearing into the cave. Finally, I used my power to pick us all up into the air, placing us back safely on the ground.

Immediately, the three of us zipped into the cave. Rounding the corner, we quickly saw a most terrifying sight. Jasmine had the baby in her hand, with the other hand just barely above the infant's chest.

"COME ON!" Jasmine screamed out. "WHY WON'T IT COME OUT?"

Jasmine grew angry once realizing that for some reason she couldn't get the essence she came for, tossing the child back towards the woman coward in the corner of the cave.

I quickly used my powers, catching the child gently, before placing it back into it's mother's lap. Jasmine turned her attention quickly in my direction, as she began hurling large rocks at us.

"She doesn't matter to me anymore," Jasmine spoke out. "Now use your powers, find the next woman for me. Do this and I won't harm you, disobey me and you'll only wish you could die! I'll put you inside of me like I've been doing to the others."

"Look," I quickly replied as I made up a good excuse. "Quigley told me where this place was, he wasn't sure, but he thought there could be one of his wives here, I guess they've come here before, I have no idea where the others are. Quigley hoped if we did find one of his wives here, she might know of the location of the others."

"THEY'RE NOT HIS WIVES" Jasmine suddenly erupted, causing the entire mountain to shake. "I AM!"

As she threw her little power trip hissy fit, the three of us made our way to the woman and her child. Without warning, Jasmine suddenly collapsed on the cave floor, with Julian and JC suddenly waving us on to get out of there. Without a word spoken and before Jasmine started to wake, I opened up my wormhole with us jumping into the woman, grabbing her and the child in the process, with all five of us instantly arriving around twenty five to thirty feet away from the door to the cell, in the mountain where Nod is.

Walking in the deep snow was tough, but we hurried to the door just the same, with the woman quickly entering. The three of us stopped short of the door, we all knew what happened if you went in there, plus there was no need for any of us to lose our powers, we kind of needed them right now.

"Thank you Maria!" The woman suddenly spoke out from inside of the cell, the door still wide open. "I think she would've killed my baby once she figured out she couldn't have what she came for."

"Huh?" I replied confused. "Do I know you? I don't think I've ever seen you before, how do you know my name?"

"Oh yeah, I forgot, you don't remember your past lives," She answered quickly. "I'm Agony, we've met many times before and this little guy here, this is Devin, you might remember him."

"Wait, what?" I said totally confused. "Devin? Like the Devin I just had a fight with not even a day ago? How could this be Devin? You have me a little confused here."

"There's quite a bit you'll need to ask Quigley about then," Agony replied as she wrapped him back up neatly in his blanket again. "I'm not going to try to explain things to you, that just takes forever. Next time you see Quigley again, have him touch you, he can show you all of your lives all at once, that is if you'd like to see them all. But yes Maria, this little guy really put the beat down on all of you, you have to admit, he's a strong one."

"That he is," I said as Agony sat down by a now barely lit fire, it was just a few hot coals, but with her using her one free hand, she placed some new smaller sticks on the coals. It didn't take but maybe thirty seconds before once again a fire was lit.

"We're going to have to come up with a better plan guys," Jupiter suddenly spoke out. "Jasmine was quicker than we were, I don't remember being slow about things either, she's good."

"She better be good," Quigley's voice rang out as suddenly he walked out of the woods, straight for the cave. "I'd hope she would be, how boring it would be if she wasn't, not to mention how disappointed I'd be in her, she's been here a long, long time, she's not quite, but almost as powerful as I am. Speaking of power, we might need for you to travel a little more discretely, let me give you a little twinkle power as I call it. Try to use this instead of your wormholes, Jasmine doesn't know how to feel for the different power this type of travel eminates. The only thing she'll know is she'll feel them being gone, not that she can feel their power, but she'll still feel a difference as they leave. I'll explain it all in my touch, enjoy the ride everyone, you know I am. Thanks for bringing my woman and child to me, one down, four more to go, as Darius will bring back the final woman."

Quigley quickly disappeared into the cell, shutting the door behind him. I could hear them laughing a little, I could tell Quigley actually cared for this woman and her child very much, as I listened to his goo goo, gaa gaa's repeating from his mouth over and over, all kinds of baby babble, it was almost serene to hear this come from him.

I opened the wormhole back up, we all walked over to it, but as we did, I closed it, instead trying the new type of travel I'd just been taught, in just an instant, we found ourselves back at the lake house, as this is where I wanted to go. We waited for Jasmine to show up, but after a few minutes, we knew she wasn't coming, she couldn't feel us just like Quigley said. This gave us the time we needed to come up with our new plan, a much better one at that.

(HAPTER 21

"Alright," I spoke out as we walked around the back side of the cabin. "I have no idea what to do next, I'm just not sure I can do this by myself, Quigley was too vague in the directions, told me that gifts are meant for all to enjoy. I'll need both of your help on this one, that crazy little weirdo just never gives you all you need to know does he? I do think we could all die in the process of saving these women, so if either of you want out, then now's a good time to go. I don't care what happens to me anymore, if she kills me, she kills me, but she won't get what she wants, I'll see to that by myself if I have to. I promise to hunt you two only when there's just the two of you left, I'm very sorry I even have to, Jupiter, you know I love you, well Von, I love you as well."

"Hang on a second there Maria," Jupiter quickly jumped in. "I don't ever remember saying anything about leaving your side. Do you really think I'm afraid of death? You're the love of my life, I'll die for you, if not with you."

"I'm only your father by donation, to which the DNA was altered," Von said with a chuckle. "Yet, I find I've grown very fond of you as well. I've never had the privilage of getting to know my Great Grandmother as well as I have this time."

"HUH? What did you say?" I asked quickly in disbelief. "I'm your Great Grandmother? How? I don't understand."

"Well," Von said with a smile that quickly spread across his mouth. "See Darius is getting ready to become a father, it's always a girl, her name is Shadow, she's my mother. Believe it or not, but Lars' is actually my father, at least, they'll be these people once their all grown up, I'm just very old. So like I said, you're my Great Grandmother, a really cool one at that, I really enjoy seeing you in action. So, whenever you do have to kill me, just relax, I'll be back soon. I've really enjoyed being able to get to know you like this though, I've never had very much contact with you in the past, Grandfather was always afraid I'd alter his designs. That is, until his mind saw something terrible happen. He had to stop this atrocity from becoming a reality, as the world depended on him. This is when he finally included me in his wonderful plans, it's taken some time for them to all play out, but here we are now, just as he said we'd be, he's maybe a little on the childish side sometimes, but he always give you the answers, you just have to think about them."

Jupiter suddenly walked away from us, not saying a word, as he rounded the corner of the cabin, he looked over his shoulder at Von for a moment, before speaking out.

"I can't believe this," Jupiter rang out. "I'm *so* done with all of this, Maria, why don't you and I just do this by ourselves. This man has lied to me for hundreds of years, befriending me, gaining my trust. The entire time he lied to me about how he came to be in our world and who he truly was to me. I don't think we have time for liars right now, I can't trust him anymore."

"That's a hell of a way to talk to your Great Grandson," Von yelled out. "I mean come on, what was I suppose to do? Grandfather forbid me to talk to anyone except him or Lars about what we were doing. I couldn't tell you anything, don't you see? I wasn't trying to deceive you, I had to make sure I wasn't the reason Jasmine became aware of our plans."

"Quigley this, Quigley that, why does he have to be involved in everything we ever do?" Jupiter replied as he began walking back to us. "What we're doing right now, what we did last night, last week, last year for that matter, he's set everything up to fall right in order. Now, here we are, having to figure out what it is he wants us to do, this is bullshit. It'd be nice if someday Quigley wasn't even a thought in my head anymore, but he'd probably just save a space up there and have it reserved just for him."

"I'm sure he already does," I laughed. "He seems to have everything else covered, why not the only spot in your mind you could ever escape to? Leaving his nasty little thoughts all over the place, you'd need towels to wipe it all up."

"That's just gross Maria," Jupiter laughed back. "Alright, I'm done being mad now, sorry about all that, your theromones are becoming stronger, which seem to be making me more aggressive than usual."

"It's okay hunny!" I replied. "I noticed that back in the suite. I have to admit though, what Von just revealed was quite a bit for me to take in as well. I've gotten used to surprises over the years though, seems our lives are full of them."

"I really am sorry I couldn't tell you the truth until now," Von spoke out as he looked at Jupiter with a sincere look on his face. "If I could've told you, I'd have done that long ago, I never meant to lie to you, I was given no choice in the matter."

"Alright, alright," I jumped in changing the subject. "We have a problem here, I feel as if Jasmine will find a way to find us, even if this twinkle power is supposed to be undetectable, I wish we didn't have to make so many trips, I think it'll make it easier for her to find us if we do it one by one."

"Now," Von spoke out with a little grin appearing on his face. "If you think about it, Grandfather already told you what to do, you just have to think like he does. He said that gifts are meant for all to enjoy right? Did he say anything else?"

"No, not really," I replied confused. "Only how to use the twinkle warp he does, well, he called it twinkle power."

"Hmm, twinkle power," Von said as he rubbed his chin. "You sure he said this? He calls his warp a warp, but if he said power, then he gave you something to share with us. Just grab hold of our arms, then concentrate on the instructions he gave you. If he did what I think he did, then we're all good to go here."

Von and Jupiter walked the rest of the way over to me, extending their arms. I don't know what came over me, but for some reason, beyond my control, I suddenly grabbed both of their heads, slamming them into each other.

"Hey now!" Jupiter quickly said as he grabbed his head. "What the hell was that for?"

"Wow," Von spoke out as he grabbed his head as well. "Talk about your instant headache, was that really necessary?"

"I'm, I'm so sorry guys," I spoke out in a startled voice. "I don't know what came over me, I didn't mean to hurt either of you. It just happened as I thought of the directions Quigley gave me."

"Well then," Von replied still holding his head. "Knowing grandfather, this was how the gift of his power was given. Now if you'd be so kind as to grab our hands, we'll see if his instructions get passed on to us as well now, if not, then I think you've had your fun, but you'll have to concentrate a little bit harder."

I reached out, taking both Jupiter, as well as Von's hands in mine. We stood there for a few awkward moments before a sudden rush of info not only filled my head, but theirs as well. Unlike Jupiter and Von, I was given an even better gift, as unexpectedly a new type of energy surged throughout my body, one very different from what I'd ever known. My fingers tingled with an electric sensation, I felt like I could just reach out and zap a person if I chose to. I could no longer hold my body on the ground either, as I hovered over it a good foot. I could hear thoughts better than ever, even being able to hear the thought as it was being made. My vision was way different, I could zoom my eyes in on things now, like a telescopic lens, which I quickly found out. I could see a squirrel around a hundred foot away or so, I concentrated and within moments, my eyes zoomed in all the way to it. I could see where it's pupil ended and the white began of its eye, as well as the earmites which covered the inside of its ear. The reddish grey fur covering its long skinny body, looked different from an average one, as if it were a crossbreed between a red and grey squirrel.

"That was interesting," Jupiter replied as he stretched his arms out while a quick yawn came out of his mouth. "Boring, but interesting. So all you and I get is this warp thing huh? Maria once again gets all the cool powers, I don't think Quigley likes me much, he never gives me anything like he gives her."

"It's not a popularity contest," Von said in a defensive voice. "The guy already knows who to give the powers too, because he already knows the outcomes of all the senerios possible. Trust me, he knows what he's doing, it has nothing to do with how he feels about us."

"Hey," Jupiter said quietly. "Just saying, I think he has his preference, it's pretty evident. At least we'll all three be able to pickup a woman at the same time now, I can feel one only a few hundred miles away right now as we speak."

"That's funny," Von replied. "I feel a woman as well, but she's halfway around the world right now, I don't feel anyone close by."

"I think I understand," I quickly belted out. "I don't feel either of the two women you both seem to feel, I only feel one that's just a couple of miles from here. I think we all feel different women so we can all get to our targets without having to deal with Jasmine. Think about it, we're doing it all at once, that would have to confuse her, even if she did feel us."

"I see what you're saying now," Jupiter spoke out informatively. "We should get to each of our targets immediately. We can't waste any time once we find them either, grab them and go, no matter what. Let's all meet right back here once you've finished, we'll still have at least one more woman to find."

"I'm glad this power came with instructions," Von laughed. "We should feel blessed that he gave it to us at all, to be honest. I've never known him to do this for anyone, that is except once before, long ago, but that's another story."

"Well then," I laughed. "I guess I should feel honored. Let's get this over with already, I'm curious to see how traveling like this feels."

The three of us looked at each other, each one of us concentrating on our targets. Jupiter was the first to twinkle, disappearing almost instantly, followed closely by Von. I stood there a few more seconds, that is before I got my attention on my target just right. As I blinked my eyes, with the back of the lakehouse in my sight, as my eyes opened back up from blinking, I was now in a place that didn't feel very familiar.

The cliffs surrounding me towered above, making me feel small in my new surroundings. Trees grew out of these cliffs, which created a natural canopy, sort of a tunnel looking effect. I hovered over a path which lead towards where I felt the woman's power coming from. Upon making my way about forty feet from where I first arrived, I found a place where a crevice in between two colliding cliffs lead all the way to the top of them. Making my way through the rocky little maze, I finally found myself at the top. A small shelter which didn't look very sturdy could be seen about another fifty feet away.

As I made my way there, I could hear what sounded like muffled screams. I quickly hurried as fast as I could, opening up the flimsy doorway, with it falling to the ground. To my thankful mind, she wasn't in distress from anyone trying to do her any harm, but because she was in the middle of having her baby, with the head already protruding from her.

She was a beautiful woman as well, such as Agony, but with gorgeous black curly hair, the curls held their shape, bouncing up and down as I startled her upon entering. She looked at me with a painful smile, before pushing again.

"Hey, I'm very sorry about this," I said without trying to be a rude person to her, as she laid there with her womanhood exposed. "But I have to get you back to Nod immediately, you and your baby's lives are in danger."

"WAIT!" She yelled out as she bit down hard on her own teeth, grinding them together making a horrible sound. "HE HAS TO BE BORN ON EARTH, JUST A FEW SECONDS LONGER."

"Works for me," I said as I watched the child's slimmy shoulders pop out of his mother. "I think one more push will do it."

With the woman baring down hard, she gave one last hard core push, with the baby sliding safely out of his mother onto the floor of the shelter.

"Now can we go?" I asked without even waiting for her to pick up her baby. "Jasmine is looking for you right now as we speak, she wants the child's essence."

"Well then, she needs to find another baby," the woman replied. "Mine is already born, she can't get his essence now, it's safe and sound inside just where it belongs, in my little Raven."

"So you're Raven's mother?" I quickly asked. "I'm Maria and you are?"

"I'm Misery," She replied. "I already know who you are though, you and I go way back."

"Well Misery," I spoke out quickly. "I think we should get to Nod before anything bad could happen. I know you're not worried about her taking Raven's essence, but is he immune to her just killing him? Does he have the power to not be effected by such a thing?"

"Quigley thinks she's going to kill the babies?" Misery suddenly asked in a worried voice. "How are the others? Are they alright?"

"To be honest Misery," I said as I grabbed her by her arm. "I really don't know yet, we have a plan in action, but until I see the others, I won't know if they were successful."

"Then what are we waiting for?" Misery asked as she picked Raven up off the shelter's floor, holding him tight against her body, quickly using her fingers to pinch the umbilical cord in half. "Let's go girl, the sooner this night ends, the happier I'll be, that is, once I can come back here with Raven, I love our private time out here, he's so much fun to watch grow and of course play with."

Holding her arm tightly, I concentrated, this time much quicker. With another blink of my eyes, we found ourselves directly outside of the cell door, which was still shut.

"Hey!" I spoke out loudly as we approached the door, with me trying to look inside once arriving, but with the fire so dim now, the shadows swallowed up most of everything. "Come on you idiot! The baby's starting to get cold out here."

Suddenly, the door to Nod began opening up, with Quigley standing in the entryway as it opened. He made his way directly over to the door, using his powers, the key came flying across the room, out the window and inside the lock on the door.

"You want to turn that Maria?" Quigley suddenly asked. "Or do I have to do everything around here?"

I grabbed the key, twisting it counter clockwise instead of

clockwise like normal locks, hearing a distinct clicking noise. Misery couldn't wait to get in, as she instantly grabbed at the handle, reaching over me in the process, kind of booting me out of her way.

"Sorry about that!" She spoke out a she entered the cave. "Wasn't trying to be rude, just wanted in."

Just then from behind me, I could hear voices, I quickly turned to look, to which my happy eyes saw a gorgeous hunk of a man. Along side my Jupiter was a woman with long dark brown hair, she carried a baby as well.

"Guess you beat me here huh?" Jupiter said as he walked towards me. "That's alright, I take it I beat Von, so at least I'm not last. This is Vicious by the way, she's holding Sven right now, you might remember him. I now fully understand what an elder is, it actually makes sense if you think about it."

"What makes sense?" Von suddenly spoke out as he quickly approached, coming out from the treeline, a woman which could only be described as looking exactly like Cleopatra walked along side him, carrying a child such as the other women. "I didn't get to hear what you were talking about, we just got here. By the way, say hello to Savage and her son Marley."

Jupiter and Von made their way over to me, with each of the women and their babies entering the cell. We watched as Quigley had them all go into Nod, with him following closely behind them, shutting its door behind him upon entering.

"So!" I spoke out as we watched the door close. "Do you guys feel the last woman like I do?"

"Yes I do!" Jupiter spoke out happily. "I'm ready to get this over with, how about you guys?"

"I've been ready," Von replied. "Not really looking forward to the outcome, but I'm ready as I'll ever be."

"What's that supposed to mean?" I quickly asked as we all got closer to each other, grabbing hold of each others hands. "Why wouldn't you look forward to this night being over?"

"Oh, it doesn't matter, it's nothing really," Von replied. "It just signifies something different for me, that's all."

With that said, I concentrated on our last woman of Nod, with a simple blink, we disappeared from the cell's area, destination to be found out momentarily.

(HAPTER 22

"WHERE DID THEY GO?" Jasmine screamed out to Julian and JC as they cowered in the cave's corner, Jasmine grabbing at her head, as she began standing back up on her feet, immediately pacing frantically back and forth in front of them. "What did you guys just do? How long was I out? You helped them escape didn't you? I can hear you, I hear you just fine now, traitors. I won't tolerate this kind of behaviour. I tried to give you two a chance to be loyal to me, even after hearing what your minds have been saying. This is how you repay me for being nice enough to include you in my little adventure? I could of just took your essence's in the first place? Wait, I can feel a difference in the power around me, they're almost done, how long was I out for?"

"Quite a while to be honest and yes, I did help her," Julian replied as he stood up. "I'd do it again, what you're doing is just wrong!"

"Me too!" JC said as she stood up, grabbing hold of Julian's hand, holding it tightly in fear, as well as unity. "You're a baby killer, you disgust me. What you did to those girls in Michigan was wrong, they had nothing to do with any this."

"THEY HAD EVERYTHING TO DO WITH THIS!" Jasmine screamed out. "You have no idea what's really going on here, or what all power I need to bring my baby to life. Look at me!"

Jasmine quickly pulled up her shirt slightly, exposing a pregnant belly, which looked to be around four to five months along.

"My belly only grew like this after I consumed those girls," She continued. "I've figured this puzzle out now, I just need a child of Nod to complete this cycle, but as I just found out earlier, it must be inside of it's mother for me to extract it's essence. I wouldn't have done anything to you guys, I was actually going to have you two do something completely different. You two were to be the new creators of the vampire race, Quigley has his pets, I want mine! I think I'll play with my babies more than he does though. I was going to wait until Maria destroyed so many that only you two still stood, that's when I was planning on killing Maria and anyone else that's with her. This would've ended good for you guys, but no, you had to turn on me, I think you'll both deserve the outcome I now have in mind."

"Do whatever it is you feel you have to do," Julian replied. "I won't watch you attack anymore children."

"I'm with Julian on this one," JC joined in. "If helping you means we have to hurt anymore innocent children, then count me out as well. Do your worst, it'll be better than watching that sick grin you get on your face when you're killing kids."

"Do my worst huh?" Jasmine spoke out as her face began changing into an evil one. "I don't know if it'll be my worst, but I can try. Given the fact I know where your powers will go once I consume the two of you, this should make my job easier, I'll just transport myself wherever it is your powers find her at, this won't be anything she'll expect, even if Quigley has intervened, your power will fly to her fast, as will I."

Instantly, Jasmine threw up her hands, with Julian and JC slamming back first into the side of the cave's walls. They didn't hit the ground though, as she had them stuck on the wall.

"Is that all you got?" Julian replied as he attempted to remove his hand from the rocks surface, with his hand slamming back up against it. "Come on Jasmine, I thought you were powerful."

"Shut up Julian!" JC blurted out, as the back of her foot started being pushed into the wall. "Jasmine, I'm sorry, please, give me another chance."

"You already had it," She replied, making sure to smile that sick grin she knew JC liked so much. "You didn't do so well."

Suddenly JC began screaming out in agony, as Jasmine began using her powers to slowly push her inside of the mountain. JC shaking violently meant nothing to her, as she looked at Julian, making sure he was watching her horrible act.

"Stop, please Jasmine, that's enough!" Julian screamed out. "Let her go!"

"Hmm, let me see," She replied as she stroked her chin. "If only you had said pretty please!"

Jasmine walked up to JC, putting her hand out as if she were going to pull her out of the wall, pulling it back quickly right before JC could grab hold of it. Instead of a popping sound though, Julian heard loud crunching sounds, as Jasmine continued pushing JC inside the mountain. Jasmine was quickly becoming covered in JC's blood, as soon you could see half of JC stuck behind the rock of the mountain. The look of total agony engulfed her face, as her head sank into the rock behind her.

"AHH, NO, PLEASE, IT HURTS!" JC pleaded. "I"M SORRY, I'M SORRY!"

"Not sorry enough," Jasmine replied. "You forget, I can hear you!"

A few more crunching sounds echoed in Julian's ears, before a loud pop could be heard, as the rest of JC's body went into the mountain, encasing her in the rock forever.

"There's more than one way to get someone's essence," Jasmine spoke out as she turned, facing Julian who was still stuck on the wall. Holding a blue orb in her hand, Jasmine stroking it a couple of times before smiling at him.

"You're the beast, not Maria!" Julian spoke out with hate in his voice. "You won't get away with this!"

"A beast huh? Been awhile since I was called that," Jasmine laughed as she rubbed her belly. "I wouldn't call me a beast, maybe a little on the edgy side, but a beast, I guess you could actually say maybe."

"Killing other people's children," He replied, still trying to get his hand off the wall. "In an attempt to give life to your own, only monsters do things like that, how can you be blind of your own deeds."

Without warning, once again that sick drained feeling started to overcome her, so without even answering Julian, she began using her powers to do the same thing to him, as she did to JC. Stopping just short of his essence popping out of him, Jasmine sat down watching Julian bleed, squirming in pain.

Almost all of him was in the mountain now, the expression on his face said it all, the word painful wouldn't even come close to describing what he felt right now. The part of his body in the mountain, looked like an etching of a person, as it was rock with his body's outline. Grey in color, forever to be etched inside of it, reminding Jasmine of rocks that have been engraved.

"See Julian," She suddenly spoke out as she still looked at the orb in her hand. "You got it wrong, I'm not a beast at all, but I am a bitch through and through, that is, once you decided to get on my bad side. Now, I need a drink, you stay right here, I'll be right back."

Julian tried to make a sound, but his chest being so far inside of the mountain made it impossible for him to get air in his lungs to speak. He watched as Jasmine went into her wormhole, orb in tow, returning with a couple of bottles of bloodwine and one glass just a few minutes later.

"Now, Where were we?" Jasmine asked as she poured herself a glass, still looking at JC's orb in her other hand. "Oh yeah, I was just about to squeeze you into the mountain the rest of the way. Thank you for being so patient with me, I'll resume everything momentarily, that is, once I have a little wine."

Julian squirmed, making disgusting noises as Jasmine sat down, taking a couple of small sips from her glass, with much of her power returning immediately.

"You know, you're really making some disturbingly gross sounds, making my wine not as enjoyable as I'd hoped it would be," She began as she raised her glass up to her mouth, stopping short of drinking. "If you and JC hadn't let them go, I wouldn't be put into the situation I'm in right now. See, I can feel that at least three other woman are now gone, which only leaves two of the women for me to choose from. If one of those women happens to be Life, then I'll only have one woman left I can use. See, I have to use a woman who's carrying Quigley's baby, not Darius's. You've put me in a spot for sure, no worries though, like I said before, you and JC will help me find her."

Tipping the glass one more time into her mouth, Julian finally managed to scream out in pain as she slowly pushed him the rest of the way into the mountain. The popping sound echoed along with Julian's last screams of pain, as another blue orb appeared in her hand.

She sat there for a moment, still sitting on the rock in front of where Julian now stood embedded. Taking one last big gulp, as she stared at both orbs, which she now had hovering in front of her

"Well, here goes nothing," Jasmine said as she grabbed at the orbs, holding them inches from her body. "Things didn't have to be like this Quigley, you made it this way. I know I'm ready for this revolution, are you?"

Pulling them the rest of the way into her, she began squeezing hard, with them not wanting to go inside of her at first. Suddenly, with a horrendously loud cracking sound, both orbs entered her body, trapping their owners inside of her like the others.

Ever so quickly, Jasmine filled her glass back up, slamming it down as fast as possible. As she took her last swallow, she finally felt it, she knew exactly where Maria was now, Jasmine wasn't really sure why, but for a moment, she could even see out of Maria's eyes, which let her know that she was with one of the women of Nod. If there was going to be a time for Jasmine to act, now was definitely it, the woman she saw was Death, Lars' mother, to which she was still very much pregnant. What made it all the better, was the fact that Lars has always been Quigley's favorite child.

Opening her wormhole, she grabbed at her bottle, standing up slowly. Staggering as she walked towards it, getting a little light headed in the process, she grabbed at the wall, nearly dropping her

bottler of bloodwine. She quickly steadied herself, placing her

back against the wall that now housed Julian inside of it. She

tipped the bottle to her lips, taking a huge drink of it before tossing

the bottle aside, staggering her way into the twirling void.

CHAPTER 23

It took hours for Darius to find his way back to where the door of Nod was. Taking a wrong path once he climbed down the cliff, caused him to wonder around for hours in the lush beautiful forest. Making his way down what would barely be considered a trail, moving all kinds of thick branches out of his way, he suddenly came into a clearing, instantly, realizing he'd found the entrace to Nod, as the door was opening up, with Quigley and four of his wives carrying babies.

"What took you so long?" Quigley spoke out as he walked up to him. "You almost missed all the fun, I was starting to think I'd have to send out a search party for you. I've been back here for almost an hour now, you got lost didn't you?"

"I wouldn't call it lost," Darius replied. "After all, I'm here aren't I?"

"And not a moment too soon," Quigley chuckled. "Are you about ready to go on your adventure? I bet you're full of excitment just thinking about it."

"Oh yeah," Darius replied sarcastically. "Really excited, yay!"

"Well you should be," He said as he began laughing. "After all, you'll get to see your precious Life, plus your child tonight."

"Huh? What?" Darius stammered. "I don't understand, I thought I was going to save some prince or something like that."

"Well now," Quigely giggled. "What fun would it be, if you saved a prince and wasn't rewarded for your services? Save the prince and you'll soon have your queen."

"Alright," Darius spoke out as he began to grow angry with the riddles. "What are you getting at, I'm sick of this, just get to the point here. Are you saying they have Life held captive or something?"

"Dumb as a box of rocks," Quigley murmured. "I'll have to fix that next time around. Now listen, Stain Casey is the prince I spoke of, he's been locked in a jail cell for the better part of today, one of the people he met while in there is Life, she's very pregnant and about to have your little girl. I think if you help Stain in his moment of need, he'll make sure to give you a reward, do you got it now? If he doesn't offer one, that's when you can demand it if need be."

"How is this guy claiming his thrown?" Darius asked as he looked at the door to Nod, thinking about Life. "You said earlier to just throw his attacker around, if the guy's stronger than Stein in the first place, how do you intend on him winning?"

"Well, his name's Stain, but you really do love to spoil surprises don't you?" Quigley barked out, turning towards the door, walking up to it. "Stain is a special person, he'll get way stronger than his attacker once he changes all the way."

"All the way into what?" Darius asked curiously. "Is he becoming a vampire?"

"No, something even better," Quigley said as an evil grin crossed his face. "A werewolf! Not just an ordinary one though, my strongest puppy, the purest of the pure blooded is what he is, bringing in a new age once again for my pets. See Darius, just as all the vampires must die before your mother creates the first one again, the same cycle must happen with my puppies. This all just happens in a different way, a much more fun way, oooh, just talking about it is starting to get me all excited."

"So how soon do I need to help Stain then?" Darius asked. "What exactly do you want me to do? Just toss his attacker around like you said earlier?"

"Pretty much!" Quigley laughed out. "He's an idiot anyway, who knows, maybe your tossing him around all over the place will knock some sense into the guy. Probably not though, he's one of those types of people that's on a power trip, with no lights on upstairs if you know what I mean."

"Which light needs to be on?" Darius replied happily. "I'll be glad to turn it on for you."

"I doubt you could find it," Quigley laughed histerically. "Then again, sometimes I wonder if the lights are on with you as well."

"Oh, man, I know what you mean now," Darius said as an

odd quirky smile crossed his face. "Ha, ha, you're a funny guy, so, I guess it's about time to call me bicycle boy, or something like that now huh?"

"Nope," Quigley replied as he used his powers to open up the door to Nod. "I don't think there's a need to anymore, you just beat me too it."

Walking on the dusty gravel path, we made our way through the door, stepping once again back into the dark and damp cell. You could still see a slight glow in the cave cell, with many hot coals of an earlier fire still burning hot, the red coloration casting itself onto the door.

They walked across the cell, stopping just short of the doorway. The door was shut, which meant it was locked, but with a maroon colored twinkle in his eye appearing, the key quickly flew from its permanent spot on the big rock, straight past them and out of the cell's barred window. Suddenly a clicking sound could be heard, as the door suddenly opened up.

Instantly a very strong cold wind gust came inside, making

Darius remember why he didn't like the cell, as the cold air poured around his body.

"WOW!" Darius suddenly said as he crouched down by the hot coals. "That really sucked! I didn't expect a cold gust of wind to hit me like that. How'd you do that anyway? The key thing? I thought you didn't have powers in here."

"Well now," Quigley replied as a huge evil grin began crossing his face. "I never said that did I? Hmm, that actually seems to be the popular thoughts of some, what a shame that they're wrong. Now Sporto, it's time for the main event, are you ready for a night to remember?"

"As ready as I'll ever be," Darius replied. "But shouldn't I go outside first, you know, get my powers back?"

"Now, now, I have to time this just right, I wouldn't want Jasmine to feel you quite yet. Plus, what fun would that be?" Quigley asked as he quickly grabbed Darius by the arm. "Remember, I'm a Rollercoaster kind of guy."

With that said and with a sudden maroon twinkle in his eyes,

Darius instantly found himself in a very heavily wooded area, covered in deep snow.

"What the hell was that?" Darius asked confused. "I just felt like I was riding in a car with my head hanging out the window, then all the sudden here we are, wherever that is."

"Did you like the trip?" Quigley laughed. "My doggies love it, I like taking them on trips, it helps to keep them obedient, I designed this warp just for them. Sorry about this little surprise, your powers should catch up to you here in just a few more moments. Which should be right around the time Jasmine feels where your mother is at. Honestly I already know that Jasmine doesn't want your child's essence, but in one instance, as I watched in the falls, I witnessed her killing your daughter out of rage. This isn't the path we're on, but alterations to reality can always occur accidentally, with one wrong move, everything changes instantly. Now, once your powers do arrive, I'm going to send you smack dab in the middle of a fight, just be ready for it, try and stay calm, no talking until the fights over with and don't use your powers on anyone. Just toss the guy around for a few while Stain changes the rest of the way, he's been cut short on time. I told Dobs twelve hours, not a second before the time was up. He's not playing by the rules right now, I guess thinking I wouldn't intervene, guess he was wrong on that thought. Stain will fix everything though, I have faith in the boy. Well enough said, time for you to go."

Within a blink of his eye, Quigley transported Darius to his destination. With what felt like a semi running into him, greeting him the moment he arrived. Making him slide backwards a good ten feet.

Upon getting his first real look at where he was at and what had just run into him, he instantly recognized the area from the one he saw at the falls. A young man which resembled Stain lay all bloody on the ground behind him, shaking violently, rolled up into a tight ball screaming out in agony all the while.

In front of Darius stood a beastly creature, a massive bodied werewolf, who was already coming back at him again. Without thinking, he put his hands up, which caused a massive blast to come out of them. The beast flew back at least sixty feet or so, before slamming back first into the base of a large pine tree, landing on the ground with a thud, as the tree fell on top of it.

"Thanks!" Stain managed to speak out.

"You're welcome!" Darius replied without thinking.

Darius looked back at Stain, who was now starting to transform into a creature as well, his head looked odd as it began filling out. His whole face began protruding oddly, making him almost look like some of the people on hieroglyphics, with it finally just popping out hard and fast, with a perfect wolf shaped mouth. This is when the hair began growing, with Stain flipping out, suddenly getting out of his little ball, jumping up to his feet, ripping his clothes off.

"IT'S SO HOT!" Stain growled out in a now beastly sounding voice. "THIS SHOULD COOL ME DOWN! DOBS, I'M COMING FOR YOU!"

Suddenly, the man named Dobs came exploding out from the tree on top of him, running full steam back in their direction.

Before Dobs could even jump at anyone, Darius used his powers to transport himself to the immediate back of Dobs as he charged forward, grabbing his back feet as he ran. Doing this caused Dobs to go tumbling head first, over and over again, with him landing about ten feet away from Stain.

As Dobs lifted his head off the ground, his face turned into a face of total fear, as he watched Stain stand fully erect, now in his completely formed werewolf body. He was massive, at least twice the size of Dobs. His hair was now a dark brown color, with a slight wave in the way it laid, with almost a rockstar look to it, very thick as well, not scraggly like Dobs' was. Just the sight of him brought fear deep inside of him.

"Now it's your turn to ring the bell for food," Stain growled out, as the base in his voice rumbled straight through quite a few people, which were in the area watching the fight, vibrating so much that some snow fell off a small tree nearby onto them. "That is, unless you bow down and kneel, yeilding the throne to me peacefully, we can do this one way or the other, it's your choice, choose wisely."

Dobs got to his feet, standing there, sizing Stain up. After a few quiet moments, he pointed directly at Darius.

"I can't make a choice with your attack dog standing right there with you," Dobs finally spoke out. "What? You have to have help? Some Lord you're turning out to be, can't even fight me fair and square. Remember this people, our lord needs others to fight his battles for him."

"I don't even know who this man is, let alone control what he does," Stain replied as he took a step forward, placing himself in between Dobs and Darius. "I thank him for his assistance, but he can leave now."

"Not without who I came here for," Darius replied. "I think you know who I'm speaking of."

"Ahh, so the woman wasn't a liar after all, huh Dobs?" Stain said as he began laughing. "I take it you're Darius, I've heard so much about you. If you go into the cave behind us, you'll find the holding area, who you're looking for waits for you there, but leave now, I got this!"

Darius instantly began making his way to the cave, turning his head just before entering, taking one last quick look. He knew a fight was soon to happen, as they began slowly circling each other.

Upon entering the cave, Darius could smell the foul stench of rotten food, which almost gagged him. Dried blood covered the caves walls, with many different shapes actually being made out of it, as if someone drew many pictures on top of each other with blood. The floor was dirt, but a very fine dirt, not one pebble could be seen in it, perfectly smooth and soft to walk on.

As he made his way down the cave, it suddenly opened up to a large area, which had many tunnels. Darius stood there for a minute, thinking about which way to go, before just doing the simple thing.

"HELLO? LIFE?" He shouted loudly. "CAN YOU HEAR ME?"

"DARIUS!" She shouted back. "I'M OVER HERE, JUST FOLLOW MY VOICE."

Darius rushed down the tunnel from which he could hear her voice echoing from, with it opening up into an area that looked like a slaughter house, with many small eight by eight jail cells, all of them had at least one person in it, some having up to four. Getting towards the far end of the area, he finally found who he was looking for, with her pushing their baby out as he arrived.

"It's a girl!" Life spoke out with a smile from ear to ear, as the baby slid the rest of the way out of her. "Her name's Shadow, would you like to cut the cord?"

"Awe, baby, what have they done to you?" Darius asked as he looked at Life's tattered dirty clothing and all of the dirt smudges on her face.

"Nothing that really matters," She replied as Darius quickly used his powers to cut the umbilical cord. "Will you please take us home now? I *really* don't want to be here anymore."

"Of course I will," He said as he reached out his hand, transporting the three of them straight back to Quigley.

"Ahh," Quigley spoke out gleefully as he looked at an actual watch on his wrist. "You're back, right on time too. Fantastic, this is going to be turning out alright even though you botched things up tonight."

"Botched things up?" Darius replied confused. "I did what you asked, you were right by the way, Stain is a massive beast."

"Yes, he is!" Quigley replied as a sudden grin came to his face. "Yet, in your using your powers, plus telling him he was welcome, you've made him look weak to the others, you made it look like he needs help to rule the pack. I'm afraid it'll be help he'll get, but this will lead to some major problems for him. I do look forward to watching everything, I always like playing with new toys, the revolution is revolving."

"I'm so sorry," Darius spoke as he realized what he'd just caused. "I didn't mean to use my powers, it was more of an accident, when he said thank you, I just replied out of habit."

"It's alright," Quigley giggled. "I already knew you'd mess things up, I expected nothing less, so I planned accordingly. Enough about that though, let's get back to Nod, the real party is just about to start."

Quigley grabbed hold of both Darius and Life's arm, who held on tightly to her baby. With a sudden maroon colored twinkle, the snow that had just begun to fall suddenly had nothing in its way anymore, as they disappeared into the night.

CHAPTER 24

Upon arriving, we instantly began scanning the area for signs of Jasmine, quickly realizing we were inside of a long extinct volcano. A crystal clear lake was directly behind us, with a small forest completely encircling it to the walls of the mountain. Vines grew all over the place, protruding out of the ground in some spots, hanging majestically from the entire canopy encircling us, reminding me of wooden spiderwebs.

Directly ahead of us, around fifty feet away, was a small entrance which lead inside a cave. We quickly made our way to it, with me being the first to arrive outside of it. Branches were in front of the entrance, so I moved the branches out of the way, quickly making my way through. Immediately I saw a beautiful woman with dark brown hair sitting on a large rock, still very much pregnant. Before I could even turn to say anything to either Von or Jupiter, who'd just entered the cave, I felt the sudden rush of not one, but two surges of energy suddenly hitting me.

I stood there in disbelief for a few moments, just staring at the woman, who was now smiling at me. I immediately realized these two surges of energy came from my old friends, Julian and JC. Feelings of sorrow quickly ran through me, as I wished I would've been able to at least thank them for helping us. It appeared that in doing so, they were both punished.

As I turned back towards the entrance, where Jupiter and Von were still standing, I immediately noticed Jasmine's wormhole opening up in the distance, through the branches of the entrance, with what looked like a drunken woman emerging, as she staggered out of it.

I wasn't going to take any chances, so immediately I sent an extremely powerful blast of nothing but dirt at her, gathering it up in my mind into a hard ball before launching it. It landed with an enormously loud thud, as it shattered into a huge puff of dust.

"Good shot girl!" Jasmine said as she coughed, the dust still thick in the air. "If your aim was to suffocate me, you're doing a great job of it. If you were trying to hurt me though, you might want to try using something just a little bit harder. I myself would recommend rocks."

Upon her finishing her sentence, suddenly hundreds of rocks began being hurdled at us, flying through the air at incredible speeds, slamming into the three of us over and over again. No spot on us was safe, with even a couple of large rocks hitting me in the face. Jupiter and Von unexpectedly jumped in front of me, sheltering me from the onslaught. Jasmine's laughter was none stop, it sounded like she was having the time of her life right now, which really began to upset me. The more I heard that laugh of hers, the more I wanted to rid her of the enjoyment she was feeling at our expense.

Thanks to them protecting me, I was able to collect my thoughts enough to use my powers once more. Ever so quickly I used the air around us, creating such a strong gust of wind, it knocked the branches clear off of the caves entrance, hitting her so hard that she flew about two hundred feet back, before skipping on top of the water, finally coming to a wet end, as she went under.

Immediately the three of us ran over to the woman, who was still just sitting there smiling like nothing was happening. She looked up at us, winking at me.

"Finally!" She spoke out calmly. "I just love a surprise ending don't you? I'm so ready for this. Glad you could finally make it here, I hoped it would be soon."

The woman raised her hand up, suddenly pointing behind us. I turned to look and with the water flying extremely high in the sky, Jasmine came exploding out of the lake. She didn't look very happy either, as the water streamed off of her.

Jasmine suddenly threw what appeared to be a fireball at us, with me quickly grabbing hold of everyone and with just a blink, we were all suddenly in the snow, only about fifty feet from the cave cell's entrance. The wind blew hard, causing the snow on the ground to temporarily block out the view of the cell, once it cleared up, we began moving quickly up to the closed door. Making our way up to it, we quickly noticed it was shut again, with no sign of Quigley anywhere.

"QUIGLEY!" I shouted through the bars. "WE'RE HERE!"

No answer was heard, suddenly from behind us, Jasmine's wormhole opened up, with her still dripping wet, stepping through into the snow.

"GET AWAY FROM THERE!" Jasmine shouted as the air blasted us all back away from the door, each of us flying in different directions. "You're not getting away that easy."

I threw my hand up, causing the snow to twirl hard around her, blinding her for a few moments. Jupiter and Von quickly zipped over to her, with both of them grabbing her from both sides, like a human sandwich.

I grabbed the woman by her hand, the look on her face was disturbing, as she still had this crazy looking smile on it. It was as if she was oblivious to the dangers around us, or it just didn't matter to her, either way, it bothered me. Once again, I made it over to the door.

"QUIGLEY!" I shouted through the bars. "WHERE THE HELL ARE YOU, WE NEED YOU NOW!"

Suddenly Jasmine, broke free of Jupiter and Von's grip, using her powers to throw them far off into the forest.

"Now it's just you and me," Jasmine said as she began walking towards us. "I'll have to make this a quick fight though, sorry if you feel deprived."

Instantly I used my powers to pull a large tree out of the ground, tossing it at her without her noticing until it was already landing on top of her.

"HEY YOU LITTLE WEIRDO!" I said as I turn my head and shouted in the cell once more. "OPEN THE DAMN DOOR!"

Suddenly the tree began to shake, as Jasmine tossed it off of her, her eyes glowing neon blue. Instantly the woman of Nod flew into the air, landing on the ground at Jasmine's feet.

"I win this round Maria," Jasmine said as suddenly a fireball of incredible size came flying at me. I had no time to react either, I just crossed my hands in front of my face, waiting for the massive blast to hit me. Instead of the blast blowing me off the face of the earth, to my surprise, my body absorbed the energy like a sponge.

I could feel it now, the tingling in my body from earlier tonight, it was strong, it had a sort of hum going on to it, I felt like a god. Looking at another tree directly behind Jasmine, a sudden burst of lightning flew from my eyes, exploding the wood as it hit, causing a large branch to fall, landing within inches of her.

"I've been really easy on you, I wasn't supposed to harm you, but I will do the world a favor, so I'll go ahead and destroy you now," I spoke out calmly. "After all, I *am* the Destroyer."

Jasmine knelt down to the woman lying on the ground next to her, placing her hand directly over her belly.

I began concentrating my energy, building it up like a bomb inside of me. My job was to Destroy, she was now going to find out why. Just as I was about to release my blast of unknown power on her, the door of the cell suddenly flew open.

"That's enough now, Maria!" Quigley spoke out as he

suddenly appeared at the doorway. "Let Jasmine do what she came here to do, stand down."

"What?" I said as I couldn't believe what I was hearing. "You're going to let her take your own child's soul? Why did you even bother having us save the others if you were going to do that?"

"Let's just say I wanted to see just how far she'd go with this whole thing," Quigley said as he gazed directly her way. "Now I see, now I know, she's willing to go all the way, well, soon she will know what all the way really means."

"Know what?" Jasmine yelled out. "Know how hard I've worked to get this all to pan out? Know how I had to kill the one person I love just to experience the love of our child? I thought I actually killed you, I stabbed you with that dagger, I really thought I'd lost you. Yet you stand there not being happy to see me, but here to chastize me instead for wanting to be a mother."

"I don't have to do that Jasmine," Quigley replied. "You'll be the one that has to live with your actions, actions I'm telling you not to do right now, will you finally listen to me? You don't know what you'll unleash, I do! I guess if you do, you do, but remember, I warned you."

Jasmine looked at Quigley momentarily, with a sudden look appearing on her face which looked like she was going to stop. Suddenly a large pop could be heard, as an evil grin quickly appeared on her face, as she used her powers to extract the final orb to her puzzle. It didn't look like the others, much larger and red in coloration.

"Put it BACK, Jasmine!" Quigley demanded. "I'm warning you!"

Jasmine looked directly at his now angry, livid face, as he stood there inside of the cell, suddenly using her powers to slam the door in his face, pushing her prized red orb quickly inside of her.

With a sudden thunderous crack, the door of the cell flew open, Quigley standing there, his eyes glowing dark maroon, with a dark red glow emanating from all around his body.

Jasmine trembled in fear as she didn't believe he had any powers inside of the cell, he'd never used them before, she immediately realized he could have stopped her at any time. He was just watching another one of his programs he'd so elegantly designed.

"COME HERE!" He shouted as he threw his hand up, Jasmine being pulled across the snow and into the cell with him. Straight into his hand she went, which, quickly and firmly grasped her around her throat. "I told you not to do that, you should've listened."

Instantly the entrance to Nod began opening up, the rumble of it opening echoing out from the cave cell. As the door opened, there stood five of his precious women, all holding their babies, with Darius next to them.

"Whatever it is you decide to do with me is fine," Jasmine spoke out as she rubbed her now fully engulfed belly. "It'll all be worth while here very soon."

Quigley looked at Darius and the women standing at the door

with him, their babies in their arms, nodding at them with an evil grin on his face.

Instantly they all walked of out of Nod, through the cell and out the door without saying a word. Jasmine just stood there, frozen in fear as Quigley's grip on her was almost too much for her to bare.

As the last woman walked out, to Jasmine's surprise, Death, the woman who's baby's essence Jasmine had just taken, came walking in, a huge evil smile on her face. She made her way past us, walking straight into Nod. Upon entering, she turned looking straight at Jasmine.

"We're going to have some fun times girlfriend," Death spoke out. "Welcome to my world, we have a new game to play, you're going to just love it."

Without another word spoken, Quigley began walking over to the entrance, dragging Jasmine behind him, as he still had hold of her throat. As he began walking through the doorway, when he suddenly stopped, quickly tossing Jasmine inside, instantly turning back out of Nod, stepping back into the cell.

As Jasmine got to her feet, the door of Nod began closing, Quigley turned, facing Jasmine, looking right at her as the door slowly closed.

"Don't worry Quiggles," Death spoke out as she came up behind Jasmine grabbing her by the shoulder. "I'll take good care of her, she'll absolutely love motherhood, I know I will."

"You two enjoy your time together," Quigley announced as the door shut tight. "I'll see you in twenty four years, then your lesson shall really be taught. You know Jasmine, you didn't have to do any of the things you did, I told you I was giving you a baby. I was just joking when I said the baby was in a frozen state, to be honest, there's nothing I could do to stop him from coming. I did want to thank you for stabbing me in the back like you did, that was really lovely, I enjoyed every moment. I'm just a piece of meat to you after all, one that you'll carve up if you feel like doing so. Or am I just a sperm bank to you? The world will never know. I look forward to our next adventure though, it'll be one with life altering results, I promise. Never again will you not listen to the all wise, all knowing, master of disaster, least we forget sexual dynamo, which is Quigley!"

I could hear Jasmine screaming for Death to get away from her as he headed out of the cell into the deep snow outside. Jupiter and Von both suddenly came busting out of the woods, quickly stopping in their tracks as they saw no battle in progress anymore.

"Show's over everyone," Quigley suddenly announced. "You have to admit, it was a real nail biter there at the end. You guys can go back about your business now, it'll take you quite some time to kill every single vampire on earth. Even if you get a few hundred to drink my special blend, you'll still be busy for quite some time, probably pretty close to twenty four years or so."

Quigley turned, as if to go back into the cell, I couldn't believe that's all he had to say. After the hell we'd all just been through for him, then to let her take the child's essence anyway, absolutely infuriated me. It was as if we did everything such as he just said, for a nice little show for him.

"Stop right there!" I said as I used my powers to slam the cell door shut before he could enter. "You're going to explain yourself to us, no riddles either, or I'll make you destroy the Destroyer, do you understand me?"

"Whoa now!" Quigley replied as the door brushed his nose as it closed. "That was interesting."

Turning back around to us, his wicked smile glaring at us as he stared at me, he began laughing such as he always seemed to like to do.

"Destroy the Destroyer," He giggled. "Now that is one senario I've never thought about, how interesting could that turn out to be? I guess the world shouldn't find out, but hey, you never know. I do have some answers for you though. Would you like to hear a story?"

"If this story has the answers, then sure," I replied as I crossed my arms. "You should try to get to the point though, I know how your stories can be sometimes."

"Ahh, yes," Quigley laughed as the cell door came flying

open from behind him. "This story is about a woman, not an ordinary one though, a very powerful and special one. She always liked to cause chaos, changing the way certain things were supposed to be played out. This caused many problems for the person which designs the show we all live in, for giggle's sake, we'll call him Quigley. This show has many alternate endings to it, as the show never ends. Well, the designer has been tasked to keep everything in check for the rest of the world, as punishment for his crimes against society. This woman constantly trys to change little details of the show, which causes a landslide effect on other issues. The designer has never harmed her for her actions, as he couldn't find it in him to hurt the one he loved most. Now the designer had long stopped designing her path, but one day just out of curiosity, he looked into it once more. To his horror, he could see what a series of events would lead to, which forced him to take action against her, plotting and planning for hundreds of years. He made sure to analyze every single move anyone could ever make, which is brilliant, if I do say so myself. Upon watching every senerio, the designer found that a situation had no choice but to occur. He informed a few people whom he trusted most and they would soon become involved with him in his master plan. He could only give them sketchy details, but just enough for them to help and make things look normal to the woman. Well this woman unleashed her sinister plot, but thankfully, the designer knew just what to do. He placed the woman deep inside a mountain prison, to which she would not be released for a period not less than twenty four years. During this time, the situation shall arrive, which will become most unpleasent for many."

"So what's this situation you're speaking of," I asked curiously. "Is it a bad one?"

"A bad one," Quigley laughed out loud uncontrolably. "I'd say, remember this series of events the designer was trying to avoid? All the paths he designed were designed to make sure it happened. It really didn't matter what the designer did either, as all paths lead to the same place, it has to happen. This situation will change many things in the future, it was much more fun for the designer to watch it all happen, as he looked forward to watching it all play out. Such a shame that he's the only person who knows the outcome of it all."

"So, what's this situation?" I asked once more. "When will it happen? Are you wanting us to help you with something?"

"Not at the moment I don't," Quigley replied with an unusual smile. "As for the situation, he has a name, it's Quinn, he's my son, Jasmine just gave birth to him a moment ago in Nod, while I stood here talking to you just now."

"That's a wonderful thing," I spoke out happily. "You should be happy about his arrival."

"Oh, I didn't say I wasn't happy with his arrival," Quigley laughed. "I'm just not happy with the situation he'll eventually put me in, you shouldn't be happy at all, with his arrival, you'll lose someone very important to you."

"So how long do we have?" I asked as Jupiter and Von now stood beside me.

"Twenty four years from tonight," He replied as he walked

into his cell. "Now if you don't mind, I'd like to take a nap in my room here, it's been awhile since I've been alone, a nice nap in here will be a welcomed thing. Oh yeah, thanks for not using that lightning attack on Jasmine earlier, if you would've done that, you would have ruined the whole thing. The baby would've been killed and I wouldn't have such an interesting show to look forward to."

"I could've stopped this situation from happening?" I shouted out. "Why did you stop me? Just for some cheap thrills?"

"Pretty much!" Quigley could be heard saying as he once more began laughing. "You might not want to get too soft there Maria, I'll have a new ride for you to go on, so far it looks even better than the Rollercoaster, get ready for Quinn's Reign. Ahh, the revolution truly begins now, what fun we'll all be having once everyone wakes up. As they say, choose your leaders wisely, I already know you will Maria, even if I have to help you make your choice, such a sad choice it will be at the time for you. Ah, to be in love, what a wonderful feeling."

We stood there for a few moments, taking it all in, the wind still whipping around us.

"Well," I suddenly spoke out as I grabbed Jupiter and Vons hands. "I guess we better get started, I feel like twenty four years is a long time to wait, might as well have some fun while we do."

My wormhole instantly appeared in front of us, it's swirling color so inviting as always. I looked at the door to the cell one last time before walking in.

"See you soon enough!" I spoke out as we entered it, Quigley's laughter was heard echoing through the wormhole as we arrived at our destination, all ready to start our new adventure.

Coming Soon:

Ring Bell For Food (The Savage series, book 1 of 2)

The Awakening (The Magic series, book 1 of 4)

Quinn's Reign (The Rebirth series, book 6 of 6)

Quigley (The Quigley Chronicles, book 13 of 13)

A Special thanks to my wife Jennifer for putting up with me while I write, who's insite has forced me to be more descriptive as well. You're an inspiration to me, I love you very much!

Another Thanks to Corie Harris for letting me use her name in my books. I hope you enjoy your character as much as I enjoy writing about her.

Another special thanks to my cover designer, Jade Phillips, for doing such wonderful artwork for each and every one of my books. Thanks again Jade, if you haven't been told this today already, you're awesome!

Last but not least, I wanted to thank my children, for always giving me the space and time I need to write without so much as a complaint. I love you all!!!

CPSIA information can be obtained
at www.ICGtesting.com
Printed in the USA
BVHW03s0608120818
524220BV00027B/181/P